Dead Fashion

By: Jayson Nichols

Copyright © 2023 Jayson Nichols.

All rights reserved. This book or any portion of this book may not be reproduced or used in any manner whatsoever without the direct written permission of the publisher or the author except for the use of brief quotations in a book review.

ISBN: 978-1-304-97490-7

Imprint: Lulu.com

Printed by Lulu Press, Inc, in the United States of America.

First printing, 2023.

Lulu Press, Inc

Morrisville, North Carolina, 27560

https://beacons.ai/jaysonnichols

Dead Fashion

*Language and readers discretion is advised. This might not be the right read for those who cannot stand violence or the acts of violence. Mental instability should also be noted and accounted for when reading. If you do not feel well mentally, seek help! This is a work of fiction! Everything and everyone depicted in this novel are very loosely based on real events or people and are mostly made up! This is historical fiction, fiction based on historical events including brands, organizations and things popular of the time period. Everything was imagined and produced by the author and has nothing to do with real life events. Basically, to sum it up...
THIS IS FICTION! Enjoy!*

For my wife and all my lovers, pray they never meet.

Dead Fashion

Dear Diary

    I am nothing more than a meat sack. I have no remorse and no further statement to describe myself with other than one word. A word I happen to love, I love the feeling of this word, I love the hatred you need to say this word, I love this word without a shadow of a doubt… That word is *sick*. I am a husk of a human. You can touch my skin and feel a human but there is no human under me. Under me, Karen Wall there is nothing, I'm empty, I'm disgusting and foul. Ok so maybe there are other words to describe me but fuck it, the point is without other people or another thing or something, I'm nothing. There's an idea of me, but that idea is different from mine. My goal is to fit into a 21st century, sharp society that not only thrives off of self interest but also isolation. Especially in times like these where everyone's stuck in a spot in their life where they just wanna take a gun to their fucking skull and pull the trigger. I'm a- ah fuck who am I trying to impress with this fucked up complex sentencing and language? I could care fucking less about people who can't handle their own minds, the weak die and for a good reason.

    I'm fucked up in the head and god dammit I like it, I've killed, I've beaten, I've stole and just about any hanious act someone can perform, I've probably done it. So far it's been slow, God dammit I wish there was an easier way to do these things, but not too easy, I don't like that. Everyday I crave more and more and eventually I'm gonna FUCKING BREAK! Sorry sorry I'm trying to hold back more than usual and usually it's not a problem but recently like I said before I'm starting to crack like a fuckin' egg over a frying pan and honestly… I like it.

Dinner at Ozymandias

"Hey Karen, are you gonna participate in this conversation? We are having dinner, ya know we never go out and-" I'm trying to self indulge and listen to the new song that came out by The Weekend but my dumbass 'boyfriend' keeps trying to talk to me. We've been dating for about 2 weeks now and tonight is it. I can't stand this guy, in a way you could say that tonight 'we break up'. Now usually nobody notices my airpods in my ears mainly because most people have some sort of headphones in and are lost in their own thoughts, but since we're at dinner this guy thinks we need to talk but unfortunately to his conversation I hear Blinding lights and watching him talk the entire duration of song shows that I dodged a social bullet.

"That's crazy babe, ya know these airpods I got are so awesome I can listen to you and the music and I don't notice a thing it's as if there is my own personal background music to this conversation, baby you should get some of these." complete lies.

"Yeah maybe but I can't stand music Karen, I haven't liked any songs since One Direction's last album sorry this new music generation is ass, there simply is just no reason for those." What an idiot. Does he know who he is talking to? You know maybe that's not the best thing to say to a musician in this "generation" but that won't matter I won't see this guys face after tonight, I just need to get him out of this damn restaurant, I mean I don't have a lot of money so a good dinner at a fancy restaurant like Ozymandias is nice but I could care less, my itch is starting to go wild and if I have to listen to this guy talk about how this killer virus in China was discovered and some sort of drone strike in Iran I'm gonna fucking lose it.

6

If he's lucky my itch won't completely take over until we are back at my place, maybe he will die somewhere nice.

      He keeps trying to talk to me and I keep responding with "That's crazy babe" and a fake smile. While he tries to continue his bullshit I think about lyrics for the next song I'm trying to make. I just hit 1000 listeners on spotify and I'm celebrating by releasing an album within the next month. I don't have a lot of followers but my followers are what you could call simps. Thinking of lyrics will be difficult with this chatter and it makes me want to skin him alive. The more this guy talks the more I want to take a rubber band and put it around his testicles until his balls turn purple and flick them off. I stop concentrating on the lyrics of the song as they get louder and louder telling me to cut him alive. I can only think about the act of murdering this fool right here right now. I start trying to concentrate on other things to take my mind off of it. This cunt is still going off about how President Trump is ruining things and needs either to be removed or assassinated but I quit listening the moment we stepped into this restaurant. Speaking of the restaurant this is probably the nicest place in the whole damn metropolitan area. Located in downtown Minneapolis the restaurant is packed full and the chaos is insane. The lighting is dim yet somehow bright enough to see every detail and sweat gland on everyone's face. The tables are spatially placed just barely far enough to not be considered *invasive*. Everyone is wearing nice Gucci and other high brand clothing attire including my "boyfriend" who is wearing some high end suit and tie like it's a fucking wedding. I'm wearing a tight shirt and a hoodie with a Nintendo 64 logo on it. It makes no sense since I'm wearing a tight shirt and want to show off my tits but it looks cool and gets me more looks than just being a hot chick. I did my makeup in a more dark style since it's in fashion for zoomers currently and I'm trying to fit in and look like a dumb uneducated zoomer and by the looks I'm getting it definitely was the play.

Dead Fashion

I'm starting to think this was a bad idea, not just the dinner but dating this guy, he's at least my 20th boyfriend since moving back to Minneapolis about a year ago in 2019. The funniest part is I don't even remember this guy's name, I've created an entire execution in my head but cannot for the life of me remember his name. Fuck it who cares,

"Hey babe, let's skip dinner. Honestly I'm not hungry and would rather do more ya know fun stuff." I make an erotic gesture of me sucking his dick and within moments he's ancy and ready to leave. My seduction skills have increased over the past borderline legacy of victi- I mean boyfriends and I know how to use my body and the fact that I'm a female to my advantage. I'm only 21 so luring targets in a metro area like this is easy.

We sort things out with our waiter, who is furious because he won't be getting some large ass tip because we didn't order anything yet and we leave the restaurant and get an Uber. Our Uber arrives in 10 minutes and after rubbing up on this chimp and seducing him for what feels like hours while listening to the new Megan Thee Stallion single that released a few days ago we arrive at my apartment. We get into the apartment and before I can even hardly open up the door we are already making out and he's trying to take off my clothes. I can tell by his mannerism and his body language that this guy is a total virgin. I was gonna kill him before we even got to the bed but now I guess I'll fuck him. Not even because I feel bad that he's a virgin but it's more of the fact that feeling the bulge in this guy's pants he is packing at least a 8 or 9 incher. I really want to do this badly so after fullying undressing him and myself I play around with him, teasing him badly. We have sex and for this guy being a virgin I can tell you he's the best person I've had in bed. It turned out to be 9.2inches in fact and was actually decent. I really like this guy and for a second I almost think about keeping him alive and tied up in my room so I can use his dick but I realized that it would be stupid to let this fuckhead live his life any longer.

He lays on the bed almost dead asleep, I can make any guy break within minutes and this guy while doing a good job was no different. He came all over my brand new sheets I got for my bed and in what seemed like gallons of his gross baby batter. I decided to scoop as much of it up as I could before it harden and ruined my perfect fucking bed sheets even more. I decided the best way to take this guy out is torture and asphyxiation. I grabbed a grocery bag I had laying around and filled most of the semen up with it but kept some. I grabbed the semen I left out and I doused my fingers with them after taking off my beautiful long fake nails. I grab handcuffs and cuff his left arm to the bed and do the same with the right, he starts to notice something and starts to come to but before he can do anything I punch him in his face, He screams in terror but only partially as I duct tape around his mouth (one hole gone). Then I take my two doused fingers and shove them up his nostrils. He breathes in his own gross sticky semen and I start to laugh as I watch tears come from his eyes. Then I put the bag over his head and tightly duct tape around his neck (all holes covered). Then as he suffocated himself I grabbed a hand saw and after mutilating his perfect dick off his body with all the blood and nasty left over skin getting all over my sheets that he ruined and I then strangled him until he completely gave up his soul to the devil. I cut his body into pieces and put them into bags, I then leave my apartment and place them sporadically around the city and after almost 4 hours of bullshit and trying to find a way to get rid of my sheets I successfully get rid of everything including most of the smell as well. It's 2am and I'm fucking beat today was a good day I finally got to relinquish my blood lust, it's getting worse and worse and is slowly starting to take over but the dopamine I get after satisfying it gives me a rush better than any of the shit the homeless fucks in this town get. Finally got my second pair of new sheets (I always buy my sheets and pillow cases in pairs of matching kinds) and put them on my bed, then I put his mutilated still somehow perfect cock in the freezer. Finally I lay my head down and can finally rest without the blood lusting urge creeping in on me and crawling under my skin, life for a moment stops and everything is perfect as the world turns dark.

My Apartment

I wake up listening to my playlist, my google home is blasting early 2010's mix and payphone from Maroon 5 comes on. It was a fun song I used to listen to when I was younger. I'm fucked up from the Xanax I took after merking some fucking homeless loser sitting next to the US bank stadium. The stadium is beautiful and clean and trash like him don't deserve to be within a mile of it. I drink a full cup of water next to my bed and when that still isn't helping I resort to my vape which I'm hoping a few hits will stop the pound in my head. My head is running at one thousand miles an hour but my body and everything else feels like I'm in slow motion. I sit on my phone while laying in bed watching a video on how a Donald Trump drone striked a guy in Iran. I was gonna ask who cares until I realized that this could start a war with the US and I'm not trying to get drafted if I get drafted I'm clapping Trump's dumb ass. No offense to him he hasn't been doing a bad job but some of shit he's said and has been doing lately has pissed me off. I don't know whether to call him my president or dictator and with this being an election year it's the perfect time for him to get his shit together.

My plan is Bernie Sanders wins it since he said recently that he will be running for president and with what happened in 2016 with Hillary Clinton cheating her way into the nomination and Bernie getting screwed over when he should have won gives this the right opportunity for him to become president. Free health care and no more student debt in America would be great, I wouldn't care about student debt since I never went to college. I went to Japan in 2018 instead and lived there until about Sept. 2019 until I decided that Japan wasn't like how Anime portrayed it or how I had envisioned life there. I ended up getting some good experience for my career, I learned Japanese almost basically fluently and got to live in a Metropolis where you feel like you're worthless and tiny. It made me realize that society and how the world works right now makes us feel small and worthless with how big our cities are and how some people like Jeff Bezos have hundreds of billions of dollars while I'm sitting on food stamps with $290 in my bank account. At least I have a home, I know how to stay tight with money and get things. Japan was fun but I wanted to move back to Minneapolis and the metro area because I felt a pull to come here. I can't explain it but this is where I feel whole and complete. I like it here more because the city is smaller and it's harder to get away with murdering someone in an alley. You start making papers faster and all of a sudden you are the talk of the city. In Tokyo that would never happen. I lived on the southside of Tokyo in the San'ya Neighborhood and at first it was awesome. Endless amounts of murdering and torturing and no one would ever know. Plus the chicks and dudes my god, asian men and women get me higher than any American drug. plus the endless amounts of cocaine and Hookah got me rampid and would make the murder sprees faster, more exciting, however non-memorable as everything was so fast, plus another problem was there was no challenge, I don't want to just fulfill my bloodlust, I want there to be meaning behind my killings. Whether it's keeping homeless people out of the city or killing someone who has some sort of value I not only want to make sure I get known but I want a police officer to knock on the families door and have to tell a family they have lost someone, I want grief, bloodspill is only a small, but significant part. I want to plan and execute someone who has value and isn't just some Japanese bum sitting in an alleyway knowing no one will go into that alleyway for weeks, however it's still fun every once in a while. I want to- fuck it this Xanax has got the best of me I'm too fucking tired to keep going you get the point, I moved back here, it's a new year and I'm laying in bed knowing damn well I aint got shit to do no work for another day and I'm just enjoying myself baby.

The Next Day

    I wake up after falling back asleep only to find that I only managed to get 4 more hours of sleep. It's now 11:16am on a Tuesday and my head has finally stopped pounding. The Xanny is wearing off and I get up, take a shower and find myself fondling my own body while looking at myself in the mirror. My wet and long Darkish brown hair glissens in my lights over my bathroom mirror.

    My face is rough and has black heads in places as I don't like to use a deep cleanser because it dries my face out, but I'm still beautiful and sexy regardless. My green eyes (rarest eye color) also reflect so well, as I make eye contact with my mirror self and see my dead expressionless face. Then I apply dark eyeliner and eye-shadow until everything around my eyes is dark like my soul. My teeth are decently white and kinda crooked, not a million dollars worth but still very acceptable; They are tolerable and complement my eyes enough for me to be somehow semi satisfied. Then I get to the bread and butter of myself, the reason men even stay with me or go after me, my body. I make my way down my chest until I get to one of my best parts, my tits… I stare at them as I fondle them gently, they are double D's and are a light white with a decent tan around the nipple. My tits are great but they hurt like a bitch, plus they give me back problems as well because of the amount of weight in the front, plus I suppose bad sleeping positions don't help but mainly weight. Then I go to my arms, I shave them sometimes because hair rarely grows on mine but still pops up enough to be considered Bigfoot and my arms are skinnier but are muscular as I work out everyday, it's one of the best ways to defend myself against stronger men and women when needed. I have to be strong yet keep the appearance of looking like an innocent young lady who can't fight back. The biggest trump card I have in my entire arsenal is the deception of looking small but in reality being stronger than most men. My nails are fake and long, they are painted pink and white, pink on the top part and white on the bottom. Then I move to my silky white flat skinny stomach, where my innie belly button with a belly piercing rests and looks super sexy. I get to my silky smooth legs I shave everyday. My thighs are meaty and nice, thick thighs save lives and fun fact I've actually suffocated a chick with my thighs before so I guess the saying is full of shit. Then I make my way down to my feet, my toes are painted and are short, they are purple with a white hearts painted on them. I'm due for a pedicure here within the month but for now everything works out. I look at my body as a whole. I'm 5'8 and could beat most men and women in a one on one fight just to pure strength. I look over my body and I'm happy, I'm sexy, strong and I feel extremely amazing for some reason today and I think I wanna go out and find someone to do it with tonight, I don't feel a bloodlust either, maybe I'm turning a new leaf all of a sudden, maybe god is up saying turn on the sanity in Karen… Hahaha oh fuck man I'm hilarious, guess I can add that to my list of reason why I'm fucking awesome.

5 weeks later

I'm listening to the new sample of Drake's album coming out this summer while writing some lyrics for my next song which by the way is a banger and it's called The Chemtrails for my small YouTube channel, The Akuma.

I really enjoy using Japanese in my rapping style. Most people can't understand it but it ends up sounding good either way and people like me, who know the words will enjoy hearing it. I personally think it needs some tuning and the beat is semi finished but I like what I have so far and hitting 10k listeners was the small boost I needed to keep going so I

Dead Fashion

figured I would try really hard for this one. I got my first check from Spotify and YouTube music, in total in two weeks I made $89.56. I was very happy when I received my check I- *KNOCK KNOCK!* A knock on my door? This concerns me because it's 1 in the afternoon on a Monday and I only have three people I would consider myself friends with and none of them know where I live. I sluggishly move to the door and after struggling with the crappy apartment door for 20 seconds I manage to get it open. A man in a beautiful suit and awesome shoes is standing there, he's about 6ft tall and has decently longer black hair with some waviness to it. He's got a nice clean shaven goatee and has cheekbones like a motherfucker, he may be in his late 40's I wanna say but damn I wouldn't mind taking a peak at what's underneath his suit.

"Hello I'm detective McDowell but you can call me Lawerence or Lars." I look at him trying to play it cool but I'm completely in love with this guys voice and him, I'm also trying to hide the fact that I'm still a little fucked up from the xanny last night but I'm sober enough that only I can really notice it.

"Um what seems to be the problem mr- uhhh-"

"McDowell."

"MccDowelll!!! Yes, that's it." I'm a fucking IDIOT oh my god I wanna kick and scream and cry, how did I forget his name literally right after he told me it? Karen you incompetent invertebrate jelly!

"Please like I said, call me Lars." He smiles gently and I can see all of his teeth perfectly colored white and straight, fuck this guy is making me wonder why I made all the life decisions I made. "I'm looking for Karen Wall? She should live at this address right?"

"Your lookin' right at her."

"Oh good, good like I said I'm detective McDowell, working through a missing persons case out of the MPD (Minneapolis Police Department) A guy named Christopher Stevenson." Oh ok that's what his name was great I remember him now. "He was last seen three blocks from here with a gal named Karen who supposedly lived here. Checked it out and found Karen Wall born December 8th, 1998 living at 4808, south 38th st Minneapolis, MN, Apartment #17. We have reason to believe you are a suspect so would you mind answering a few questions for me?"

"I suppose." I say unwillingly.

"So all of the information I stated earlier is correct right?"

"Yes."

"Ok so where were you Jan 6th?"

"I went on a date with… Chris to Ozymandias and after the dinner service was poor I left with him and he came here and well we um let's say had fun to say the least."

"Fun?"

"Ummmm yeah?"

"Describe this fun to me." He's kidding right? Isn't obvious I fucked him?

"I fucked- I mean we had sex and it was consensual too! I wasn't drugged and neither was he, like I said we we're having dinner at Ozymandias when the food and place was boring so we left came back here and had sex, then I woke up the next morning and he was gone, he had left and then proceeded to block me on all social medias and blocked my number then I never heard from him again. He was what you would call a… sex dipper or as I call them men haha. He basically fucked me then disappeared, never heard from him again. I also had only known him for about two weeks but I felt something special, I-I really thought he was the one." I start to shed a tear which is completely fake, then I say "Could you give me a moment?"

"Of course." The detective smiles then allows me to shed more tears. Then I "compose" myself and continue on.

"I never really met someone like him, it's been 5 weeks and I figured he was an asshole in it for the sex, are you saying he's missing?

"We believe so ma'am. He hasn't been seen since the night he was with you. Did he leave anything behind by any chance? Some sort of shirt or pants or something if you guys had intercourse I would imagine the last thing he was thinking about is trying to keep everything perfectly clean without a trace."

"No I looked and there's nothing, he didn't really have much with him either. Listen, is there any way that I can help?"

"Your statement is enough for now we are going to check local footage and security cameras and see if we can see anything, unless you have anything else to give us then I suggest you remain calm and let us do our job ma'am."

"Ok!" I put my hand on his shoulders and then said "Detective... Please find him!"

"We will." He thanks me and walks out and away, I shut the door and smirk with a quiet laugh, what a fucking idiot, god dammit if he wasn't so hot I would of merked that fool but whatever. I need to finish my song and get it out, the president is supposed to make a speech tonight on the recent coronavirus cases and how it's spreading like wildfire. I'll probably watch that then go fuck some idiot homeless loser up either way I would say so far this year has been amazing. And with this guy poking his nose into my business, it should get interesting.

It's over

Fuck fuck fuck fuck fuck fuck! I fuckkkkking can't, fuck balls, I cannot believe this fucking bullshit, agghhghghghghghgghgh! I was working my usual cringe ass stupid no brain shit pizza place job. I work a 12-10 shift every Wednesday - Saturday when they decided to fire me because even though there were no orders being made, writing song lyrics was not ok and my stupid boss screamed, yelled and hollered at me then told me to get out. I was in tears and rage built up so badly. This low life no good piece of shit fuck face decided that I was incompetent, ugly, fat, and retarded. FUCK

YOU JOE! Joe's pizza, more like Shit face's pizza. Fuck him, fuck pizza. Fuck Joe, FUCK EVERYTHING. I'm jobless and soon to be just as bad as the homeless cunts in the city, I'm not making enough from my music either. I'm done with everything I cannot bear to have this happen to me. I need to get my music going faster I need someone to produce me, FUCK FUCK FUCK, it's all over…

The Diamond In The Rough

The air is frigid and tense in the very crowded conference room of the Mystic Casino Hotel, in Mystic Lake, Minnesota. The room is very long and can hold maybe 15 people, but there has to be about 30 people in the very low lit conference room. It is around 7pm and there are guys who look like they have had a long day and some who look like they haven't even scratched the surface and are itching to get back to giving the Native Americans more money. The executives, investors and higher ups of the massive record label DP records gather and chatter waiting for the current CEO Isaac Damocha to speak to them about the current status of the now failing record label. The chattering stops and the air gets even more tense as the oldish, graying Damocha walks into the conference room and all eyes point to him as he walks to the front of the room to the head of the oblong table.

"Ladies if there are any, I don't see any but maybe one of you is a woman who knows these days, and gentlemen today on March 11th, 2020 we are reaching the end of quarter one and-" He stops what he is saying and looks down with his hands on his hips, the nasty coarse hands touching such a nice suit, it almost is crime to look at. He starts up again. "And I gotta be brutally honest with you guys… it isn't looking good." within a second of him saying that all the old men and young investors erupt into chaos throwing papers and screaming and

Dead Fashion

shouting. "Guys, guys, guys, GUYS!" The room goes silent. "STOP IT FOR A SECOND WILL YA?" Someone shouts from the crowd of people.

"You told us at the end of 2019 we were fine and that the lack of production was because you were creating a plan!" And the room erupts again. "LISTEN! I know, I know, I said that and I know what I said exactly, but you gotta remember things don't always work out that way, I mean for christ sakes guys, we are standing at the cusp of a possible pandemic here, the President of the US could announce any day a lockdown, we are trying to be as cautious as we can." The room continues to get louder and Damocha's secretary comes over to him and whispers in his ear. He then motions with his hand to try and get them to calm down, and after a few seconds they do. "Now just because things aren't looking too good and things may be the lowest they have ever been, it doesn't mean we don't have a plan."

"WELL THEN WHAT'S THE PLAN THEN?" Got screamed from the crowd followed by a bunch of "YEAH'S!" Damocha, not knowing what to do, decides to make up a plan on the spot, this is something he is quite good at, he's a very good bullshitter, this is how he even got his position, although he will never admit it.

"Now I have been here at DP for a long time and I ain't gonna let it go to waste, we helped create records like Funky town, and for fuck's sake artists like Lizzo and Prince! I mean, could we be any more successful? Sure recent success has been low and we don't have people flocking to our doors anymore to sign with us or produce with us, but it doesn't mean we don't have something. So everyone I would like to announce Project Urban X! This is a project to get back to our jazzy routes of things. We will be focusing on rebranding towards a younger audience, no more of this trying to please everyone bs, we have something immaculate brewing, something good. We will be seeking out and signing young artists who are from the city, born and raised, and have a deep connected root to the heart of Minneapolis! We will be not only focusing on diversity, but also including more women too! We already have five artists who could hit a top 100 on billboards who are ready to sign with us and in fact within the next two weeks will have them signed and ready to produce, even with this virus running around.

However we must remember that no matter what we think of this younger group of people, they are what will make us money, NOW! WHO WANTS TO MAKE SOME FUCKING MONEY?" And the group of people screams and cheers and Damocha stands there, realizing that he now has about two weeks before he loses his job and needs to come up with something quick. The whole idea was bullshit just to fuel their little fires and get them less hungry "OH! AND ONE MORE THING… FREE DRINKS AT THE BAR ON ME FOR THE REST OF THE NIGHT!" They all cheer even more and stand up and start hugging each other as if Nasa has just landed on the moon, this should certainly hold them over for a while. Damochas Secratary walks with him as he exits the room and walks into the massive hallway.

"Sir, umm, might I ask what exactly Project Urban X is?" He stops and looks down for a moment, before turning around and quietly speaks to her.

"Well let's just say it's an illusory, something you tell your kids, so they will stop crying ya know?" He looks at her and she looks super confused. "Ok fuck me, it's not fucking year ok, it's fair dust!"

"So you lied to all of those powerful people?"

"I didn't lie to them, I just misguided the whole truth."

"Sir, what exactly does that mean?" she asked as she looks like she is about to quit her job and become an alcoholic.

"Um, can you do me a favor?" He gets close to her. "I want you to call that young girl who raps in Japanese and English and has been blowing us up with emails and letters for the past eight months."

"Um, sir…"

"Yes?"

"I thought she was blacklisted, like she isn't supposed to be messed with?"

"Well sometimes you have to poke the sleeping bear."

"Ok but what should I tell her?"

"Tell her… That we want to meet with her regarding a potential signing."

"Sir why?"

"Because, this is the start of Project Urban X."

"That's insane, surely the company isn't that desperate for talent."

"We're not, I just think she could stir up enough controversy, that we could at least go over all her music and have a discussion with her."

"I don't think that's a good idea."

"And those thoughts are the reason you are secretary and not the CEO." He says as he smiles at her and walks away to go get lost in seemingly endless amounts of slot machines.

DP Records

It's been three weeks since I've been fired, my former boss (deceased) has been found and I saw his stupid body on the news with the headline saying sickening murder on 31st st. Damn right it was sick, that's the whole point, a sick death for a sick delusional person. Fire me?? Fat pig thought he could fire me, idiot. But I'm running low on cash and 2 late on rent notices so I need to figure something out. My song Somewhere over the Chemtrails has 50,000 views now. I'm very happy but at the same time I know it's over. The youtube pay ended up being about $114 so I'm literally about to become the thing I hate the most, I guess the saying is true, you either die a hero or you live long enough to see yourself become a villain. I've tried to find other jobs but I cannot find anything that pleases me, I wanna create music, and be creative. I don't want my creativity squished and squashed into thin particles. I want to be creative that's the problem everything is shutting down, No good jobs and the only places I can work are places in which

I'm dead inside since they are jobs no one wants and I'm not qualified to work anywhere else, there isn't anything for me to do, I'm so angry, not with myself or that pig Joe but the world, it's such a shithole, it forces me to live in a society where I'm forced to be uncreative, be in a dead end job, and not enjoy life. Words can barely describe how I feel. I just wanna kill and smash everything that gets in my way, ughh, I'm about to be homeless with severe depression and anxiety, not the best combo and I think I might decide to end it. I'm contemplating it, I really am, there is nothing left for me in this world god dammit I can't believe I've become this. I'm too pretty to die though, I can't die, I need something in my life right now, murder is not enough, I need something better, something that makes me happy, someone help me.

"Ms. Wall I'm very concerned with your marketability."

"My marka-what?"

"Marketability, it's a word we use to describe how well or easy it is to become marketable as in how many people would feel a connection, and if they like you, and are willing to buy your music and products. Karen, your music's all right."

"Thank you Mr. Damocha." Mr. Damocha is the CEO of DP Records. It's a recording agency located on Samoa Avenue southeast Saint Paul. he's in his late 50's, he's graying up and is a tad puggy. So far he has been a dick, but I'm being as nice as I can be although slaughtering this fuck wouldn't be a bad idea if he wasn't so famous.

"No Karen that's kinda all you have going for you, your music is alright it's tolerable and maybe could become popular with teenage girls and a specific group of them, but to be honest the market isn't that big for your type of music. Your rap could be good but then you refuse to do American hip-hop and want to do J-rap which to be honest doesn't seem like a smart decision."

Mr. Damocha I understand but it's what I want to do, I want to create music that I love, I know with a little boost and help I could become popular. The market doesn't seem like it's there but trust me it is, once people hear it they will like it. I

Dead Fashion

want to innovate the American music industry and it's time to bring J-rap and Alternative hip-hop into the mainstream in America. Please Mr. Damocha."

"Karen first off the oversized black shirts and long black jeans are unmarketable, the black eyeliner and dark makeup is also quite difficult to work with. Second, your music is ok, but the audience for hip hop is already so select. On top of that your fuck all non professional personality is horrible marketing. When I get a email for a business inquiry with a total of 11 fucks and 3 shits your lucky I didn't block your damn email like the rest of the industry and record labels have. You don't think I keep in touch with them? I was already told twice not to even respond to you but I felt a random urge to at least give you a shot. You see, everyone deserves a chance, even someone like you but you're difficult Karen… you really are. To be honest I don't know whether to throw you back out with the trash or this city or give you a chance." Fucking what? No way he just said that shit? He's lucky I don't put a fucking dagger in his eye. I grind my teeth and become a tunneled vision maniac on his neck and all of a sudden blood starts oozing from his body then I rip his head off.

"Karen!" He snaps his fingers "Earth to Karen! See this is another problem you Gen Z and your ADHD, how can I expect you to stay focused enough and on task to finish an album?"

"Mr Damocha trust me, please I'm a hard worker and when I get that spark I soar, just give me a chance to take the world by storm, I'm popular with Gen Z, trust me I'm one of them I know. I can do awesome. I just need a producer, a studio and good equipment. That's all you gotta give me. I'll do the rest with just one chance, please. "

"Maybe you would do good or maybe you won't but bottomline is you're difficult to produce."

"Mr. Damocha, my music is good enough though with a little money and a studio, think what I could do, I'm already semi popular and I haven't even used anything other than a iPhone and computer imagine what I could do with proper equipment and a producer, please please please. I'm at rock bottom, I have nobody left and without a job soon I will have nothing left. I encourage you to think about it, please the only way I can go is up Mr. Damocha." He sits staring at me then back at my record, he looks at my YouTube channel analytics and then sits and pondered for a moment before saying:

"Karen."

"Yes?"

"I'm willingly to make a deal, I think we can produce you-" I jump up and scream "WOOO FUCK YEAH FUCK YOU MOM AND FUCK YOU JOE!!" I realize what I did and look over at Damocha with fear and embarrassment as I start to sweat badly and my cheeks get red. I think about just merking him and then a voice in the back of my mind says do it, but I barely hold myself back and get back to reality. "Oh s-sorry." I say quietly as I look down. He is in shock but laughs after a few moments and with a smile says: "You're something else Karen I'll tell you that, but I'm not finished, the deal is I'll give you studio time to produce an 8 song album."

"Ok fuck yeah that's the compromise that's what I want, shit is easy bruh."

"Haha no listen the compromise is four of them have to be regular rap and the other 4 can be your J-rap you like, we will market it and see if A. You become popular and B. If you become popular we will see what is liked more, whatever is more popular you will be forced to make that type of music until your contract is done, got that?"

"Ummm sure." I think about it and realize this is my chance to show how much I can influence people and spread my music and Japanese rap, I'm skilled and fluent in Japanese and also in Japanese rap and fuck maybe I make a buck or two so I don't starve to death as well lol. I feel like I'm relatable and people will like my music but I just need that initial start. I need just a small push like a boat going into the water, I just need the initial push to float instead of being beached and stuck in the sand.

Dead Fashion

"I look forward to working with you. I hope you succeed, because if you don't it's my ass on line, I'm taking all the risk here, in fact I'm taking so many risks I shouldn't even be doing this but there is something special about you, something I can't quite put my finger on but I believe the spark is there."

"Thank you, thank you, thank you." I get up and shake his hand and as I'm about to walk out of his office he goes "My secretary will help you with your contract."

"Oh shit ok what I just gotta sign a paper or some shit?" He looks away from his computer and looks at me then bursts out in laughter.

"Not just a paper try like 50 papers don't worry she will help you, when you're finished she will escort you out and then we will call you to set up a studio time." Fuck you Paperwork… and Damocha. My smile fades as his ugly ass secretary with a Jew nose opens the door for me stupid haircut as well. This is gonna be a long afternoon but hey at least I won't be broke anymore… hopefully.

The Day

"Do you know who I am? I'm the bitch who's gonna BURN YOUR HOUSE DOWN! I'm The Akuma mother fucka I make The Akumas of hell look like children, stupid bitch you can't get damn sesame chicken and orange pork right??? Dumb broad you're lucky I don't stab you in stupid little old bitch throat!" The Chinese lady looks at me with a stern face or what I would see as a stern face under her mask as she doesn't understand a single word I just said. I take my mask down and say: "you don't know what I'm capable of you dumb old-" I stop myself, I'm very upset not only because they messed up my order but also because I'm being forced to wear a mask. I get it Covid is in the area, 82 cases a day right now but still this is fucking bullshit, I'm just trying eat some Great Wok. It's days like these that I feel like my life is a thriller, slasher movie and I for a moment contemplate splatting blood all around the restaurant but with all the Covid shit up and the stupid glass it would be hard and worthless. I leave the restaurant and walk back to my apartment. I'm about halfway home passing run down shithole buildings on empty streets. No one is out because everything is borderline locked down and other than the occasional person or car there is nothing. It's quiet and almost blissful for a moment Downtown Minneapolis feels still almost like a mosaic of Picasso or some famous other artist I don't know. But to intrude on my peace and slice through the silence to make come back to my modern psychotic senses, my phone starts to ring and after looking at it I realize, it's Jew nose…

"Karen? Or The Akuma?"

"Yeah you're talking to her!"

"You sound busy, I'll-"

"You hang up this phone and I'll march down to DP like Julius Caesar on his way to Egypt."

"Uh, well hey! I'm assuming from your response you know this but, this is Shelly from DP Records, I'm calling to say that with Covid restrictions, it has limited us with what we can do. Which means-" FUCK FUCK FUCK! Are you kidding me? Of course Covid would fuck everything up my one shot, my one FUCKING shot. Dammmmit I wanna kill the Chinese bastard that made this stupid fucking virus and lobotomize his ass. "We still are able to get you a day of studio time 7am to 7pm 12 hours due notice, but unless you are in the booth you must wear a mask and other than the producer and a equipment technician no one else is allowed with you? Now have you worked on your songs as per requested via the contract?"

"Yes I'm actually super ready to spit." I'm so fucking hyped right now I could kill somebody!!!

"Un-huh.. Well, does April 10th work?"

"Fuck yes! Haha are you kidding me I'm ready now!"

"Okayyy I like that enthusiasm Ms. Akuma, but you gotta chill out a little bit." Ms. Akuma, I love it, that's what everyone will call me now it's perfect. "April 10th 7-7 got it? That will be your first session, then depending on the circumstances we can get another session set up. So you got all of that?"

"Yessss!!"

"Good, producer Mike Clemons, one of our best producers, has heard some of your work and will be with you that day. He's taken a liking to you and is a very busy man so Mr. Damocha has asked to be super respectful and do your best, you're on thin ice." Ok, fucking bitch, no need to sour the mood.

"Got it, sweet thanks Jew nose- I mean Shelly!"

"Karen, if I may, some words of advice for you?"

"Haha, no thanks!" I end the phone call and I jump up and down, mentally of course this isn't the ending of an 80's movie, but this is perfect! My music is done, a real producer is involved and cash flow, fuck yes, I think I need to go cut some losers head off with… an axe? Ahh no, that's too lame and easy. What about a scythe? No! That's too… weird, hmm… I got it, a chainsaw, ha what could go wrong!?

Monday April 6th

It happened, the dream again. An empty office with maybe hundreds of hallways and no desks, no computers and not a single soul, bright lighting and only the hum of what seemed like air ventilation. It felt and looked like an office but no one was there, no one was working and nothing. This is the third time this has happened in almost a month. I wander the halls with nothing ever happening. It silences and feels like an eternity. Except tonight something did happen. Wandering like usual wanting something to happen and or someone to come to me. Occasionally I can hear the cries of people. Sometimes it almost sounds like the endings of all my victims in their final moments. One of the lights went out in the hallway. I walked under it and then in silence, I closed my eyes and heard Joe, my former boss, screaming in agony and then the memory of me picking each of his fingernails off his hand plays almost as if it's a movie. I open my eyes to the sounds of screaming in the distance. It's a foreign scream as I have never heard this one before. I remember most of the screams but this one was not one of them. The scream very distant started to get louder. Then the lights started to flicker and even though I panicked I did not run. I stood in place waiting and then rustling as if hundreds of footsteps sprinted toward me and was loud and brash and shook the ground, then the hallway started to slowly turn completely black as the screams got to its loudest and then everything around me went black as the screams sounded as if they were right in front of me then all of a sudden a creature of 50 maybe 60 faces I only saw it for a moment jumped and screamed at me. The scream was foreign because it was all of the screams and sounds made by my victims as one scream. Then abruptly I woke up and was sweating so badly I looked like I pissed myself and maybe I did. My heart was racing and my breathing was shaky. Cut to the present and now I'm sitting on my couch shirtless with just my bottom part of my underwear on sipping red wine to calm me down. I look at the clock and it reads 5:48am. My TV is on, and I'm watching the early news.

"Well Covid ya know has really messed things up I mean Hennepin county has now had 300 total cases, the quarantine is working a little bit but people need to get back to their lives. When can we expect to see that?"

"Don't worry Diane like I said earlier Covid is rampant but the virus with the help of the quarantine should not be a problem. So far it's been three weeks and we are looking at this virus being gone, not eradicated but not a problem by middle June. When it warms up a little bit we should start to see a drop and we can expect to get to our normal lives by early July, so don't worry."

"Thank you for your time Dr. Stevens."

"My pleasure". Early July huh? Wow that would be great right now stuff is bad I hate being mostly stuck at home, I work out almost daily but the gym has been closed so right now I've occasionally jogged each day. I've watched a lot of news, played a lot of video games, watched stocks and have had more gas station food now then I did in my entire life.

Dead Fashion

White zero sugar monsters, pizza, gas station sushi and everything else that's junk I have borderline living on, with the occasional Chinese food, McDonald's and Taco Bell, but this isn't like me. For the past three years I had done nothing but eat a healthy and balanced diet and occasionally mixed these things in. In four months I have started to undo three years of work to my body, to become the best version of me. This is horrible I can feel my muscles weakening, I can feel the fucking flubber filling the lining of my stomach that you see them remove on my 600 pound life. The monstrous amounts of shit going down my gullet, the disgusting and vile being I have become, I'm worse than I have ever been. I'm at my lowest and I mean fucking lowest. I need to get back on track starting now! But… Red wine at 6 in the morning is sooooo fucking good and it really hits the tiny itch in the back of my brain.

    I wait a little bit and then WCCO's morning show comes on at 6 and I watch it until about 7 and then finalize some of my lyrics for the 10th, I basically have nothing to do, so apart of me wants to go back to sleep but the other part of me knows if I go back to sleep I will only have the dream again, so I take two Xanax and then I become so high I don't remember what I'm doing, then I pass out, is this what life should be like?

    Later…

    I woke up at 4:30pm with my head pounding but I didn't have the dream so that's a plus, but still I feel like I can't even breathe. I manage to fall out of bed and onto the floor, then I puke white… weird shit up and it makes me wonder if it was from the shit I'm eating or the drugs I have been numbing my brain with. Then I clean it up with some bed sheets lying on the floor; I need to wash them, but the smell reeks throughout the house so I use febreeze that I normally use when the smell of bodies lingers and then the smell goes away for a while. Piles of my clothes sitting next to my door that I need to get out of my apartment and into the wash along with garbage scattered throughout the apartment. I really do not want to go to the laundry room on the other side of the complex either, but

I'm starting to think I have no choice, but being so lazy is fun. The sun shines onto my face, but it doesn't feel right, it feels fake, everything feels fake, almost not real, the drugs don't help to suppress this feeling I suppose.

I go to the bathroom and when passing the mirror I see my ungroomed appearance. Normally I care a lot about how I look but for some reason I don't really care, a very strange feeling. I walk out of my apartment still looking the same and make a quick trip to Casey's where the girl working the counter side eyes me and for a moment I imagine dragging her body out out of here and throwing her off the Wells Fargo building and trying to hear the splat on the sidewalk, but I do nothing about it because I don't have the strength or mental to do it right now. I'm conflicted because I'm scared of nothing yet feel fear, but I don't know what.

J&R Public Accountants

"Hey Mr. Rocker, this is quite a surprise. I was just finishing up some lyrics when you called, most people don't want to meet in person these days now that we are in this "pandemic" so this must be serious." This mask is killing my face and is making my nose itchy but I pull through it, like a goddess.

"Oh it is Ms. Wall, I'm concerned with your finances this year... Specifically your gains."

"Well, Pilates helps."

"No I'm not meaning your muscle gains or your weight gains, I'm meaning your income. It doesn't make sense Karen when we did your taxes about a month and a half ago you were on the brink of bankruptcy just like you are every year yet somehow you get a magical sum of money classified as a "Donation" in a yen format that gets wired and transferred to your account and this sum is always the same amount, ¥9,075,822. Now this is somehow always overlooked and is never noticed each year but I see the same amount even calculated for inflation too. And I wanna know what it is!"

"It says right there" I point at the word in front of the sum on the sheet of paper. "Donation."

Dead Fashion

"Karen don't bullshit me, I've been doing this for almost 22 years now, people don't 'donate' money to someone, especially since it's the same amount every single time. You classified as being below the poverty line this year making barely $35,000 a year working at a fucking pizza place and yet you live alone… in the heart of city, I mean of course not high class but still you live off nothing. Karen this irregular income will eventually get flagged you know that."

"Well what can I do to stop having a random person wire money to my bank account? I've already had over ten meetings with the bank about this and when we tried to trace it back the bank can't find anything and we are assuming it's someone with the wrong wire transfer who is giving me the money, hence it's a donation."

"Not how that works" he says, breaking eye contact with me and looking down at the papers. "Karen I'm trying to look out for you-"

"Oh, look out for me? Oh wow, you're such a strong and brave man Mr. Rocker! What next? Want me to drop under the table and 'thank' you for your hard work, protecting me from the big bad IRS?" I say in a very obvious baby tone.

"Karen, NO! I'm just saying, you're using this money to stay alive so I need to know where it's coming from, Karen please."

"I told you I don't know! What more do you want from me motherfucker? I'm a struggling musician. I use anything I can to stay alive, trust me if I was so worried of the IRS, I would not be in this fucking country, it doesn't matter anyways, I got a record label to sign me so… Soon 90k will look like nothing, it won't even be noticeable. Soon I'll be making five times, maybe even six times more money in one month than you will make in a year."

"Un-huh Karen if you won't tell me at least listen to me."

"Oh hear we go again, HAHA." I lean back in the very still office chair thinking about what this guy's head would look like on my shelf.

"Karen 90 thousand is not a lot of money for this area, that will barely make you through the year the way your living in the city, so here's my advice, move into the far suburbs just barely outside of the main suburbs and live and work from home, save more of your money, your basically living by doing nothing don't get used to it but work around it, don't waste your money on bills and other random crap live cheap and you'll never have to work a day in your life and you can continue with your music. And who knows maybe you'll get a hit and go big. Although in this day and age it's very unlikely." I stare at him for almost 15 seconds, dead stare emotionless, no empathy, my ears start to ring as he says something but the ringing draws it out. I finally break into my voice, not breaking my dead stare, but starting to smile.

"Thank you so much for the idea, but right now my label is in the city and I need to stay here." I say softer, holding back the urge to strangle him and for a moment I imagine my hands around his neck and choking him out until he becomes a meat sack, but then I quickly flash back to reality with the flash of his death in my mind. "I get it as my accountant. You need to look out for me but I don't need you to. So do me a favor and finger fuck your bussy because I'm done with you. Worry about your own damn money because I DON'T NEED IT!" I say firmly.

"Karen, don't do that."

"Do what?"

"Base everything on luck, it never works ok? Look, I've seen people lose everything because of luck."

"Rocker, do you know what I want to do? I want to-grab you by your ears and scream as loud as I can into your face and tell you the same fucking thing I've been saying since the first minute we started talking, I DON'T NEED YOU TO LOOK AFTER ME!" He quickly stands up and slams his fist on his desk.

"KAREN! DON'T FUCKING DO THIS TO YOURSELF, THIS WILL RUIN YOUR-"

I get up and quickly put my airpods in my ears to drown him out, then I flip him off with my back turned to him as I leave his office. I can hear muffled screams but Dancing Queen by ABBA drowns him out perfectly. Yep, I'm feeling frisky today. It felt like the 70's today. The song continues as I walk through downtown, and seeing very few people around and the buildings and the fresh air just made me feel a certain type of way, almost like I wanna overthrow the government with a little bit of Montana forest vibes, a very… very weird combination.

The Wrecking Ball

It's the night before my big day, the day history is made. The day I become an icon and blow the world up. I decided to celebrate by bar hopping until about 2 A.M the morning of my recording session and then go to the hottest club in the metro area, The Wrecking Ball. It's honestly a really stupid name but everyone loves it and maybe I can find someone here to have some fun with. I'm starting to think that people in this town have some sort of disease as everyone seems to have this weird feeling almost as if they are brainwashed into "being normal".

"I never quite understood how a society like ours functions with the terrible deeds and terrible things people do in their daily lives yet somehow everything is some perfect happy family society. Everything feels like an anime where the world is perfect and everything is good. But how can a world feel like that when the truth is it's evil and corrupt. How can a society which treats the poor like shit and homeless like animals somehow manage to become the dominant life form on the planet? It all doesn't make sense humans are… So irrational and stupid yet we are the most intelligent life form, how?"

"Look lady, I just need 19 dollars for the drink. I don't need a psychology lesson."

"19 Dollars!!!! How in the fucking fuck does that work?"

"Well we aren't supposed to be open because this "virus" shut everything down so we are getting taxed out of our minds plus we are basically ruining this shit illegally now are you gonna give me 19 or what?" I hand him a 20 and he slides me my drink at the bar. I smile at him and grab my drink plus my dollar and then as I'm walking away I imagine smashing this bottle over his bald grotesque head and then sticking pieces of the glass in his eyes but I restrain myself so as to not get caught. I decided instead to scope the place out and see if there are any chicks and dudes who are worth my time and after spotting a super hot chick like I mean the hottest chick in the city I strut towards her and she eyes me and I reach the standing table she's at and start to talk.

"I thought the U.S didn't have a Monarchy yet I somehow see the Princess here in front of me."

"Haha that's a good one. I've never heard that one before, what's your name?"

"Karen."

"Veronica."

…

"You must think I'm stupid or something huh Karen?"

"What? Why would I think that?"

"Because I'm out here in this club while Covid is going around destroying our lives, you must think I'm some freak Conservative who is against abortion and is a Trump supporter don't you?"

"Well let me ask you this Veronica, are you fat?"

"No."

"Do you drive a truck that is suped up to sound super loud and annoy the shit out of everyone you drive by?"

"No."

"Do you wear overalls and own some fucking stupid farm?"

"No."

"Do you wear trucker hats?"

"No."

"Then there's your answer, no I don't think you're some fat pig republican who thinks Covid isn't real, and that you are a bad person. We've been in this Lockdown for three weeks and nothing seems to be getting better, the entire world is at a halt and with there being nothing to do or see or play with or eat, it's kinda fucking hard to live life. In fact I see this as you being an intellectual, you are going out and getting your party on to defy the odds and the corrupt government ran by that orange oompa loompa douche bag to come out here and get it all out of your system before anything gets over the top. I think this is amazing and I think your way smarter than all those fucking losers staying at home."

"Karen… You have a way with words, I guess I-I never really looked at it that way. Do you think I'm attractive?"

"Woah what the freak, where did this come from?" I lean back a little.

"Oh I knew it I'm sorry I just thought maybe you were into me or something, my bad."

"Well what if I told you I am though." I now carry my distance close to her at the standing table and caress her hand on the table. She looks at me and a slight smile and blush goes over her face, fuckin right this bitch is into me. She leans over the table and I do too, she smothers her lips into mine and we make out over the loud EDM playing in the background and our kiss goes to a full blown make out with our glasses spilling, people are us start to scream "Hellllll Yeah."

"Oh that's hot as shit."

"Damn I wish I was the girl on the right."

We leave the club really late into the night, I don't even know the time anymore and we manage our way back to her apartment, luckily she's rich as fuck clearly and only lives a little bit away from the club in some fancy sky high apartments and while I'm a little drunk I am sober enough to see and understand everything around me and this bitch is hot as fuck and has got money. We arrive at her apartment making out as we go through the door she gets undressed and she has a perfectly tan body, medium sized eyes with black and dark blue eyeliner and shadow. Her hair black and her nose small and perfect, so delectable. Her tits are immaculate, her C- no D cup tits are also perfectly tan she must use a tanning bed instead of natural light. Her tits are so perfect and are mesmerizing as she flops onto the bed and they bounce around and the bounce speed along with the way they flops at the downward motion via gravity shows that her left tit is slightly bigger as judging by this information it must weigh around 9.4 pounds, while her right tit also perfect is slightly smaller as the speed on the downward motion is slightly slower meaning less weight and her right tit is only about 9.1 sadly. They are perfect, my god they even have a birthmark on the right tit. Her body is amazing as well, skinny, shaven and has a nice plump ass. We do the thing I've been trying to do all night with her and it was the best experience I've ever had with a women, honestly might be the best ever almost made me rethink my life choices and become a full blown lesbian and marry this chick and have some kids and live a nice life, but I'm too far gone for that. I fall asleep as the sun is coming up and once again that itch and ache that keeps tormenting me finally ceases after all of that plus two tablets of Ecstasy of course.

RINGGGGGGGG! I wake to my phone going crazy and busy as I'm in my room. This revelation shocks me more than my phone buzzing sporadically with the sun shining right at my eyes through the window of my bedroom, but I play it off. I missed my phone twice before grabbing it and sliding it, it's an unknown number.

"Hello?" I say sluggish.

"Hey Karen this is Mike Clemons the producer working with you at DP, just a quick question the studio is open and I've been here for 25 minutes without you showing up."

"Oh sorry I stayed up really late at this chick's house, she was-."

"I- don't need the details of your hookup, can you just be down here in the next 25 -35 minutes? I'm mixing some of these beats you made and honestly they are some of the best

Dead Fashion

beats I've seen someone make for the genre, especially at this studio, helluva a job girl."

"Thanks, I'm goated. What can I say"

"So see you down here?"

"Yes captain!"

I'm still not understanding how I got from Veronica's to my house last night, there is no number in my phone, no pictures or videos which I usually take either of us fucking or their mutilated bodies so it's quite odd. Also the club I went to last night must've got caught because as I was walking to the studio I walked by and the building looked abandoned almost as if no soul had touched it in years, strange.

I go to the building and as I get to the studio it seems almost like an underground place, the walls are just brick and from the outside, you would never ever think that it was a studio for recording, let alone anything at all other than an abandoned building. I walk into the building from the broken down concrete sidewalk, the buildings around are in shambles and with this Covid going around they definitely aren't getting any use. The building on the inside is very nice and actually well maintained, the walls are painted half red on the top portions and black on the bottom portion. I arrive in an entrance room, one that is very beautiful. It has a bunch of nice red leather chairs that look like they cost more than my apartment. There is a glass desk with a lady sitting at it. Records up on the walls along with little trinkets and other items scattered all over the place. It smells like a mixture of lemon and weed and some other very strong smell I can't quite put my finger on… maybe pomegranate. I walk into the booth where a guy and two other casually dressed men sit with a huge mixing station. The one guy who greets me is Mike Clemons, tall, older but not as old as Damocha and is in amazing shape, must have a rigorous workout routine for an old white guy. He says that he's excited to hear what I've got. I recorded the first song Dice of a Generation is what I called it and when I finish I go to Mike and the other guys.

"So what did you think?"

"Well Karen it's definitely something. There is something here although I think we need to remix the beat."

"The one I provided is not good enough?" I chuckle nervously, "I spent almost a week mixing that one, it's supposed to be my best one."

"Well no it's fine it's just it could be a lot better if we remix it, here you can sit with us and do it as well, I think we got some fire brewing up here but I think it could be even hotter ya know?"

"Oh ok." god this guy is cool and is the most supportive guy I've met in this industry yet!

2 hours later…

"Karen, it's been two hours. I think we need to scrap the beat, we can re-record a new beat. Seriously, this isn't working."

"I didn't come here just to get put down. I spent weeks on this, you don't get it!"

"Ayo Kev leave the booth real quick. I need to talk to her." I watch Kevin/Kev leave the room and go down the hall towards the lobby. "Karen, take a seat."

"Why? I don-"

"That wasn't an option, it was an order. What's wrong with scrapping the beat realistically?"

"Well it's mainly because I like it and I-" SLAP! Mike slapped me across the face and for a moment I thought about smashing his entire skull into the glass panel that separates the booth and the studio itself, but I have too much respect for him and quite frankly I am not in a violent mood today, he's lucky.

"Karen don't lie to me, give me the real reason or do I need to give it to you? I get it, it's your beat, you mixed it and made it, however you gotta remember where you are. You are in a studio ok? Not your stupid apartment studio setup either, you are in a professional studio in a professional setting, now you could leave right now go back to your depression-filled life full of bullshit and making music for a literal shit hole corner of the internet and throw shit at the wall until it sticks or you could let us help you out, make a good ep and song for that

Dead Fashion

matter and bring you into the spotlight, you got the talent you just gotta rely on other people."

"I can't." I said softly.

"What?"

"I said I CAN'T!" I damn near break into tears as I look down towards my legs. "When I was growing up, I didn't have anyone, no parents, no siblings to rely on, it was all me, I never had anyone who I could trust in helping me, everyday the same shit and fucked up world, every goddamn day I was neglected and beat like a fucking slave, I've learned to trust no one for anything, because it never works ever, that's why I wanna keep this beat."

"Karen it's ok I'm only here to make you better, now you may not trust us or hell me, but let's do it this one time, redo the entirety of it. Just let go. Here you know what? Take this.

"What the fuck is even that?"

"It'll calm you down, maybe make you rethink shit."

I take it then after a bitter taste hits my mouth I ask again. "Dude what is this?"

"The best ecstasy you'll have in your life."

"What the fu-"

...

I wake up naked in the recording booth with shit everywhere including my bra hanging on the microphone, the lights are off and it's basically pitch black except for a few small lights still on. I try to get up but my head is pounding and I'm so light headed I feel all the blood rush from my head, it's like I'm in slow motion. I look over to the side of the small couch I'm laying on and see a big piece of paper with something written on it but my vision is so blurry It's hard to read. Finally my vision kinda starts to get back and I see the piece of paper and grab it. Attached is a key taped to the back and the paper reads: "Karen your one crazy bitch I'll tell you that, never seen anybody party like you do, your clothes are in the booth somewhere ha u crazy as fuck. Also here's the key to lock up, you'll love the new beat for Dice of a Generation btw."

That… motherfucker.

Saturday April 26th

After days of recording and re recording and re recording and… fuck it you get it. We finished the 10 song debut album/ep as a testing waters for audiences. I let the few people that follow me and keep in touch with The Akuma/me and let them know I have a big project coming out and to spread the word. The album was set to release on the 24th and we needed to start building up hype. DP got some smaller interviews and even got Dice of a Generation to be played on a bunch of radio stations to promote it. Mike and I finish up some of the final stuff and we continue on with our lives, until premiere day. Fast forward to the 24th and the "EP" as we called it is released titled "The Red, White and Black" and after a week, listens on spotify, youtube and apple all together plus a few other smaller services ends up being around 350k listens fucking beast only one ep got me some heat, what can I say I'm just a fucking beast I guess. Fast forward to today where I got called into the record label. According to the lady at the front desk who was different from the jew nose, it was urgent and I needed to get there ASAP. Of course she had one of those bitchy, nasally voices which kinda put me in a bad mood, but I digress.

20 minutes later

"Karen you are such a bitch, you never talk to me or hell any of us!" My Mexican friend Erica tells me over facetime as I make my way to DP, I'm walking with my brand new generation two airpods in and I am not paying attention to her, as I am admiring the perfect spatial audio these things have and how awesome the noise cancellation is too.

"Sorry I am in a hurry trying to get to work!"
"Aren't you like a music artist?"

Dead Fashion

"Uh, duh c'mon you are literally one of my only friends, yes I am a music artist, have you listened to any of my stuff I've been sending you?"

"Karen I don't like that weird shit you make, I'm proud of my sister for making it, but I ain't a fan sorry."

No need." I say as I continue to speed walk to work, it's still a little chill out "I don't need your lame ass opinion anyways."

"Hey calm down now sis, who was the one who bought you that nice studio mic, for your birthday two years ago, so you could start making music?"

"And I love you for it, doesn't mean I don't get to be a bitch to you!" I say with a smile, looking at my reflection in the darkish phone screen seeing my beautiful lipstick "Look Erica, when the whole covid thing blows over, we need to grab drinks, can I count on you for drinks?"

"As long as you're buying, Ms. Famous Musician!" She says in a mocking baby tone.

"Ok now I draw the line and I'm hanging up sorry." I wave to her.

"Wait I-" I end the call before she can continue.

...

I arrived at DP records after taking an uber which btw was the worst rideshare I have ever done. The guy didn't speak good english and worst of all he was Somolian! Like I'm already in a bad mood then trying to rush to the office while he can't speak a lick of english is hard even with GPS. And For the record I'm not racist I just hate people. I lived in Japan for damn near 4 years, I learned Japanese fluently and became a... nevermind. Point is I just hate people in general, most people piss me off and whenever I look at someone I don't go: "eww their skin color is different than mine" I usually go: "I wonder what their head would look like in my freezer."

I walk in and I'm immediately ushered to Damochas office, not even getting time to put my mask on, where two gentlemen in matching black designer suits sit with Damocha and Mike.

"Karen please sit down." Damocha urges me and I do, I sit right next to Mike in clear view of everyone. The room is so stale and the air seems thick, everyone with blue standard masks and seems like there is something big going on. Damocha says looking at his desk "Karen this is-" and before Damocha could finish he is immediately cut off by the guy on my left in the suit.

"Karen The Akuma, it is a pleasure to meet you, I would shake your hand except well I'm not trying to spread anything."

"Then why did you fly here instead of just doing this on FUCKING ZOOM?" Damocha gets a little hostile. The room is silent for about 15 seconds after that before I finally break the silence.

"Please just call me Karen, it's super easy and has fewer syllables." He replies to me

"No I will not, no offense Ms. Akuma but your real name carries no value to us."

What type of villain ass monologue is that?

"Oh um ok? Why exactly am I here then? And no offense to you Mr. fancy suit guy, it's just you're quite slow so pick up the pace." Damocha and Mike both stare at me like this dude was about to blow this bitch up like Hector in Breaking bad.

"Ms. Akuma, we are here for business" the first guy says.

"Business involving you." the second guy says in a way deeper tone, this guy should've been the one talking the entire time. I put on a smile and say:

"Great you finish each other's sentences, the wonder twins should be afraid of you two."

"Damocha if you don't get your talent to stop talking back this deal is through."

Damocha was sitting in his chair smiling before realizing that everyone had their eyes on him, he got serious and said with the smile now gone: "Karen please just listen." I sigh.

Dead Fashion

"My name is Gary Stevens. This is Sylvester BrockMoller but everyone calls him Brock for short. Ms. Akuma, we can make you big."

"What are you talking about?"

"We are looking for a small independent musician to do music on The Tonight Show starring-"

"JIMMY FUCKING FALLON? You're kidding right, this is all fake and you guys are firing me right?" I look over at Damocha shaking his head no while smiling. I stand up and hug Gary and he starts screaming get off me, clearly he's anti-social but whatever a hug from a woman never hurts so he should suck it up. "You guys were complete dicks, why? Why not just say hey we are The Tonight show join us and none of this needs to happen."

"Ms. Akuma this is a big deal please keep this serious, we just had Kesha on last week and we want you to perform Dice of a Generation live for The Tonight Show. Only thing is you would perform it from here since the show is being ran from home right now and you would just have a quick segment just the song and maybe talk with Jimmy for about 5 minutes and call it a day, bring your listens up, make some new fans, it's only a win-win for you.

"Let's do it, I'm fucking ready aghhhh." I said as I was so pumped up my blood pressure was probably 220/140." "So when do we do this?"

"Well you would perform on the 29th for the mid weekly series called What are you doing Wednesdays, it's our biggest episodes of each week and will get you the most traction, so you would do that on the 29th but we can start the paperwork right now and get it done.

"P-P-Paperwork?!?!?!" 'Yes we have to." A tear comes down my eye.

Monday April 28th

"Good Monday morning I'm Christine Evans on the morning show here at WCCO, our big story for this morning, more remains of Local Italian business owner Joe Romano were found, he was 51 years old and police say was slaughtered in the night after work. No security camera footage was found with him or the attacker in it and as of this time there are no key suspects. Johnny good morning, what can you tell us about this sickening act? Was it premeditated or not?"

"Well Christine that's a good question because while yes the body was dismembered and put into different trash bags that doesn't mean it's premeditated, see this happens all the time ya know."

"Un-huh."

"You know somebody gets upset or ticked off and murders somebody then realizes what they've done then try to cover it up, however the precision with the time of the kill plus where it happened made it look like whoever did this had been planning for some time. In fact the knife wounds weren't chaotic like they didn't know what they were doing. The knife wounds were all in very vital spots to make sure he went down quickly, most of the time even marine or military members don't do this type of precision work in hand to hand combat let alone a civilian."

"So are you saying this maybe mob work or like maybe even mafia."

"I'm not saying that, I am saying whoever did this is sick and dangerous and knows what they are doing."

"Thank you John."

"Thanks Christine."

"Now here's Mark with the Weather."

Sick huh? That's what they think, Interesting.

The Tonight Show

I sat in my room. I was told my makeup needed to be very nice but not over done so for the past four hours I've sat here trying to get it perfect. Black eyeliner, a little blush and dark red cherry lipstick complimenting my hair which I curled to perfect curls which took most of the time and while this only took me about thirty minutes I have redone this about nine or ten times now. I finally am not happy but I'm about 10 minutes from being on so I need to let it go. Sometimes I wish I had an actual manager. These things would be easier, then I also realize they probably wouldn't live long enough to be my manager.

10 minutes later...

I joined this very secure zoom call with about 45 people in it, all probably producers and other people of that sort and all I hear is them giving Jimmy his next lines while a commercial for insurance plays on the show. The audience which is a fake sound bite since no one is actually at the studio due to Covid so all you hear is the fake sounds of clapping you could probably find on YouTube when you look up clap tracks for tv shows or something along those lines. I sit waiting for my introduction and as I do I feel like I'm being watched, which isn't possible since I'm not on screen yet it feels weird and my palms start to sweat along with my body and I feel like I'm going to explode, my body is burning. "Karen, Karen listen to me you can do this." I say to myself, the music queues from which I finally hear "Ok Karen you are on in 1 minute." And just like that 2 minutes had past in a matter of what felt like 2 seconds

"Hahaha welcome back America, our next guest is someone you might not have heard of." Oh fuck, oh fuck.

"Now when I heard her music I was like wow this girl has some talent, I got it recommended to me when I was on my treadmill, doing incline walking... while having a milkshake," *audience laugh track plays* "So I saw this lady and to my eyes I figured oh wow it's another one of those small artists which let's face it a lot of them are not the greatest, but something felt different about her and next thing you know my figure reaches over the song I don't know if you guys have heard of it called Dice of a Generation? I clicked it and played it. Yes I did, and let me say the words she was saying and rhythm spoiler alert. She's a rap artist and it was beautiful, so I decided to get her on the show. Everyone please welcome thanks to Zoom, Karen/The Akuma." *Clap track plays,* I see myself pop up on the screen and my heart drops as maybe hundreds of thousands are watching.

"Karen it's a pleasure to have you on this show, now of course you know our day to day lives have been hindered by the uh... big C" Laugh track plays again.

"But I want to fully indulge myself into the world of a small artist like yourself and how have you been affected in this time?" everything stops and slows down and I feel like I'm about to burst, everything around me is blurred and for a moment I almost feel fear. Not because I'm scared to say anything but I simply look awful, my makeup is a little messed up, I could care less about what the world thinks of what I say, I'm more scared of what the world thinks of my body.

"Uhh well it actually hasn't affected me that much to be honest with you."

Jimmy looks baffled on the shitty zoom call and kinda looks to the side, maybe at some producer or something before speaking again.

"Really? Covid hasn't messed up your workflow or even ethics like there's gotta be something ha right?"

"Well no I'm a hermit I really am, and I don't really do much other than sit around and record music, I guess maybe the partying but other than like the nightclubs I don't do much that got affected."

"Ok so now with Dice of a generation this is a statement about covid right, correct me if I'm wrong but when I listened to the song one part spoke to me." What the fuck is this guy talking about? " 'Quittin' time, maybe it's a new-age, crazy ain't it? History repeated with a fresh new coat of paint.' Now that really spoke to me because in this time that we are living in it seems like this is a problem, history right now is just repeating itself and right now sorry to get political but our current administration isn't doing anything about it."

"W-what are you talking about?" I laughed, "The point of the song is about how our generation is shunned and put off and away treated differently like we are some sort of mad and dumb group of people and I wrote a song about how I felt in that situation mainly because I was sick and tired of being treated like a baby. I just felt like our generation doesn't have

Dead Fashion

any of us who are an inspiration to young people, nobody stands up for themselves anymore and I just think somebody needed to put some fuel to the flame."

"Incredible well Karen I'm sorry we are gonna have to cut this short due to time slots being so short so if you wanna listen to The Akuma's new Ep, 'The Red, White and Black' it's on almost all streaming services for music and we are gonna play her biggest song Dice of a Generation as the end of the show Karen thank you so much, I would shake your hand but I uh- ha" Laugh track plays.

"But I-" The screen closes and I am removed from the zoom call... "What the fuck just happened?" I say outloud to myself as I get removed from everything. That was awful, Why was he trying to make everything about that bullshit covid, and also why the fuck was he being so weird. That was just awful. I feel like I just lost brain cells after that maybe I need something to fuck me up or I need a nap, hey maybe both? Oh yeah and I need to talk to Damocha maybe in person so I can shove a foot up his ass for allowing me to do this, like seriously after doing that I feel like I need to kick my own ass for being an idiot and spending time being nervous and getting ready for some big load of shit. Ok seriously I need a sleep.

May 3rd

Some time has passed and the listeners while they spiked for about two days are now proceeding to drop again. Everything is so strange right now, like everything is so fast paced. I used to only get a bloodlust for people during the night and could almost be completely uncompromisable in my day to day, but something is off. For example The Tonight Show, I remember guests having massive segments on his show. I mean how else would the show be run, however I felt like my time was super short. Shorter than usual. When I asked Damocha over the phone since all of a sudden we care about covid protocols and he said it was because it was all in the moment however that just doesn't feel right, I know normally when your in the moment things go fast but, when I rewatched my segment it was only about five minutes long, ridiculous. I'm very distraught and cannot handle things anymore. Which leads me back to what I was saying, I'm getting unhinged almost animal like. When I was in Japan this wasn't a problem. I was killing at one point 3-5 people a night, and now I think I get it. Being cooped up and nobody going out it's hard to relieve my… tick. I'm at a loss while writing this because even up until not just a month ago I was fine, so it has to be covid right? Surely I'm not making assumptions and pre diagnosing myself. Anyways today has been slow so far and- *ring ring* Fuck off.

I grab my phone from out of my pocket and look at the caller id… Mom, fuck me to tears.

"Hey mom, what's up?"

"Sweetheart, I was with my friend while getting my nails done at the salon, a very nice new place in town we should go, they have beautiful wall coloring and the lady is super nice."

"Mom get to the point."

"Anyways, so I'm there with her and she says to me 'your daughters the emo girl with the blackish blonde hair who dressed like some boy who's going through depression right?' and I replied 'yes'

"What the fuck Mom!?"

"Hold on sweetie. Then she said 'well I heard someone who sounded like her on the tv and she looked just like your daughter' so I googled your name and I saw you on a TV show."

"Yes mom, I was on the tonight show."

"With Jimmy Fallon right?"

"YES WITH JIMMY FUCKING FALLON MOM! Who else would it be? Joseph Fallon? The younger, more asinine brother who only speaks in moon runes?"

"Karen Jackie Wall! Do not raise your voice at me missy. I was just asking a simple question. Stop being a goober."

"What?"

Dead Fashion

"I said stop being a goober."

"... Holy shit mom you're stuck in the 90's, who the fuck calls someone a goober?"

"Hey don't you talk shit about the 90's, if the 90's weren't so badass you wouldn't be alive."

"The only good thing that came out of the 90's was the music and me."

"God Karen you're so obsessed with the damn music, first Japan and now this."

"It's my whole life and always has been Mom! And don't bring that up, I don't wanna talk about that right now."

"Kare Bear, I think you should come to Washington this winter and spend some time with us. I mean for crying out loud we haven't seen you for almost 3 years, you went to Japan then back to the twin cities right as we moved out here. We think you're avoiding us."

"I am."

"Don't be like that, come spend time with us out here please just this winter, one time Karen."

"UGH! Fine, if the travel restrictions clear up a little I'll come out there and spend a week or two with you and dad."

"Promise?"

"Yes mom I promise, you have my word."

"Yes, Yes, YESSSSS! Sweetie, it will be so much fun."

"Sure will."

"Oh and by the way have you started making money now that you're on TV?"

"Mom... I am not just on TV! I am making music. But as a matter of fact I am starting to make money at a decent rate compared to working slave jobs. I signed a three year contract with DP records in the cities, they are one of the biggest record labels in the state, nice people (lie) too that do good work."

"So are you making more than in Japan?"

"Mom! I said to stop! Fuck, you just always gotta hit the wounds don't ya? No, Japan was a can of worms, not even close to it. I hate that, I won't go back to that... place."

"But you made more money like more than what me and dad were making in fivr years."

"Yes and I still receive small amounts of money from them, but that work was awful, the NDA and no breaks and forcing me to do a bunch of things all because some FUCKING JAPANESE GUY WANTS TO…. nevermind, I DON'T want to talk about it!"

"Hey, Hey, that's alright sweetie, it's in the past being an icon over there is different from here."

"I know and that's why I completely left that brand and restarted, it was easy since I knew what everybody already wanted so I just redid it as an 'up and coming artist' and it worked and I'm more happy now." I also get more pleasure out of murders in the US anyways.

"That's good, I'm glad Kare bear but have you been eating well at least?"

"Well if Ramen, Taco bell, and Chinese are good then I would say so." complete lie. Yes sometimes I do occasionally eat those things but I have a very well balanced and nutritious diet that is not only good for the body but also helps me build up a stronger physique. I'm not an idiot, but everyone else is.

"Eh… Well at least it's something. As long as you're staying alive haha."

"Gosh mom you're a hoot."

"Thanks sweetheart." After about 15 seconds of complete silence I realize that I have spent almost 10 minutes on the phone and that I need to wrap this up like a birthday present, so I do the old midwest goodbye.

"Welp mom, I got some stuff to do so I will talk to you later."

"Ok sweetie I can't wait for you to come down this winter, I'm so excited I get to see my baby!"

"Me too mom, me too."

BORED

After about a week my life was kinda boring, I basically did nothing for the entire week other than workout, this is gotta be a new personal best for an amount of time with no bloodshed and I'm not even lying. It's been about three weeks without a kill and I'm very distraught. Everyone is being a bunch of bitches and being scared to go out, at first it was great because only the pussy's didn't go out but now everyone is all spooked. This Covid thing still doesn't quite make sense to me other than the fact that people are getting infected by it. And now there is all this political talk and it's kinda pissing me off. I can't go five minutes without hearing something on youtube or the news about Donald Trump this and Joe Biden that. I don't give a shit about an oversized oompa loompa and a man that doesn't even know half the ABC's. Maybe I would give a shit if Bernie or Yang was still in but there is no one left to care about. And at the end of the day it's all old white men... well kinda white men. Trump got those oompa loompa vibes like I said but it is annoying.

  Anyways in better news I finally am gonna move out of this shitty ghetto ass apartment and found a new one just barely outside of Frogtown, it's about 1k a month compared to the $500 I'm paying now and is just a little smaller but is way fucking nicer and is a little closer to the studio though the way Damocha was talking I might have to studio from home, which if that's the case I'm fucked. But when it comes to money I'm livid, my album is doing alright. It's slowed down now but last week off the commissions I made 4k and this week about 3k and after getting a 150k signing bonus for just dropping the album it was due. My apartment is $1200 a month and is the nicest solo place I've owned. In Japan I stayed in my shitty apartment mainly because you really can't live good without spending millions which was just unfair you fucking pricks; This apartment also has good travel next to it, being almost right next to the bus station and few food places along with a grocery store. I was thinking about moving out to Brooklyn park and spending a shit load but live in a really nice community and place but I decided I'm not a fag and won't do that, I'm too much a big city girl to fuck around with shit like that. Damocha did check in with me and when I told him about the apartment he offered to pay for it for the first few months which I said yes because A. Free living. And B. I'm a manipulator who uses every little thing to my advantage. So I am officially moving in at 2320 Marshall Avenue, St. Paul and while it's expensive it's also really fucking nice. For now I'm brainstorming ideas for my next EP or song but I'm going mentally insane not having a good kill in a while. I'm not gonna go merk a dude or woman on the street. I need a lure victim and I might need it soon before I jump off a building. I did get an idea though even through all the bullshit insanity thoughts I have, I heard on the news a while back about me being sick, as in the murder of my old boss at the slave job and that word sick really caught my eye, I might need to kill over this thought though.

3 Days Later

I'm basically in nothing but my underwear, it's a decently chilly morning and quite nippy. I'm contemplating making ramen for lunch here in an hour or two or if I should order something on doordash; Taco Bell, Chinese, I don't really know I have the taste buds of a pre teen and the mind of a 40 year old going through a midlife crisis, that's the right age right? Ah who fucking cares, I mean at the end of the day I borderline mentally unstable. Motivation is the hardest thing and sometimes I don't even have a motive for things, my motive is no motive. But that doesn't really make sense, surely there is a motive, maybe it's that I'm insane, maybe the motive is I cannot function without drugs and violence. Maybe I am trying to fill a void in a bottomless pit. At least that's how it feels, the only way I can describe it is trying to claw my way out of a pit where all I can see is a dot of light. I know there is a top but I don't know how far. It's as if I am making no progress as if the dot of light never gets bigger as getting closer to freedom seems impossible. To what this represents I do not know, what this could mean is I perhaps feel trapped where I am, but that is simply not true, I lived in Japan and even a few other small towns so I am not trapped, but maybe I'm looking at it the wrong way. Maybe my direction is wrong, maybe all this time I was clawing upwards on the side towards the light when maybe I should be going the other direction. Maybe the small light is a facade, an illusion to a place that looks fine but is not what I want, maybe I need to go downwards, rather than up, maybe this is the universe telling me that I am a demon and always will be; The Akuma is the key yet I never really realized it. All this time I was copying what others were doing and while it was working, it was only working so well it was not the right key for success. While I was going the same way as everyone else trying to become the best it wasn't right. I need to go in the opposite direction and go my own path. Everyone is trying to go to Heaven, when the key is to go to Hell.

"So Mike that's why I'm saying I need to get into the booth, I need to drop this solo."

"Karen, listen I get you had this sudden change of heart and this massive good work day but one song right now will not get you into that studio. They are barely letting our biggest artists in for some recording of massive releases and one song will not go over well, even if we got you in the song is not dropping without mixing and being looked over."

"Ok! So I will do that then."

"Karen you cannot."

"Why not? I did it before I can do it again, I just wrote this entire song today and this is not only the best I have felt in months, but also this is one of the best songs I've written, I really feel like this is it, I mean Mike look at this, tell me this isn't only fire but also really to heart and my audience would eat this shit up."

"Karen right now I get one day in the building, I am at home for the rest of the time, the reason we couldn't meet up and we are calling rather than face to face ya know."

"Brother!!!! Just help a bitch out, on your day there I'll sneak in without Damocha knowing and I'll record it real quick and then dip out of there."

"I'm sorry but Covid protocols say-"

"Mike, Covid protocols can lick my ass I do not care, I am going there and we are recording this and I will drop this banger myself. Even if this goes against the contract I feel something about this one, it feels right."

"OK! OK! Let me figure out a little plan and we can try and drop this, this is definitely some of your best writing, however if this doesn't translate well into music I'm not working with you ever again. Got that?"

"YES! YES! YES! Mikey-"

"Don't call me that!" he sighs.

"MIKEEEEYYY! Thank you, thank you, thank you, I promise this is worth it, you wont regret it."

"I better not."

The Next Day

Buzz, buzz, my phone is ringing somebody is calling me, I look at my clock and it's 9:42 in the morning and I am still trying to enjoy my massive super comfy bed but of fucking course I can't have anything good in life, my life sucks ass but as they say, life never gets easier, you only learn to handle the hardness better, haha dick joke, got ya bitch! Anyways I pick up the phone and my crusty eyes open up but squinch as I forgot to turn the brightness down on my phone, but my eyes adjust finally and I see who is calling. It's Mike.

"KAREN!"

"Holy shit Mike! It's 9 in the fucking morning and I am still a little hungover please calm down, fuck man.

"Karen" he says in a softer voice "I have figured it out."

"What do you mean you figured it out. How to get the song recorded?!?" I jolted out of the bed, standing with nothing but panties on, I grab a soft white robe and put it on as he explains it."

"I've been up all night thinking about this, at first I was just doing this as a friendly thing but now I'm doing it because I spent way too much fucking time trying to get this to work and I've done it. I come in on Thursday and I plan on coming in at 11:30, I have talked with some other producers who come

Dead Fashion

in and out of the building and they said that Damocha because of Covid is not there!"

"Holy shit, Holy shit!"

"I know Karen right? That's what I said, so anyways I sit and ponder and then realize that the desk lady doesn't ever check in the make sure we need to use the booth, she always lets me go, so it's a shot in the dark but if we come in at the same time we might be able to just say we are going in quick and I'll drop the track and spit on top of it, it works out completely!"

"Fuck me sideways, YES YESSSS! Ok but about the beat we need it, and I won't have time Thursday is" I look at my iPhones lock screen, it says Wednesday "Tomorrow."

"I know, I know however that's why I stayed up all night, me and my good Friend OP a guy I know in the rap scene mixed and made something just to rap over, we can just record the lyrics and then we can add the better beat later, we just need a little template and we have it, we are lock and loaded all we gotta do is pull that damn trigger."

"Mike… I fucking love you, so we are doing this then? Like for real, for real?

"I'm ready." I start to smile as my coffee continues to brew. For the first time in a decent amount of time I felt real happiness, something feels really weird right now and feels like something in the air.

"Mike you're the best, so 11:30 tomorrow?
"Yes, meet me outside, I'll be waiting."
"Ok."

• • •

I look at my clock 1:48pm, "Oh fuck!" I said to myself as I looked at my phone, 14 missed calls all from Mike, "I called him back, for the first time since I can remember as my heart dropped."

"KAREN! ARE YOU FUCKING KIDDING ME? YOU ACTUALLY DITCHED LIKE THAT!"

"Mike, I can explain."

"Ok, you know what? Go ahead explain why I just spent the last 48 hours setting every domino up for you to knock over only for you not to show your face, let's hear it Karen!"

"I slept in."

"You slept in?"

"Yes."

"KAREN I'M GONNA FUCKING MURDER YOU! AND I'M NOT KIDDING." Try me bitch, he couldn't take me even if both of my arms were broken, weak ass fuck.

"So what? Why are you so upset, yes it's unfortunate and yes I'm sorry but why are you so mad? We can just set it up again."

"Why am I mad? You're kidding right, all this prep work and you blow me off because you got high or some shit, we discussed why this was a big deal!"

"HEY! Don't talk about me like that... If I was gonna do drugs I would do something that's actually worth going to jail for!"

"Whatever. The point is you just made me waste the last two days trying to get you to be a financially successful artist, but no! You wanna blow it all off because you're a zoomer. Your entire generation is like this, god I should've known not to even help you. You have no drive Karen, you don't! How are you gonna keep living if you can't get up a little earlier for your job."

"You know what?"

"What?"

"I'm done, I'm not gonna do anything with you anymore or Damocha and his stupid rules, I'm done with it all, Don't call me or talk to me, I'm done!"

"Karen, you signed a two year contract, you are not done. The moment you stop writing songs and singing them Damocha is coming to your house with a lawsuit that runs you dry of every penny you have in your bank account. So I suggest a proposal."

"Ewww I'm not marrying you, nasty."

"Karen just fucking listen." So aggressive daddy.

"Even though I'm very upset with you, I am willing to forgive you, and let this entire thing go, ok?"

"You were literally so upset about five minutes ago what happened?"

"Well I realized that you need to make money for me to make money and if I get upset and quit working with you, then I can't support myself or my family."

"You have a family?"

"Yes I- stop side tracking me."

"Haha ok, sorry."

"So when this whole covid blows over, we can continue, as of now, just relax because according to your contract even if you are not producing anything, you still get the same monthly pay and royalties."

"Wait, how do you know my contract so well?"

"Well let's just say me and Damocha are very good friends, and maybe let's say I don't know some guy who produces music, saw massive potential in you, and threw a bone for you, specifically on the financial side."

"Mike… You somehow piss me off and then five minutes later I'm so happy I know you."

"I get that more than you would think actually. So anyways as I was saying, just write some music and bounce ideas in the background, and I guess instead of going behind people's backs to drop music, let's just enjoy some paid time off."

"Honestly, now that you put it like that, it sounds very, very nice. I need some juul pods and food in my tummy cuz I am about to fucking explode."

"Whatever Karen, just enjoy… being young I guess, you never cease to amaze me."

"Yeah I get I'm the greatest of all time."

"Shut the fuck up Karen."

A Little Break

Do you know how boring life is? Even before Cockvid I was still bored out of my mind when I wasn't working or had time off. I get so upset that I say this and everytime I say what I'm about to say I want to jump off the Burj Khalifa, I think I actually liked working blue collar jobs. Yes, making music is fun and is what I'm most passionate about... maybe, but honestly working ovens for pizza, working at McDonalds cash registers weren't that bad. Sure the pay was lame and the jobs are annoying but at least I'm doing something. When I'm making music I feel certain way but that's the thing, I'm not always making music, when I'm sitting watching YouTube or hell even the fucking news I feel empty, I only feel whole when I am making music, when I'm not singing or writing, I feel... awful. When I first started back in January I didn't feel this way, I felt like I was always whole because I was trying to achieve something, but once I semi achieved what I wanted, I feel worse, I feel like I'm missing something, I want more and more now. It's almost like an addiction I can't quite fill. Whenever I get what I want it doesn't please me, I want more and more on a larger scale. When I take one person's life I don't even feel full anymore. I used to kill to feel but after I lost that I started to sing to feel but now I feel nothing. When I'm alone with my thoughts I feel nothing empty, void of emotions, I'm like a robot with no feelings at all, some would feel frightened to not feel anything and for a moment I thought I was. Then I remember that feeling frightened is feeling anything and I don't even feel that, I'm a mess, I'm losing my temper slowly, what is wrong with me?

  A little break has now felt like a long break, it's only been less than two weeks yet little over 15 days has felt like a little over 15 years, well maybe not that much but it still feels so long. Everything for the past 5 months has felt super fast yes life is boring but seriously like my god I have nothing, everything fucking closed and the things that aren't closed are those hillbilly republican shops that if you dont look like a 45 year old man with a 2003 chevy pickup with a trump sticker on the side and trump flag your not welcome. Pretty annoying so

Dead Fashion

yeah I guess I still get to enjoy my food tho, every couple of days I splurge on some chinese when I'm not on a strict 2k calorie diet and when I get my cheat days. However since Covid I have started to invest in more home gym equipment, mainly just some small lifting stuff I can put in the corner of my living room while I try to live through boredom, I have kept a decent routine for working out mainly body weight stuff, rather doing a bunch of lifting and running I cut that down in exchange for calisthenics. I currently have a small boost income that I got which is quite odd considering everyone is losing money right now; I have bought a fake fighting dummy for only about 300 bucks. It's so great honestly, and because of this for the past month all of my exercise has been focused around fighting this dummy, which by the way I named Damocha because why not name it after my boss lmao. So kickboxing, knife fighting, punching and just about any form of fighting that will help me get better at easing my mind from my own insanity. Instead of killing people I've been taking all of my itches and anger out on Damocha and it's nice, I get upset after a guy beats me in NBA 2K (Yes I game, I totally forgot to mention that my b) or when I get stuck on a lyric or song title I go fucking nuts and balls to wall on Damocha. It's been less than 7 days since this human colored dummy arrived with it's expressionless face and already it's almost unrecognizable. He's still in very good condition even after I've fucked him up badly multiple times so I'm very perplexed, this was probably the best thing I've ever boughten. However the easing of my insanity is starting to wear off, I'm starting to get an itch for the real deal again even though it feels real enough, I want some blood or maybe just a scream. I tried recording myself screaming and then having it play on loop while I stab the shit out of Damocha but it just doesn't work the same way. I need a real scream and some real pain, it's simply just not as fun. Although I am getting a little more reserved with my kills and myself, I no longer feel like my first option is to kill, maybe my brain is growing and maybe I'm becoming more mature but I don't have a sudden urge to mess anything in my path up anymore as the first option, maybe I'm becoming a better person...

    HAHAHA YEAH FUCKING RIGHT! You think I'm getting better? A couple of sentences just made you feel completely different didn't it? You actually felt I was growing as a person into something good and that the remainder of this story was me deciding I want to be a better person didn't you? Your such a fucking loser lmao HAHA I would never... ever do that! Anyways working out has honestly saved me, sure I'm still so fucking bored but at least it's not as bad, oh god I don't know what I would do if I was going broke again, I think I'd probably kill myself and I'm not kidding. OOOOO also my new doorbell came today, I was so excited! I got a ring or whatever where I can see whoever is at the door, but get this... I can hear them and record them! It has automatic detection, 24/7 surveillance and uploads all visits to the cloud after notifying me on my phone, I can also talk to people through it as well through my phone, it's kinda epic not gonna lie. I installed it after having a mental breakdown trying to get everything to work but once it was in working order it was so nice and I started to feel like I accomplished something with my life. I am at a point in my life where I'm 21 and feel like im 41 where I do a tiny thing and consider it an accomplishment, ridiculous how life just slaps being gay as fuck in your face and it's so annoying. Like when I was younger I dreamed of being an astronaut or being a youtuber or being a professional gamer, I figured I would be some worldwide known thing and sure I definitely have a niche audience but I am in no way how I thought I was gonna be. I always thought my parents were lame and uncommitted and that's why we weren't mega famous rich billionaires who owned an estate, but in reality my parents were just lame, they weren't uncommitted.

    Now I am way more committed to success than either of my parents were and to be quite honest I'm smarter, better and stronger than they ever were in their prime. I didn't go to college and put myself in thousands of dollars in debt and I still make more money than they probably did at my age, I didn't

Dead Fashion

marry at 19 and have a worthless kid- wait I just called myself worthless? Whatever point is I don't have a fucking whining ass baby walking around sticking it's finger up it's nose and making messes all over my house and I sure as hell am not staying committed to any man for more than half a year, I can't stand most people let alone spending the rest of my life with them, like Jesus fuck me in ass I would rather get shot- no get hit by a car going 100+ miles per hour than live with and fuck the same person over and over; simply is so too cringe and annoying to deal with. Holy shit it's 10pm already I guess I need to do my work out now. Today I have stomach crunches and push ups. I can do roughly 900 stomach crunches and about 100 push ups before totally collapsing. I might push myself a little farther today and go for a 1000 and 110 push ups. I put on my tv to go to watch Shrek (My favorite movie and helps ease my mind while working out) when I accidentally had the news channel WCCO 5 on as I forgot to switch it from cable last night and usually some shitty show like the good doctor or some random show is on at this hour, but the tv was not on one of those shows. It was one of the craziest shots in television history in front of my eyes. I had never seen something like this on WCCO. It was a picture of a man on the ground while a police officer was over top of him and that picture stood on screen as the newscasting lady spoke.

"Tonight a story breaks out in downtown Minneapolis as man on 38th and Chicago has been suffocated to death by Minneapolis police, The suspect was in custody for supposedly stealing from a store however witnesses say the man had done nothing wrong and had no signs of aggression or of any wrongdoing, the story is still coming out as this is breaking of just a little over an hour ago, police have not given a statement but social media has gone rampant. Over to you Mark."

"Yeah Christy I'm standing nearly 15 yards away from where the man was killed, um there are at least 50 people outside of this downtown store and police have been called down to hold everyback. Currently the police are maintaining the police but if you listen behind me you'll hear shouting and screaming and all kinds of things. The people are very unhappy with not only the police officer who did this, but the city itself for allowing this to happen. The number of people has been increasing since we've gotten here and so far it has not been good. Right behind me in fact is the man who was killed, just on that curb over there, things are escalating very quickly and soon we might have to get out of here as things don't look like they are getting better, back to you Christy." I shut the tv off and sit in awe, this is… awesome! People yelling and screaming at the police while they gather in a mass crowd my god how lucky I am to live in this city. Sadly though it probably won't last long so instead of a workout I think I'll take a nice little walk downtown and see if I can have a little fun while it lasts.

I Am The One Who Knocks

It's been three days since the guy was killed. I lurked around downtown and even saw the crowd. Normally in these situations it all dies down within about two hours so I was surprised to see they didn't leave and in fact the polar opposite of what I expected to happen actually happened. I figured everyone would get mad and then go home but more and more people kept showing up. I eventually left because I got bored of chanting for some guy I didn't even know the name of. I did a little research last night and found the guy's name, some George guy. A black man who I had never seen in my life and who apparently was shopping at some store or something that detail is still a little unknown he used a fake bill and then some cop decided to choke this guy out by kneeling on him long story short a person took a video and then all of a sudden this man was going viral, first in the metro area which was early last night where I saw it on tv and then I refreshed twitter some more and saw that he ended of going viral in the states and then in the world because for some reason US politics and problems become world problems and now long story short you have people coming from everywhere protesting in downtown

Dead Fashion

Minneapolis. I turn on my phone to see twitter going nuts and with videos and all these tweets my god. I closed the app. I can't stand to look at that anymore, I can hear chanting from across the city so many people are here and it's getting farther than most of these small protests I've seen, maybe it's time Minneapolis saw a little riot. I think maybe that would change a lot of peoples perspectives on life and how to live it. Another thing that actually made me smile is the people. All these people left their covid restricted lives to protest for something they care about, it almost makes me give a shit about what they are protesting. Look people die everyday but when a guy who is supposed to protect the people does that than oh boy you got some clean up to do, I think today is a good day to relax and just smile while I wait for some action on either sides, let's light this fucking candle.

"Karen honey, are you ok?" my mom says on the phone to me as I sit in my chair at my small office setup.

"No mom I got suffocated to death, I am George." I say as I chuckle a little.

"DON'T SAY THAT! That's not funny. Karen, that looks bad."

"Mom, I think it will be ok, it's just a protest, don't they happen like everyday in Seattle cause of all the homeless people?"

"Those aren't more than a gathering; they don't even really protest most times and our homeless rate has gone down."

"Probably because they realized they were living in Washington, HAHA. Also they are probably doing that anti homelessness shit with the benches and the spikes under bridges and stuff."

"I think they just go south down to California and never come back."

"Well listen mom, I would love to talk about homeless migration patterns and where to find them but currently I'm enjoying a day off trying to live my best life so-"

"Karen I'm worried look you can try to get rid of me all you want but maybe you should leave the city, go live with your auntie down in Montevideo for a while until the people leave, with that many people it looks like bad stuff could happen and they don't look friendly either they seem violent."

"Mom I not going to Monte-fucking video to live with aunt Rosie in her haunted ass house. Not to mention how lame the city is."

"Don't you be saying shit like that Karen! I grew up there."

"Yeah and I grew up in white suburbs but I still call them morally and ethically wrong and racist the way they are set up, I don't sugarcoat the subs just because I grew up there. Just because you have memories of a place doesn't mean they are good. How many times did you guys have a flood watch again, didn't grandma and grandpa's house get fucked because they refused to sell out and their house was destroyed in that massive flood? That's what I thought, listen mom either way Rosie's house is creepy she has all those old antiques and I'm pretty sure-" I lower my voice down to a whisper "She's a klan member."

"Oh Karen we grew up with conservative parents of course she's gonna be racist even though I am still a little racist."

"That's probably not a good thing to say, mom." I say quickly as I look down at my chewed off nails and look at my pc at my Nvidia stock.

"Either way just leave the city Karebear, for mom please. I don't want you getting hurt." Yeah right like that'll ever happen. I dare someone to try me.

"Mom, do you remember Walter white from Breaking bad?"

"What does that-"

"Do you?" I say firmly."

"Is that the show with the bald guy with the glasses who makes meth?" Very descriptive mom.

"Yes do you know what he said and this quote stuck with me ever since the first time I saw it."

"And what was that sweetie?"

"It goes something loosely like this: You clearly don't know who you're talking to, so let me clue you in... I am not in danger, Skyler. I am the danger. A guy opens his door and gets shot and you think that of me? No... I am the one who knocks!" I say it verbatim because I don't loosely remember the quote, I know it like the back of my hand. Because inside it defines me, me and Walter White are one and the same. Everything he does is calculated, every word he speaks he means it, every action he does, he does with intent and purpose. Just like me.

"Jesus Christ Karen, did I really raise you to be a psychopath?" Yes... Yes you did mom. Then for a moment there is a brief pause of silence and it's almost piercing like a knife.

I fake laugh "No. I'm just kidding, mom you know what, forget it. Don't worry it was just a joke." she laughed nervously.

But it wasn't just a joke, Inside we are one and the same. I suddenly feel a bloodlust again. I stare aimlessly at the wall while my mom talks in the background, but I cannot hear over my own thoughts. I only think about another kill, this sudden urge to cause violence I can only amalgamate to the recent protests and this sudden nostalgia trip for the past. I feel lethal again and feel like this time a dummy won't suffice, I'm curious to see how the night will continue now after this change in mood has been broughten onto me, this sudden remembrance brings back The Akuma inside which I cannot control and even if I could I don't know if I would stop it. It's been long enough with my dosage and I might not get a better opportunity than this, I feel ready to cause chaos to anybody who gets in my way no matter who they are. I am on the verge of a breakdown.

"Karen sweetie, are you still there?" My mind snaps back to the present and back to my mother.

"Yes mother." I say robotically, my mask is slipping but I cannot control it. I need to get off the phone now before anything bad happens. I said softly, "I think you should hang up." I continued as I stared face forward at the wall "I think I know what I'm going to do."

"Ok well be safe leaving the city do you want me to call Rosie and let her know you'll be coming?" My mother has mistaken my words as in I made up my mind to leave, she is too stupid to understand and too ignorant to know.

"No… it's alright mother, I got it."

"Ok stay safe sweetie, I miss you, can't wait to see you in December." I completely forgot about that trip. "Love you Karebear."

"Yeah, love you too." I said softly once again.

The Servants of God

It's May, late May to be exact. I'm not very sure how I feel right now, I feel… very different. I don't quite feel normal, most times whenever I feel like killing or causing problems I always feel like myself, but this time I don't feel as if I have control of my body. I feel as if I'm acting on primal instincts, looking… no stalking the concrete jungle tonight. I'm on Chicago ave, 36th st, just roughly a block from where the incident happened last night, there are so many people around so it's easy to stalk through the crowd. I'm looking for the right person, I can't quite understand it, but I believe I shouldn't just kill just any dumb protestor, I need something a little more exciting in my mind. I'm wearing all black with loose black sweatpants (Adidas) with a black hoodie and black t-shirt. I made sure I was fit for the job here and chose black everything. I'm wearing my hood over my head with a black cloth mask over my face. I have black eyeliner sporadically done around the lips of my eyes and onto my eyelids. I have two black latex gloves over my hands so as to not leave any type of evidence behind as well. I also have two knives on my body for the killing, one is this little military blade black steel I got on amazon for $120 it's about a five inch blade and is easy to

Dead Fashion

conceal in my hoodie pocket. My other knife is one of my personal favorites, it's a stainless steel karambit with a small rainbow tint on the stainless steel, it has a very cool and unique pattern that caught my eye and I just knew I had to get it. It was $200 and I purchased this from an armory store just outside of Brooklyn Park. I keep it in my black winter boots I wear all year round because I'm simply sick. I am stalking through the crowds in all black, luckily everyone is wearing masks so it's easy to completely blend in. The sun is completely set now and only the street lights shine. The people are getting angry, agitated, worse than early today. More and more people are here, it's being at a concert thousands of people are all over, some singing, some screaming and most just yelling with protesting remarks. I don't care to be honest all I care about is something to stick a knife in; something that will feel some pain. I think if I'm gonna do this I want it to be brutal and I simply can't do that here, it would draw too much attention. All of a sudden before I know it, I start to smell smoke and I hear people cheering. I look down the street and they all start moving towards a bright lit up part down the street. It's coming from the main business district downtown, something so bright plus the smell of burning could only mean one thing. Something get fucked up right now with fire. I see this as the perfect opportunity while everyone is distracted. I make my way towards the business center faster and faster. I look across the street and I see a small little restaurant on fire… "Holy shit!" I had to say out loud as I had never seen something like this in the city. It completely even got me lost. I see more things start on fire, this is now bad, now I probably only have about 40 minutes until the national guard comes and stops this whole thing, I need to act fast. I look around, I see nothing but liberals and fucking losers out screaming and moving all yelling. It's complete and utter chaos right now and while this is good and I would love to participate I'm getting more agitated by the minute and I feel as if I need to stab something right now! GOD DAMMIT FUCKING FUCK! FUCK! I stomp my foot and turn around but as I do that something catches my eye that is almost impossible to see but with my eyes is completely noticeable. Just outside of one of larger crowds a man is speed walking with a military vest on towards an alleyway and enters it. Now normally these are just psychos who think they are some fucking cool guy wearing camo but when it's something like this we can rule out that he's real military involvement because he wouldn't be alone and would be fully kitted with more than a vest, camo pants and a grey shirt and we can also rule out that he is here for the protest. Doing my research I and even if I hadn't done research you could clearly tell this is a very liberal/democratic protest and most times and I'm not a political science major, but most times those types of people who wear camo vests and walk around like tough shit are a demographic who like their guns and usually don't associate with these people protesting. So this now got a lot more interesting; I walk quickly toward the alley and see nothing, that's odd considering this alley leads to basically nothing and has a dead end at the end of it. I look around a little bit only to discover a big metal door is barely crept open, it's a heavy door and leads into the back of some run down business here.

  The place looks like it's been abandoned since I was born. I open the door slowly and as quietly as I can hoping to find this guy in here, only I hear voices coming from inside. I sneak inside and see the inside is completely stripped and looks like it's under construction. It's a big pit with a bunch of small rooms connecting above it with little to no lighting everywhere except in the middle which has a massive light on it. this place looks like the perfect little hideout and it's so close to the main business area hmm. I look to my left and see a small window and can see all the people protesting moving slowly down the block about roughly 400 yards away now. I keep hearing them talking so I decide to creep a little closer to the main part, the voices get louder and louder until I can hear exactly what they are saying. I finally see the guy but this time he is with five other dudes, six in total. Three of them are bigger, two of them are smaller and the guy I followed is about my height and

Dead Fashion

weight. I see assault rifles and bullets everywhere and I see them huddled together. The one guy has a massive ginger beard and is wearing a mock military camo outfit, some serious gear and looks like he likes to play pretend military guy. The rest are in this sudo mixed military and plain clothing style but all of them have an ar-15 in their hands and they are looking at them and playing with them except the guy with the ginger beard. I stop and take a deep breath after I realize how serious this shit is, and how seriously fun this could also be if I play it correctly.

  I figured it out, I'm not taking a singular target anymore. I need more and I need a challenge; I'm taking six lives tonight.

  "Alright guys so we gotta be careful how we do this." Said the guy with the ginger beard.

  "I say we FUCKIN rip their faces off with bullets already. Said another guy

  "Jacob calm the fuck down before I put a bullet in stupid little skull." the ginger bearded guy replied.

  "Well I'm FUCKIN tired of it I need to SQUEEEEZE this fucking thing and blow some heads off already."

  "We will, we will I promise, but remember our cause, we ain't letting these fucking monkeys destroy this nation goddammit and they have already started burning shit outside according to Bill imagine what they are gonna do else where, these fucking sick diseased things. This isn't what God would want! Because if God saw them destroying our nation like this and destroying his creation he would put a stop to it and that's our purpose gentlemen. So it's time we fucking take back our soul and nation." the ginger bearded guy said again, he's obviously the leader and well a racist. "We split into three teams of two, so Bill and Cameron you guys are gonna run up Chicago ave just outside of here and make a big fucking stir, start shooting some people maybe scream and get the people scared and noticed. Then me and Jacob are gonna be on the rooftops with the bumbstocks taken as many people as we can while they are running like a herd of sheep, it will be like shooting fish in a barrel, Bill and Cameron keep firing into the crowd and then Danny and Eric are gonna come in from the north side where they are running and that's when you guys throw the mustard gas and then start shooting through the smoke, you guys got your gas masks?"

"YES SIR!" they both said in unison.

"Good fucking shit boys, finally after about 2 minutes of this we run and take everything and get as far away from here as we can and never come back to this god forsaken city. God I fucking hate it here, there's too many of them if I was Trump I drop a nuke over this whole fucking city, that'll get rid of a shit load of libs too." I called it they definitely weren't democrats. As I looked over they dropped their guns and put all their foreheads together and then put their arms around each other's backs just below the neck and got into a tight small circle. They then started whispering what I could only imagine is a prayer of some sort and then they all stopped and resumed like nothing happened. "Ok so that's the final time we're going over the plan so-" all of sudden my phone started to ring, I forgot to silence it. OH GOD HOLY FUCK HOLY FUCK! IM FUCKING SCREWED OH WHY?? I look down it's my mom, of fucking course it is, ahhhhh that stupid bitch! The guy with the ginger beard screams "WHAT THE FUCK IS THAT? IS THAT A PHONE DID ANY OF YOU LEAVE YOUR PHONE ON THE RAILING UP TOP?"

"Nah!"

"No!"

"Why would I?"

"OK THEN WHO THE FUCK IS THERE?" He screamed. Then they all get focused with their guns and look around. I panicked! For the first time in a long time I felt real fear and as fast and as quietly as I could I ran and hid in one of the side rooms connected to the top part of the place. "SOMEONE WAS LISTENING IN ON US SPLIT UP WE AREN'T LETTING ANYONE LEAVE! SEARCH EVERYWHERE! Jacob go check outside and make sure no one is within 100 yards of this building! Kill them if you have too, the rest of us, we split up and check inside, shoot on site. GOT IT?"

"YES SIR" they all scream. I sit in the darkness waiting, my odds are very low to make it out let alone get a kill, this is bad. I thought it would be one crazy fuck with a gun but instead it's six. I'm fucked… I literally fucked and their is nothing I can do. Wait a minute, what am I talking about? I just have to be strategic about this, my percent is low but not 0. I close my eyes and steady my breathing. As I do that my heart rate goes from around 120 to 130 beats a minute to maybe around 90ish. I steady my breath quietly and listen to the footsteps. Judging from what I saw, this building is decently big, maybe just about half the size of a football field, and decently narrow but enough.

Judging from the footsteps they are all over the place and didn't stick to grouping up. The nearest footsteps are still faint so they are on the other side still and are rapidly coming this way. The one guy's movement is very clunky. I can hear him from a mile away and he is the closet on my left. To my right is one other room and then a brick wall, but in front of that room is the walkway and the footsteps are not on that narrow stretch. So I can deduce anyone will have a good shot on me. Not to mention their aim, even if I give them the benefit of being on the level of a US Marine, their chances of hitting me from that side if I sneak out and stab one of these guys is low. Especially if I use his body they will not shoot through their own man.

He is now only two rooms to my left now and will check my room in about 20 seconds. I can see the light of individuals as well so they are easy targets in the dark. They also must have flashlights and they are moving weirdly, as if one of their hands is holding the flashlight. So it's more than likely not attached, which means if these guys have AR-15's and are balancing them with a light, then their aim will be even worse. The light moves closer and I stand at the edge of the door with my back against the wall. The light moves in to check my room and for a second I breathe in through my nose as the guy moves halfway into the room. I hold my breath until the side of his body is on me and the gun is in front of my area of being shot.

I pull the knife, STRIKING his body and then with my other hand grab his gun and with the pain of the knife struck into his side he screams and his body goes semi num and he loosens his grip and I am to get the gun out of of his hand as he fires a bullet into the wall, then I arm the gun and fire two shots into his body and his body goes from a limp stand to drop and then… I breathe out.

I hear panic and chaos from the other guys rushing towards the room screaming and shouting. The gun doesn't have a bump stock or a switch so I have to be more reserved with my shots. Knowing this gun type and the mag size, it holds 30 rounds and he only fired a single shot into the wall and I fired two so I'm now at 27. I quickly grab my knife from his body and then breathe in once again and listen for the footsteps. The one guy is on the narrow part of the walkway, I get my back off the wall again and quickly with my trigger finger fire two bullets and see the light of the guy fall and hit the ground as I hear a screech. I must have hit him in the hand. What a nice shot Karen.

The other guy tries to fire from the other side and I quickly go to the wall again. He keeps firing and firing until all of sudden he stops and I realized this idiot just made a vital mistake. He wasted all of his bullets. I quickly get back into the middle of the doorway and fire three more shots and I see his light fall too along with a scream; I'm on point today considering I didn't hit the range and haven't fired a gun since the beginning of Covid. I see two more lights come from the outside door and I fire about ten bullets at the door. Both of them go down with no scream from either of them, I must have hit them in the head. I hear cries and screaming from the other two guys as they are bleeding out. I walk over to the guy closest on the walkway and shoot two more bullets into him on the ground and he dies. I breathe out.

Dead Fashion

I know there is still one more so I don't leave the room. I wait until I hear the dragging of a body, it's him, the final guy and he's distracted. I go to the doorway only 10 bullets left and fire two at their postion, but their is a piece of the railing that's sticking up blocking the shots and he hides behind it, before firing back at me around 15 shots within one second, (I fucking hate bump stocks!) I bait him out again and he wastes his other rounds before screaming. I breathe in, I run through the tiny walkway and turn to the left to shoot him, and I fire four shots. To my surprise I just finished off the wounded guy... what the fu-

I get tackled from behind as I hear a loud scream, he tries to tackle me all the way to the ground but I quickly fall onto one knee with his entire body weight on top of me and I realize he's super heavy and definitely the heaviest one, it's the ginger bearded guy. He was the only one that was semi fat and looked bulky. I push him over the top of my back and in front of me, but he grabs onto my torso and pulls me with him as he also gets a punch to my face in and I get knocked back. I'm on my back and he immediately gets on top of me and tries to strangle me with both of his hands and then pins down my right arm with his left knee. He sits on top of me and I can no longer breathe at all, I'm choking trying to get him off with one hand but to no use. I feel my heartbeat starting to rise and fear starts trying to take over in my mind but I won't let it, I try to reach into my hoodie pocket but his entire body is on it so I cannot grab my military knife that I used earlier to stab the first guy and I'm running out of time but I won't let him succeed. I always carry two knives for this reason I try to reach down into my high black boot and I start seeing black everywhere, I keep reaching just barely out of reach until he loosens more on his right side and I'm able to reach just literally a single millimeter more and grab the finger hole at the top of my karambit and quickly launch it out around my index finger and in the slowest motion I've ever felt and I watch the knife do a full spin around my finger, then come straight into my hand as the darkness almost fully covers my vision. I can feel my body weakening, I then through an act of unknown power or strength jab it into the left in his neck and he loosens his grip and his hands come off my neck entirely as he falls back off of me and screams.

    I gasp for air and the air is super rigid and nasty and my throat burns, but I knew I couldn't end there, I get up onto my knees in a really sluggish manner and then crawl to him and grab my karambit out of his neck and then stab it into his neck again and then I stab it into his head and now as my strength came back I started stabbing faster and harder and harder until I could hear the blood curdling from his neck as it tried to pump through but couldn't. I kept stabbing over and over and over and I just couldn't quit. I don't know what happened but I let loose as if with every stab I was releasing three months of pent up energy into this sick bastard. I could feel my teeth grinding as I started to growl and then started to scream at the top of my lungs and then I put the knife into his deformed bloody face for the last time, then I fell back. I started to cry, not tears of sadness, no… It was tears of joy. I smiled as I cried and could feel the darkness release from me as I laid back into a pool of blood now staining my back. I just laid there in their blood. Cries turned to laughter as I suddenly had a feeling of relief completely take over. It was so sweet, it was so pure, I was entrenched in my own insanity that I laid for maybe five minutes or so laughing over and over until finally I stopped.

    I got up and took their bodies and piled them up in a corner of the building. I then lit their bodies on fire using a match in one of the guys pockets followed by grabbing all of their guns and placing them there too. I waited until they were just mere ashes, burned skin, and bone before using the match again to set a piece of paper on fire, that I set in the building next to some of the wooden beams holding it up. I held the match to the beams to set them on fire as well and within 10 minutes the entire place was on fire.

    I quickly ran out and went across the street and looked back, the building was now getting engulfed in flames and the protesters were making their way back to this part and stopped in front of the abandoned burning building and started to cheer and scream. I was swallowed up by the crowd and quickly couldn't tell who did what. I reflect on what happened and I smile as I take my mask off and breathe the fresh air of smoke and despair. The city is in shambles and in chaos, most people are ready to give up and quit on the city while the protesters and now rioters are destroying the city. We see the national guard come in down the street maybe a mile on the horizon and as I see them I think about what the city needs, I think the people want some hope, maybe an anthem to sing and something positive that they can take away from this whole event, I think the people of the states especially this city need a song to play and listen to when remembering this time. They need it and I have it. I've decided, I'm going against Damocha and Mike. I'm gonna drop Dead Fashion tonight.

The crowds panic and start to disburse and run and panic and just as quickly as they had arrived they were gone. Within ten minutes the people disappeared into the shadows and the night, along with me as well.

Manager & Me: Life and Love of The World's Worst Human

"What are we gonna do with this kid? I mean Mike I get you and your wisdom had this strong feeling about this girl but I mean seriously this is ridiculous; She uploads a song with a whole music video from the riots, I mean for god's sake shes making us look like we're killers signing psychopaths to our record label. Not to mention Micheal, she uploaded this without consent or talking to us acting like she owns her own music, I mean this isn't six months ago little girl you can't just walk around acting like you own the place and then expect there to be no consequences."

"I get that Isaac but-"

"I mean does she have any idea what she has here? I mean after all we've given this girl and she wants to act like a punk? Disobey not only her own words but OUR CONTRACT? I SWEAR TO GOD I-"

"Isaac Damocha! You're acting like a child, stop acting as old as she is. Your letting her get to you, she's young and dumb and you know the risks of signing young artists especially ones from inside this city! Don't keep bitching about her and the things she did when you knew stuff like this was gonna happen. Yes I do agree there should be some consequences but I feel they need to be constructive consequences rather than punishment. And who knows maybe to her this will be like punishment."

"What will? What do you have in mind?"

"Well considering you signed her without her having a manager, which is always a red flag I think it's time we control our superman with a little kryptonite. We need to get Karen a manager, and not just get one, force her to listen to them.

"Micheal… this is why you're my second favorite Micheal in the world."

"I'm not your first? Then who is?"

"Well obviously the goat, dumbass. Micheal Jordan, I even got him to sign my bull's jersey back in 90 oh man what a time."

"You're not a timberwolves fan?"

"FUCK NO! What do you think I'm stupid or something? Honestly, how dare you think of me in that way. You're a dick ya know."
"Haha sorry bud."

• • •

I walk into DP records, sitting at the desk with a mask on is of course jew nose and I walk right past as she screams at me.

"Ms. Akuma, wait! First off, you're breaking multiple covid restrictions right now." she says in a panic as she chases after me as we walk down the main hall and take a left to Damocha's office. "Karen goddammit you don't have an appointment do not go in ther-" I slam his door open.
"Give me five reasons why I shouldn't put a bullet through your dense skull you fucking boomer!"

Dead Fashion

"Karen first let's get a mask on, we don't wanna go around spreading the corona right now in this horrible time."

"Fuck the virus. You send me a goddamn email with my new manager? And then think I won't be pissed? You want me to put a foot up your ass?"

"The answer to that last one might surprise you."

"Fuck you Damocha! Seriously, you have no right to do that!"

"Well… actually I do, it says in your contract on page 13 line 5 that we have all the power over your management and how you produce your music. Would you like to read the contract that you signed?" He hands me the contract and I flip to the page and look, it says it clear as day almost word for word what he said.

"You son of bitch! I'm gonna kill you and-"

"Karen you should look at this in a positive lens, you now will get even more help with music and music videos along with your social media, she will get you interviews etc etc"

"That was YOUR job!"

"It was my job, until you decided to disobey me and then go off and do your own shit and go to the riots and film it! Do you know what our investors said about you? They said you are a brand risk and that you were causing more problems than profits. The only and I mean only god damn reason you didn't tank this company and lose your job was because that music video got #1 on trending last night and has over 30 million views in two days."

"Wait what?"

"What did you not see your stats on youtube? Karen look at them." I quickly grab my phone and go to the youtube app and then go to my channel and see my analytics, 31,672,908 views in 51 hours, 250k new subscribers and ad revenue through the roof. Not to mention #1 on trending and over 30k comments.

"H-H-Holy SHIT! Are you fucking kidding me?!? I'm fucking popping off! Damocha why didn't you tell me you stupid old fuck?"

"I figured you would check your own goddamn analytics! Plus this is right into what I was saying, your new manager who I hope you will meet soon has gotten you an interview with the New York times about the song and the video. They are quote on quote inspired by your song and music video. On top of that I have rap artists and labels calling me just about every 30 minutes asking about you and your 'J-rap'."

"I haven't been this popular since… Nevermind, I'm FUCKING PUMPED! Damocha I-"
"Don't mention it." he says as he starts looking at papers on his desk. "Close the door on your way out, I'll have Shelly send over the details and do me a favor and speak to your goddamn manager, if not you're dropped, got it?"
I sighed "Finnnnnnnneeee! Whatever, give me her phone number since you said it was a her."

"Her landline or her work phone?"
"... You're fucking with me right?"
"Why would I joke about something like that?"
"Now I'm actually gonna kill you."

The Next Morning

Damocha ended up giving me her zoom since she apparently had to get a computer for the covid stuff and so I figured if she is so old that she is gonna have a landline she might as well get tortured by trying to figure out technology. Especially when he said her name was Susan, I instantly knew this was a boomer in her late 60's, pfhhh thinking a old witch will manage me what a fucking joke. I create a zoom space and as I sit at my $2500 gaming computer setup with flashing leds and a razer huntsman keyboard with purple switches and light up keys I sit for almost 15 minutes that I get so bored I start a match of league of legends, yes I'm a degenerate, and when that is done there still is no one. I swear Damocha told me he would tell her but I'm getting worried that she might have had

Dead Fashion

a heart attack and died. Not caring I go to the bathroom and grab a poptart from the cupboard and after I sit back down in my Herman Miller chair I see a very young lady with makeup done like she went out to the bar. She had brown hair stuck in a ponytail and was sitting with her legs on her chair scrunched up and she was wearing a pink tank top and super mario pajama pants. She looked only at most 30 and I immediately straightened up and put my headphones back in.

"Hey, I'm Karen. It's so nice of you to set up the zoom call for your grandma. She was supposed to be here about 45 minutes ago." I said as a big fake smile went over my face.

"Are-Are you talking to me?"

"Yeah, where is your grandma might I ask, I have some business I need to talk about with her."

"What grandma are you talking about?"

"Susan. I'm talking about Susan."

"Karen, I think you are confused."

"No I think you're confused, I'm looking for the old lady that is gonna run my life for the next however long."

"BITCH! I'm Susan." … No fucking way. There is no shot. This pretty young and well sexy girl is my manager, she doesn't even look older than me.

"No shot."

"What do you mean no shot? Karen I'm Susan. What made you think I was an old lady?"

"Well Damocha said you only had a landline and a work phone, and then with a name like Susan I just figured you were a 70 year old lady."

"Oh my god you fell for that trick too? HAHAHA I did as well when I first started working for Damocha, he told me I was gonna be repping this old country singer named Bill Davis and did the exact same plot as you just got trolled and it turns out I was doing something with this young dude from Duluth, cool kid but didn't make it too far. Also you thought Susan was an old name? BIIIITCH have you heard your real name? Your lucky the rap community doesn't go by real names you would've been fucked from the start, talking about old lady names, Kaaaaarrren."

"Hey fuck you!"

"When and Where?" … What? I know my manager did not just say when and where to me saying fuck you. Holy shit… I think this might actually work out. I've only known her for less than 5 minutes and she already roasted me, made fun of me and hit me with millennial humor. Not to mention she is one of the baddest bitches I've seen around here in my life.

"HA ok, ok. So if you're really Susan then we need to have a serious discussion."

"Shoot. I'm all ears, she leans back in her chair."

"Well for starts I don't make music for anyone but myself, I make music based on how I feel and how I act, so let's get one thing straight if you think your pretty ass is gonna persuade me into making some music and shit, it's not gonna work ok? I am a tough cookie to crack and I'm not gonna work for anyone."

"Ok."

"Ok? You're fine with that?"

"Yeah, that's exactly how I want you to act and feel. Your music should be personal and have heart, I'm not gonna force art out of you."

"Sweet, so I-" she cuts me off abruptly.

"However… I am still needed."

"What do you mean?"

"Well my main goal isn't to force you to make your art and use your talent, it's mainly to protect yourself from you."

"Um- I'm sorry what?"

"Well I just need to make sure you post the correct stuff as in nothing illegal, anti semitic, racist, anti trans, anti lgbtq+ and well anything stupid. Even politics I gotta step in sometimes, although listening to your music you have a very clear stance on your politics especially of your generation and the people around you. No I can't change that or make you change that because obviously it's needed and working, I am basically here to make sure you don't fuck up. I also will get

Dead Fashion

you interviews, like the one I did with my connection at the NY Times and other big Hollywood connections I have as well. I also have a lot of experience with other rappers and big names. Have you by chance ever heard of a rapper named Snoop Dogg by chance?"

"Are you kidding me, of fucking course!"

"Yeah I managed him for almost 5 years and made a bunch of connections before I moved up here when Damocha hired me."

"You gave up SNOOP MOTHER FUCKING D O DOUBLE G FOR DAMOCHA?"

"Yes I did. Mainly I wanted to slow down a little bit and after I had my connections I knew I could use that as leverage to get paid more than what snoop would and also living here was way cheaper than living out west. My coffee here is $4 compared to $8 out in Long Beach. Not as warm but I love it here, such a young atmosphere and a very awesome diverse crowd of people! So much opportunity and well I guess my thoughts lead me to good places because now I'm sitting here with you, who happens to fit my bill perfectly! A young girl with some popularity and a new style of rap that isn't big yet, so exciting!" Yeah right bitch, keep thinking so optimistically, I'm nothing what you think I am.

"Anyways I'm excited to start working with you Karen, we got off on a weird foot but here is my phone number for my CELL PHONE that I OWN." She gives me the numbers and I add her as 'Cute Manager-tan'. "Karen if you wanna face to face just face time me next time and don't listen to that old fuck Damocha so seriously, he's the biggest troll you'll ever know."

"Wait Susan before you go, how old are you?"

"I'm 26, I got my bachelors a year early in Digital Media Management from UCLA in 2015 and right off the chopping block I went to work for Snoop when I was 21 and boy let me tell you that was something else. Maybe I can get you guys to collab some time."

"Actually?"

"Yeah, when do you think you're gonna drop your next album? Like now you got some traction recently?"

"Well I don't really know yet to be honest. I will probably put Dead Fashion on there and I have one other song I'm working on but other than that I don't got much. I might start up again now that I do have some fame coming in I mean for god's sake I still can't believe everything, it's all happening so fast and chaotically in covid, I need time to reflect, so maybe I'll shoot for something at the end of the year let's say?"

"Perfect I'll get in touch and lemme see what I can do for ya, sound good?

"That sounds amazing."

"Perfect! I can't wait, I don't know what it is with you but something feels different ya know? This feels special, something I haven't felt around here."

"I think I feel it too, I honestly came into thinking you were gonna be some old witch who was gonna control everything I do, but you're like…"

"Chill?"

"Yeah!"

"I get that a lot, anyways I'm running late so I think I'm gonna log off though, I'm excited Karen, I really am."

"Wait what? In covid where you gotta go?"

"I'm late to my date with Ronald McDonald of course." We both start laughing "I gotta get some food in my stomach somehow. For lunch"

"Ha well good luck, and I'll see you around."

"You're damn right you will, BYYYYE!" She logged off. God I hate this chick and love her at the same time. Part of me wants to rip this chick's face off and make her eat it and the other part of me wants to be her best friend. She is making me feel things I shouldn't be feeling, although I do feel this sense of happiness is only temporary just like with the money earlier this year, I am curious to see how this plays out. Who knows, maybe for the next couple of months I'll have an amazing time. I am curious if she can pull off the snoop dogg collab, if she can do that then I think I might actually scream. I do gotta be careful though, If I get too high I might spill some shit and I know how those Cali rats be, I gotta stay alert, but for now I think I'm gonna workout leg day today, then cook some chicken and then probably gonna go out of the city and pick up this new rifle I bought, every since that night three days ago, I've been non stop thinking about shooting stuff. I got this guy who is gonna sell me this rifle and I might wanna shoot some shit with it when I get it, shit is gonna be fucking epic.

July 14th

It's been over a month since my manager and I have gotten together, not much has changed. I've been on a strict workout routine along with the occasional gun and knife fight training I do. I usually stay inside most days and write lyrics and watch youtube when I don't have anything to do and I have made two new song lyrics that I need some beats for. So while Susan continues to try and get some interviews and get Damocha to allow me to collab with some beat maker other than Clemons, I'm at a stand still. Currently I am ready to do so many things but the day just keeps drifting by. I am a little upset at myself as well, for being such a pussy, I mean for god's sake I haven't gotten a good kill in almost a month and I've been inside my apartment for the entire month as well. Basically I'm a loser, "Oh Karen it's ok to do nothing it's covid, everyone can't do anything, you think no one else is feeling the same way you are?" everyone says, but I just- I just don't accept that lame ass excuse. I mean I get it's ok to be lazy, hell I'm the laziest person I know, but I also don't think it should be normal to allow everyone to be so lazy. Someones gotta do the lame work and with this WuHan Flu bullshit I can't. I won't let myself feel ok for being a lazy sack of shit. I also will not accept myself being a fucking pussy anymore either. I haven't felt the urge to kill someone so now I'm thinking I'm turning into an old fart, one of those early generation millennials… eww. My phone starts to ring and it's Susan.

"Sup Seus?"

"Nooooothingg much… other than you just gained verification on mother fucking twitter biiiitch!"

"No shot!"

"Yes, in the sniper scope with a clear view and no wind type of shot."

"Susan you are just amazing you did all the digital marketing for me and now this? You're crazy."

"Well when you've spun the block a little bit you know how things work. Plus all your schizo postings you've been doing on twitter helped you. Your engagement with audiences 13-30 is through the roof, late gen millennials and zoomers are like going head over heels for you. Guys and girls too! I've never seen this before with an artist."

"Never seen what before?"

"Well usually a fanbase is universally leaning one way or the other… ok imagine it like this, most news sources right?

"Yeah."

"Well usually their audiences leans one way or the other, CNN is usually very liberal and ones like FOX are usually pretty conservative, so now just replace those with Males and Females. And all the other genders tend to flow into their somehow, but a lot of artists usually attract a lot of females or a lot of males."

"Ok… it didn't need to be that complicated."

"Anyways so yours isn't gender based it's more generation based. It's a trend that's been talked about before with artists like Eminem way back in the day, but even he suffered from having a predominantly male audience, well you're like the living breathing example of this theory. Your music is coinciding with the younger generation of all genders, not just one or the other. Karen this is great! It shows that your music is sending a powerful generational message. Dead Fashion is still in the top 10 of billboards 100. Now of course reaching #1 was impossible when Megan Thee Stallion and the

Dead Fashion

queen herself Beyonce dropped a song the same week however this is the first time in DP records history that they had a song in the top 10's for more than a month. Not to mention all the interviewers who got to interview you, oh and by the way you're going on Sirius XM on the 20th for another interview. Anyways Karen you should feel proud to produce such ripples in the music industry especially in this time period. Pat yourself on the back, girly girl!"

"Ha ha, I'm just excited that my music finally did what I wanted it to do. I mean for the longest I dreamed of not being a music slave for a major company only producing generic pop music that had no soul or meaning and I really wanted to do something with my music and have it have meaning, make it feel real, like from the heart, ya know?

"Yeah, and that's exactly what happened, I think this is great, Karen you're awesome, you really are. I know I said I wouldn't pressure you to make an album after this but this following and gaining of popularity on all platforms." Oh brother here we go… "I really think you should make and drop an album. I mean Karen, The Akuma is a symbol right now, for young people, I think dropping an album that not only makes a lot of money and gets super popular but also starts a mini movement. Not like what happened a month and a half ago where buildings are burning down and fire spreads everywhere, but I mean more a shift in the culture of young people. Let them know they aren't alone, that someone out there feels for them, and know them. I think young people need a face like every generation has, Elvis, Micheal Jackson, or Nirvana and Eminem. The Zoomers need someone, I really think Dead Fashion was a start, a good catalyst, but I think you could do more… way more.

"That's… my dream, I've always wanted that, more than anything else in the world."

"Then do it."

"Yeah but the beat makers still haven't got back to me."

"Well then maybe start there. Look for small independent beat makers who were the same boat you were months back. Find upcoming people and bring them with you, I'm telling you, this is a start of something big, girl. Anyways I'll let you go, I gotta do some paperwork and other random bullshit, anyways keep up the schizo postings on twitter and get ready for another album, love ya Karen."

"Bye." Maybe I do need to do another album. I mean I've always wanted to be the face of a generation, maybe Susan's right. Well I guess I better start thinking of some lyrics then... oh fuck me.

July 20th

It happened again... The dreams, it's the same thing over and over and over! I'm in this very weirdly lit place. It looks like an office building or some type of workplace. I stand in an endless loop of the same lights and patterns on the walls. Everything keeps repeating over and over. But this time something was different. Every single time it's completely silent, I could hear a pin drop from a mile away. But this time there was sound, a low deep hum, and it was persistent, it didn't ever change. I found myself walking through again and seeing everything going back and forth. Then smeared on the wall it's a giant blood stain and a corpse laying next to the wall. But every time I try to get close to see if I could recognize the body, I wake up and then that's the end.

"FUCKKKKK!" I said out loud to myself as I waited for the doordash delivery guy who is for some reason 16 minutes late and if it takes more than 30 minutes he won't get the chance to deliver another order today. It's 1:06 PM and now I remember why I just walk to restaurants or food places during the summer, but it's so hot today. Almost 102 degrees. Even Arizona isn't this hot, I mean Jesus Christ what the hell! My interview is at 1:30 and so I decide to go do everything I need to do before this big interview, since unlike Jimmy Fallon this is a real interview and not just to play a song. I use the bathroom and then stand in front of my mirror trying to think of every question that could possibly come up. I go through how it is to be super young, how it felt when making Dead

Dead Fashion

Fashion and so on and so on. I stand for what felt like 2 minutes but after looking down at my phone it's 1:17, so I splash some water on my face and compose myself. *Ding Dong* The door finally rings and I race all the way to the door and whip it open only to find some nerdy kid who looked like McLovin from SuperBad standing 6 feet away. I laugh as he takes a picture that I hope is for the order and not some nasty jack off collection of sexy beautiful women like myself. Then he proceeds with a thanks and I say nothing back as I slam the door and open up my subway sandwich. I ordered a Cold Cut Combo on Italian Bread, Of fucking course I got the footlong and the large drink with the raspberry cheesecake cookies. I sit down at my computer setup and keep refreshing my email until the email from Susan pops up with the invite link. They are surprising not normies and are using discord for audio and visuals, since it is superior to zoom (I fucking hate zoom with a passion.) I look at myself in my webcam and mess with my hair a little bit more and make sure my makeup is correct and then I put on my newly acquired Akuma Shirt, that's in the works and I will be showing it off and talking about the merch line coming. Me and Susan brainstormed this super dope hat that is black with my little Akuma symbol and then has the pointy horns like my symbol does. It's now 1:29 and I join their group and after doing some audio checks and camera checks I'm all set up and waiting. I could feel my heart beating in my throat and feel myself almost losing my composure, but I held it in. I then close my eyes and listen to my breath go in and out, in and out. I get snapped back to reality when a voice finally drowns out my silence.

"Hey Karen, this is Klark, I'm the host during the week on channel #2 What's a good baby girl?"

"Oh, um hi, yeah are you gonna call me Karen the entire time?"

"Naw, naw I'll call you The Akuma or whatever, just wanted to introduce myself over the screen, you can see me alright?"

"Yeah, I can, it's a little blurry but ya know how that shit goes."

"Haha fucking covid, well this will be the chillest interview you've ever had."

"Ha alright bet." The producers come in and make sure all the audio is getting picked up and then the video for their youtube channel and then a voice comes in and tells us we're going live in T-3. I sit and keep digging my nails in the palms of my hands. I don't why, but a real interview that's not edited or tampered with is scary as hell. I look down at my phone on my desk as a notification pops up, it's an iMessage from Susan, telling me that I'm gonna do amazing and then to remember to be myself. I closed my eyes again and now I feel very zen. I feel like wind, feel like I'm high almost and then all of a sudden, I feel composed.

"3… 2… 1…"

"Alright alright this is channel 2, hits 1. We've been talking about it all morning and we finally managed to catch ourselves a demon here today, no exorcism needed either. We got Miss Akuma herself."

"Haha Hey guys it's Karen, aka The Akuma, what up."

"Ha the sky, anyways her EP Dead Fashion has been Top 10 in the US for the past month and a half and now she's currently working on a new album as well, but Karen we really wanna know, what was the inspiration for the song? Like most artists ya know, they usually work on a bunch of songs and release an EP like this to promote something, but correct me if I'm wrong, this was completely solo?"

"Yeah this was, um I for me really, I kind of just sit down sometimes and just think how I feel, and then when I take those emotions sometimes I just dump them onto a piece a paper or like a notes app on my phone, and then I'll mess around with beats and shit ya know, then well like with Dead Fashion, it kinda felt right for the moment, it felt like something that was needed. And I really put myself together and wanted to give a good piece of art to come out of a horrible

Dead Fashion

situation. I felt like people, especially younger people, wanted something ya know?"

"I get that."

"I wanted to and still do want to show off how inspirational our generation is, I want to show people that zoomers and young people can make a difference."

"Niiiccceeee. Well Karen, how the show works is we like to take fan call-ins with questions they have for the artist so they can answer some non generic question, something they don't think about a lot." ARE YOU FUCKING KIDDING ME? DID THEY REALLY JUST BROADSIDE ME LIKE THIS?!? OH FUCK, OH FUCK. I'M NOT PREPARED AT ALL! My face goes numb and my smile fades to an expression of horror. " alright we got our first call from Jackson in Oregon, Jackson how are you doing today big man?"

"Yeah I'm doing good. I just wanted to say that I'm not a fan of her music too much, but I do wanna ask how it feels to be lucky enough for your song to blow up so much, like if I'm being honest the algorithm of youtube really helped you a lot I saw this music video about everywhere, So I was just curious how it feels to be a deadbeat relying on luck you know some of us in this society actually have to work for their money?"

"HEY HEY, Cmon now, that's just plain rude dude, how do you think she fee-"

My mind goes blank and my brain snaps as my mask slips, I speak: "Deadbeat huh? You know in life you get an opportunity… and sometimes in life people seize that opportunity, most don't but some do, I seized that opportunity. Life is what you make it, you make your own life and some people say they can't succeed because the life they were given and to be honest they are full of shit."

"Yeah but-" He tries to speak again.

" No, no no, listen to me mother fucker, hard work makes a person, if you work at your dream you can make it come true, any dream can come true with work, not LUCK! Luck doesn't exist in dreams, I made my own luck you fucking twat, I worked hard, I made sacrifices, I made risky decisions. I was piss poor broke at the beginning of this year and because of my actions and choices, I can live free now. I can live how I want and do what I want. And if you don't understand how success works or how to succeed, well let me tell you, it's not because of the life you were born into it's because you aren't talented enough to make it, your not different or better, everyone can be great and become powerful and rich and do anything they desire, but they need to work at it, start marketing and taking risks, work later and more on your projects, if you hate doing something simply don't do it, do something else, I mean for fucks sake there is no reason to struggle working a 9-5 for a corporate fuck face making 86 billion dollars a year doing nothing, seize your opportunity seize your destiny, people aren't destined for things, they are made to do things and if they don't do those things that's their own fault not the society, yes society is fucked up and it's not right that assholes can sit and do nothing and make billions but they are not responsible for your stupidity and your unwillingness to become greater like I did or anyone else did. The biggest setback to you is yourself, very few people actually are set back by other people or things. Life is what you make it and if you want to make it miserable then by all means you can live like that sitting around complaining to me about how lucky I was and how deadbeat I was, because at the end of the day I'll be sitting here enjoying my life and being free because of the things I've chosen and the work I did and risks I took. I think this shit is over, thanks Clark for having me, but I can't stand these uneducated people who shit on someone because they are more successful than them, good day."

July 21st

"ARE YOU KIDDING ME?! Susan you're lucky you aren't standing in front of me right now there would have been a chair thrown at your face!"

"Well that's a little aggres-"

"I mean come on you really let her go off the chains like that?!? You're smarter than this Susan. Now I got calls

Dead Fashion

flying in from investors that are seeing the clip go fucking viral on Tiktok and Youtube and- you know basically the point is Karen's freakout is everywhere, and now I frankly don't know what to do with her? I mean you let her go on that show when she's obviously not mentally stable enough to keep that pretty little mouth of hers from saying stupid shit. So what do you think Ms. Susan Harris?"

"So obviously Karen was in the wrong here, you're absolutely right, so here's what I'm thinking. I devised a plan to rebrand Karen. First off she needs to be able to connect with her fans and right now that's hard considering we don't know where they are and what they enjoy other than her, so I think we need to run some data collection to see exactly where her biggest numbers are. Second you're absolutely right it's blowing up on Tiktok so we need to get Karen a Tiktok account. Third Focus on Karen's interaction with her fans through social media, and finally we have Karen take a little break as in not like the last one but a real break, We'll say she's taking a mental health detox to reset the psyche and then from there get a scheduled tour started for when Covid is done, In the meantime Let's get Karen to brainstorm some music and I'll see how my sources in LA are feeling right now. However Damocha I personally think if Karen embraced this, her fans might-"

"Absolutely not, I want you to listen to me and listen to me carefully. I do not care what a bunch of snowflake zoomers think about this decision and how much of a 'Bitch' or whatever they call people these days, she is for this. I care about the people who are currently funding this company and right now they are on the verge with me because of this girl. You're lucky I'm even still keeping her considering how without any human interaction she still has managed to be the biggest pain in the ass like a rocker from the 90's. So no, Karen needs to be punished for this."

"Pfff! Punished for sticking up for herself" Susan said under her breath..

"What was that?"

"Oh, nothing."

"That's what I thought. I like your first thought: stick with it and get her to shape up, or get ready to pack her bags and leave, end of discussion."

The Talk

"Karen… time to have a chat." I'm trying to have greek yogurt, yes strawberry banana because all the other flavors are ass, and Susan decides that of all the times in the history of history, that the middle of July when my AC is broken to have a "Serious"conversation.

"Look Susan I'm not issuing any apology statements or anything like that, that pussy knew what he did and everyone knows it wasn't my fault."

"Yes, however we still need to post on your socials, something saying that you will be taking a break and maybe a little remorse for yelling at that guy."

"OH, thank god! I thought you were talking about the Mcdonald's drive thru incident, phew ok good, I was gonna say I already gave the guy $500."

"W-Uh-I'm sorry what?"

"Oh nothing anyways, you want me to take a break from MUSIC!?!? For how long?"

"Well a long time."

"WHAT!?!"

"We just need this to blow off, and so we are thinking and don't get mad about this, six months."

"…"

"Ah don't get mad Karen I know I'm sorry I tried but Damocha was all-"

"BAHAHAHA!! Are you kidding me? That's it? HAHA, oh my god you had me scared for a sec there. So-so let me get this straight, you just want me to take 6 months of no music, writing, social media, studio stuff, and I still will get my money and live my life? Sign me the fuck up, holy shit this is perfect, damn now I can go see my family in Washington this

Dead Fashion

Christmas. Susan you are the goat for getting me that much time off, damn you are sexy and good at your job."

"Well I actually tried to get you less time but-"

"Well butts, asses, tits, the whole deal either way I have a whole 6 months of even more freedom, ahhhhhhhhhhh, I'm gonna kick my feet up and do a whole lotta nothing."

"Don't get fat."

"HUHHHHH? Excuse me?"

"Well I mean since you're an idol and people look up to you to stay healthy and keep yourself nice and vital for when you come back, because well, what I told you isn't the big plans."

"What are you talking about?"

"Well the real big news, are you sitting down?"

"No! I'm flying an airplane dumbass."

"Well you would still be sitting down if that were the case monkey."

"EXCUSE ME BITCH? I'll have you know my great grandad was ⅛ black, your canceled sis."

"KAREN! Stop with the 14 year old humor, SHUT THE FUCK UP and listen for a second."

"Ok, Jesus."

"So the big thing is well, the rumor is this covid vaccine is gonna be out by around December so, we are right now piecing together a massive comeback tour, it will get you so many social points you wouldn't believe this shit."

"No."

"I'm sorry? This is every small musician's dream, your own US, to World tour!"

"No."

"What why?"

"Only the US."

"Once again, why?"

'I just…" I pause myself and think about it for a moment. "Can't do that, I just can't do it."

"Karen we are close friends you can tell-"

"I CANNOT DO IT!" It's silent on the phone call, all the hums of the broken AC unit trying to work and the sounds of the city are the only things making noise. "Listen, I just want to stick to the US, if we even can do a tour, I mean how do they know that, and if it's true how do they know if it will even work? If things go as you plan them too and let's say January we start the tour, I want it in the US and you can tell Damocha that I will not cross out of the country for any circumstances."

"Ok ok! Calm down I'll figure it out, I mean a US tour will do good anyways, it just won't be as smart if you are showing big amounts of listens outside of the US but, if that's what you want to do, then we can probably make it work, just double up the shows go to about every state, yeah, yeah we'll make it work."

"I'm sorry I just can't-"

"Hey, hey hey, whatever it is, it's ok don't worry. Damocha will be pissed, but I'll just have to stand up to him."

"I'm… sorry, thanks."

"It's alright, I got your back Karen, don't worry, like I said before, leave the ass work to me."

"Ha.." I wish I had the strength to tell her why I don't want to travel outside the US.

A Clockwork Orange

November 13, 2018

Roughly two years before that call. They stare at me like I'm an art piece, some sort of disconnected stare, right through my soul. I'm barely 20 years old, but I feel like I'm an ancient painting or sculpture or whatever the fuck those Greek fuckers made. Every single one of these guys is an old Japanese dude who probably has a failing and or already failed marriage and is gonna beat off to me tonight. Next to me to my left is a very attractive and beautiful Japanese girl who's maybe 18 at most and to my right are two girls both Japanese as well

Dead Fashion

and both very beautiful and then for some reason there is me, ugly white American alien. How in the hell did I get to this point? The main guy, a Japanese dude, comes and stands in front of us. He's probably mid 50's. He's got a graying beard and is wearing a very expensive suit, along with the other men. The guys stands tall and speaks to us:

"おめでとう、あなたが立っているなら-" Oh I suppose you have no idea how to read Japanese fine I'll translate it into english just know all of this is happening in Japan in Japanese and yes I am fluent already in Japanese it was my life long dream to become an idol in Japan I studied Japanese since I was 12 and moved when I was 20/this year, there you go, your caught up to speed, your welcome… bitch.

"Congratulations, if you stand here before me that means you're part of K12." He turns and says to his other co-workers or employees I don't know who they were. "The newest Idol group to take over Japan! Congrats, especially to the cowgirl over here who is the star of the band."

"Wait really?" I said in Japanese,

"Yes cowgirl." he looms closer to me and caresses my cheek "You see your exotic, your different, and your talented as well. It will make national headlines, shows will be sold out just to see you. We are beginning anew, now we have important stuff to get to but for now take the night off, it will probably be the last night you'll have. We'll reconvene tomorrow to get everything setup." This is it, this is what I was waiting for, my entire life has lead to being a Japanese idol, I'm finally gonna live the life I've always wan-

The next day

"BURGGGHHHH!" the sound of my throw up hitting the toilet as I look over at the scale, I'm still 5 pounds too heavy. This has been horrible, I have to lose 5 more pounds before the end of the day or I'm fucked. FUCK FUCK! I walk over to the other stalls where I see my three colleagues also throwing up. I'm on a strict no eating diet until I hit 68 kg which is about 150 pounds; Deadly diet is what it's called, nothing but throwing up and no eating. Our first rehearsal is tonight as well so we have to be perfect for it, dammit this sucks.

3 hours later

6:30pm JST rolls around and my sisters/colleagues are perfectly fine, you wouldn't have known we were just throwing our guts up into the toilet a couple of hours ago. Big bright lights shine on our faces and there are about 25 people running around chaotically behind the set. In front of us is our manager who is of course an old dude and he is giving us our lyric sheets, which are already completely done.

"Hey Manager ummm when do we get to write our own music and stuff? I got some pretty cool ideas for some English-Japanese mixes."

"Aww how cute, want me to put them up on my fridge?"

"Umm no."

"Then what the fuck do you want me to do with it?" The other girls start chuckling, and I look around to see them laughing at me.

"Sir, I wanted you to take a look at them." He stares at me for a good three seconds before bursting out laughing and then proceeds to walk away saying:

"Don't worry, cowgirl you'll learn." What the frick is wrong with this place?

We do rehearsal and after constantly getting pushed around our toes swatted at to get into the right spots and then getting some of the dancing started, we finish around 8:30pm. I'm exhausted and dead inside. Then we are told to practice singing as a group for an hour then to practice at home, and then finally in the morning we are going to be here at 8am sharp to start singing rehearsal, and then dancing in the afternoon. And that will be my schedule for the next 3 months before we start doing songs and shows. We are all showering after we are done singing and as we are cooling off in the sauna I decide to try and make some small talk with one of my "sisters" as well, we are gonna be working together we might as well be close right?

Dead Fashion

"Hey Yuuka is it? I'm Karen, I feel like we haven't really gotten to know each other properly yet and we have already done all this singing and dancing together, so I just wanted to make some small talk." I smile at her but she is still eyes closed dead faced.

"Karen is it?"

"Yes!"

"That's whiter than I thought it would be."

"I'm sorry?"

"Well, choosing the time when we are in a condensed box with nowhere to go is a great way to make a good first impression, Yes my name is Yuuka. Oh and don't call me Yuuka-chan or Yuuka-san, we are not close like that, you call me Yuuka-sama and we are not sisters either."

Well what a bundle of joy this bitch is.

"Well it's nice to meet you!" I extend my hand, but she doesn't shake it. Instead she looks down at my chest where the towel is because of the way I bent over to extend my hand.

"So disrespectful coming here with those." she says, laying her head back again and closing her eyes. Now a little offended from the disrespect she's been giving me I speak back to her.

"What are you mad that you can't get any of these?"

"Keep talking, maybe someone will hear you."

"Yeah, it just sounds like someones a little salty that I'm the lead vocalist."

"The only reason you are the lead vocalist is because to these old fucks your like a gem to them, white girl, who doesn't know what she is doing, young and attractive and will do anything to keep her job. When they saw your application they probably came in their pants because of how easy of a slut you're gonna be, and the fact you will also make them money." I stand up and go to slap her but I hold myself back.

"Just keep holding back like the good girl you are, all I'm gonna say to you KAREN, is here soon when you want to keep this job, you're gonna be in a lot of these guys crotches, good luck!" She gets up and walks out. I stand there for a second before dropping to my knees and tears start to run from my eyes. I hear the door open and another one of my "Sisters" walks in, this time it was Sakura, the very pretty girl who was the only one who smiled at me when we first met. She sits down and then gets comfy, as she does that I also get back up and wipe the few tears coming down my face and sit back on the bench and put my hands in my face. God I'm such a failure, is the only reason I'm here to be some sex doll?

"Hey! American girl, don't cry, what's wrong?"

"Nothing just that I'm far away from home and I'm also well just a little upset with my singing ability today I guess." I say as I lie to her.

"What? If you're crying then I should be jumping into the dumpster sister, you sang so good today, way better than all of us. Listen if Yuuka said anything about your singing she was just jealous. We didn't even have time to prepare and you were killing it already. Don't be ashamed of yourself... What's your name again?"

"Karen."

"Karen, listen, you did great today, don't let other people mess with your mood. If someone pisses you off or makes you mad you just take your anger back out on them, by being the better person and being the stronger person. If she wants to act like a child, then she will be treated as such."

"Thanks, Sakura, right?"

"Yep!"

"I thought it was just double checking, thank you, I will be a bigger person next time."

"Glad I could help!"

I leave the sauna and go back home to the shitty tight apartment complex I live in. It's run down, but it was the only place I could afford right now until the pay starts coming in from the job, I walk into the apartments and it's super cold in the hallways, I call the elevator but it doesn't arrive so I have to take the stairs to my floor which is the 7th floor. After a stupid long walk I arrive at the floor and open the door. A musk so disgusting comes out of the hallway I almost vomit from it alone. The lights are a deep yellow and are flickering while making a buzzing sound. The carpet is a brown color with dark stains everywhere, I walk through the hall as all the thin walls reveal my neighbors' doings. One guy is watching an American Football talk show or something along those lines. I hear the English speakers talking about the San Francisco 49ers coming up short on the New York Giants the night before. My other neighbor was listening to REALLY loud rock music and I could hear my other two neighbors right across from my door going at it like rabbits in the wild. I mess with the lock and open the door to find my shitty one room apartment.

    Clothes everywhere and it's cold as hell. I take my clothes off, drop my purse and lay in my bed. I close my eyes and for a moment I feel peace and quiet before my phone starts to ring violently. I stumble and pick it up not even seeing who it is.

    "Hello, Hello."

    "Good morning sweetie, how are you doing?"

    "Good mom and it's not morning for me, it's like 11 o'clock at night and I had a long day."

    "Oh boobear I'm sorry, but that's the cost of living the big dream out in Japan!"

    "Yeah the dream mom... The dream."

    "So how was the first real day of practice?"

    "Shit, it sucked and I threw up a lot, mom I hate it here!"

    "Well sweetie this was your decision to be fair, anyways I"m sorry you had a bad day, but once things get rolling I'm sure it will get better!"

The next day

    "BLAGGGHHHH!" I threw up again. Another day slay or so they say, it has officially been the worst day of my life, I should've just went to college, fuck what am I doing. It's about three in the afternoon and so far my body has never been through more training and physical activity in my life. I have to go to a singing rehearsal at four until nine and then now I have

to work out and eat nothing until tomorrow's lunch… YAAAA! Well now to puke my guts out some more!
9pm
I'm hurting, my vocal cords are fried and I feel like at any moment I could pass out. The other girls look great yet I know they are feeling horrible as well and now finally after ripping my vocal cords apart I can finally go home-

"Ms. Wall, could you stay for a minute, the rest of you, you are free to shower or do whatever you please." They all exit the booth and I'm left alone with the old guy who has been running the microphones. He's now looking down at a piece of paper until I interrupt him.

"Um yes what is it, is everything ok?" He doesn't even look up from the paper but still speaks to me.

"Mr. Fujikura wants to see you."

"Wait the Mr. Fujikura, the guy who owns and runs this talent agency?"

"Yes I don't know who else it could be." he says disgruntled… bastard. "His office is on floor 40 the top of the tower and the floor belongs to him so when you come off it should be hard to miss him, if he's expecting you."

"Ok, um thanks." I say as I walk out into the pristine hallway, the building is super nice and quite new. The elevator is nice and smells great and I check my phone as I wait for it to rise to the top floor. DING! The elevator opens and I'm greeted by a secretary who is packing up getting ready to leave. "Ah you must be who he's waiting for." She says as she picks her stuff up, puts her coat on and walks by me "Good luck, you gonna need it bitch." she says under her breath

"Excuse me?" She looks back and smiles but the smile fades away as she turns her head. The floor is nothing like the rest of the building, the rest of the building was pristine, but this floor was divine. It's all set up with expensive and modern art pieces with a gold and black wall finish. The entire room focuses onto a massive two door entrance that says:

"CEO Sanji Fujikura" I go up to the door and take a deep breath before knocking on it.

Dead Fashion

"Ohairi Kudasai." He says which means come in.

"Oh American girl, I'm glad the message was relayed to you." He says in Japanese. Sitting in front of me is the current CEO of this talent agency Sanji Fujikura. He is about maybe 5'11 has semi wrinkling skin and grayish hair and a graying beard. He is wearing glasses I would imagine some high luxury pair and has a silver suit on with a golden tie with white stripes. His office is all a very weird style, it looks sterile. White walls and wood textured shelves and bookcases. He has a massive window behind him that is looking over parts of Tokyo. He has a very odd white silk carpet on the floor, while the main floor is actually marble. There is a computer setup on the desk in the middle of the room which once again boasts the white and wood texture setup. His chair is some high end swivel chair and a couple of chairs with an all matte black design in front of the desk. There is a TV on the wall to my left and a door that's shut with a black finish right next to it. To the right is a wall with a ton of records and pictures of what I presume is Japanese talents over the years. Finally a massive glass chandelier sits over top of everything on a white ceiling.

"Hello, call me Karen, it's a pleasure Mr. Fujikura!"

"Oh it will be!" What?

"Come sit."

"Oh sir, I don't know I got-"

"Come sit."

"Oh um Ok" I sat down in one of the black chairs and I am now facing him.

"Tea?"

"Ah no thank you."

"Coffee, water, anything?"

"No thank you."

"You sure I can always get you water."

"Thanks, but I'm ok"

"Ok them, well... I see you have been working very hard recently, way more than the other girls in..."

"K12?"

"YES!" Does he really not know what his own group is called?

"So Karen my girl, after looking at the tapes and practices, I think you deserve a reward, for all of your hard work for us."

"Uhhh, Ok, What-"

"I'm thinking of a solo album, just you no one else, I think it would go over very well with everyone and could make ends meet for you since you are so young of course."

"OH MY GOD! Are you serious, Mr. Fujikura?!?"

"Yes my girl! I'm thinking of a 12 song album full of anything you want, for your hard work, it's the least I could do for you since you stepped up to the plate and delivered."

"Oh my god! Oh my god! Oh my god! Fuck yes! Oh sorry for cussing. Do you mind if I step out and go call my mom quickly, it won't take to-"

"Since I'm doing something for you, I'm gonna need you to do something for me."

… "Um, sure, anything."

"Give me one second, boys!" The door to the left opens and a group of men who all have a very similar style to Mr. Fujikura all come out. They are all older, probably 50's if I were to guess. Six of them all come out and are now standing around me, as Mr. Fujikura stands up and walks over to me, I stand up, but I am met with one of the old guys immediately. "So the thing you're gonna do for us is something very special, feel grateful you were chosen."

"What are you-" The old guy grabs my arms and spins me around."

"Young American meat like you, never comes around, this will be their first time on a white girl."

"Mr. Fujikura" I'm now tearing up and the mascara is now starting to run with the tears. "Please don't"

"Do you want this solo album Karen?"

"Not if it's going to be achieved through this." I'm now being pinned down to the desk.

Dead Fashion

"Ok then how about money every month, that sounds good, you'll be set for life, all you're going to do is this little favor for us."

"STOP IT! NO! PLEASE! I DON'T WANT THE MONEY!"

He turns me around and now I see six men getting naked and he grabs my face as he lets go of my hand "I wasn't asking for your opinion, that's what's going to happen!" he says softly, my hand now free I punch him in the face and he falls back, I try to run through them but they grab me and slam me back on the desk. "Oh you little bitch, you wanna play like that huh? Ok and he hits me back. I fall to the floor now as blood is dripping from my nose, he grabs my shirt and starts taking it off. "Now I really am going to enjoy this.

"PLEASE, NO! NO! NOOOOOOOO!"

Two Hours later

I get dragged out by two bodyguards and they take me through the backdoor and into an alleyway behind the building. I am thrown into a trash bag and then I hear the metal door shut as I lay there crying. I feel disgusting and nasty and all I can think about is everything they did, all of it coming back and back and back. I can't take it, I can't do it anymore. I am physically shaking. I try to get up but my legs are dead and I cannot feel any of my lower body, my mouth is sore and everything hurts. I can't, I can't, I can't. I lay for maybe an hour with the stench of trash in my face. The cold hits me harder and harder. All my mind can see is him, all my mind can see is him, all my mind can see is him.

I finally manage to get up and start to walk out of the alley, I only feel rage now, I no longer feel like myself. I get past a big trash bin before I hear a man say in Japanese "Excuse me miss, please, help me." I look over and see him sitting there by the bin. He looks like your typical homeless guy with rags on and a scuffed beanie. "Miss please."

"Please what!?"

"Help me, can you give me some cash or something, anything?"

I come and squat down by him and say "Why would I do that?" I look at him one more time and I see it, the beard, the gray beard and my mind immediately floods with… him. It's him.

"Please ma'am, anything, I'm so hungry and cold."

"What's your name?"

"Daichi."

"Well get a fucking clue Daichi, does it look like I'm in any position to help you." My mind starts to calm down just a little and I can compose myself some. "Sorry Daichi, I cannot help you." I start to walk away when he grabs my arm with force."

"Please Ma'am." In a moment's flash everything from the night flashes over and I see it all and within a moment I stare at him, but all I can feel is the rage, all I can feel is the anger. I lunge and grab him by the neck. I start to strangle him and my grip gets stronger and stronger. He tries to pull my hands away, but cannot. He struggles and winces and bloody spit starts to come out of his mouth as all of it builds and builds. It feels natural, it feels like my body is working on primal instincts, it feels… good almost. I watch the life drain from his eyes and then slowly his hands plop down to his lap and eventually he's dead. My grip doesn't stop as I keep gritting my teeth and gripping his neck for another two minutes. Finally everything hits me like a brick and my eyes go wide as I realize… I just took another person's life. I drop back and fall onto my ass. I see his body lifeless in the alley. I look at my hands and realize what I have just done, my mind shouldn't feel pleasure, It shouldn't feel good, it's horrible to take another man's life, yet it felt so good. Everything that had been building up is gone, I don't feel the stress, I don't feel anger, I only feel whole. I quickly get on my feet and exit the alley way, as I promise myself to never do that again, but that promise wouldn't last.

Walmart Brawl
August 27th, 2020

"Karen, Earth to Karen! Hello?"

"Oh shit sorry Susan."

"Jesus, that must've been one hell of a day dream. What did you find the dream guy or something haha?"

"Haha." I laugh out loud as my face immediately stops smiling as she looks away and back at the road. She is currently driving and I'm in her 2016 Ford Fusion.

"So you really can only get this face cream that you can't get anywhere else? It's literally on the other side of St. Paul, you couldn't have ordered it on Amazon or something?"

"No I couldn't, this Walmart is the only Walmart in the state that supplies this face cream and I absolutely need it."

"Whatever Ms. Perfect everything."

"Shut the fuck up."

"Haha."

"You're one to talk anyways I feel like I'm in a Stanley Kubrick movie, this car is so clean and just perfect, so sterile. Obviously you've never had sex in this car."

"It's funny you say that because I actually gave a guy a blowey the first day I got this car."

"No Shot."

"Yep."

"Your a fucking demon susan."

"Once again you're the one to talk." she says as she side eyes me and then breaks down into a laugh.

We pass the Xcel Energy Center where I hope I have my first concert coming out of covid and that's also where the Minnesota Wild hockey team play. I went to a game with my dad when I was little and I remember it was really fun and seeing a bunch of Russian names, interesting experience.

"God traffic is a bigger pain in my ass than you are Karen I swear."

"Well we literally are in the heart of St. Paul" I have no idea what she is bitching about, I find the traffic nice, it allows us to slow down and see everything around us, the infrastructure really is beautiful.

"Karen, unlike some of us in this world we don't get to sit around and do nothing all day like you do, we have things we have to do."

"I thought this was a day off for you?"

"..."

"That's what I thought, shut it and enjoy the infrastructure."

"Eww no."

"You don't like the infrastructure." Ok now I'm really convinced I can't be friends with her anymore."

"Compared to LA or San Fran? God no! Cali was way better than this. The infrastructure is so trashy and way down to earth urban, I like a more traditional style like the capitol buildings and stuff."

"I mean it is right over there down the street."

"Yeah but like I don't know how to put it St. Paul and Minneapolis don't do it for me." Damn, what a bitch.

"Well anyways just be glad you're getting to spend quality time with someone during a time like this."

"Karen it's hot a hot ass late August day while Covid is more dangerous than ever, you think I want to be here doing this right now? I would rather be home watching… Well pretty much anything, so long as I'm not here."

"So then why are you here?" I thought about this question as I asked it, if she really is so mad and annoyed by taking me why is she taking me? I know if the roles were reversed I would never in a million years take her especially if I was mad let alone if I was in a good mood, I don't like doing anything for anyone period, unless it involves a computer and me not leaving the house.

"Karen sometimes you just do something for someone, because- well because you just simply want to do it. Sure it might make you mad or angry or put you in a bad mood or take time out of your day, but you just do it, you never have done anything like that before? Like when your parents would get groceries even though they were coming from the car and were perfectly healthy yet still came inside and told you to take the groceries in?"

"Well yeah but, I don't know where I was going with this I guess." I lay my head on the side of the window and look out at the few people who wander the streets. Some masked up, some with no masks at all. We finally get out of the massive traffic block on the light and we drive past the Children's Museum and then start to cruise. "Man, I wish I had a car."

"Well maybe you can use some of the cash you got from Dead Fashion and the album, I heard from the grapevine you were thinking about getting one of those super nice apartments in the new gentrification wave downtown there."

"Yeah I was thinking about it, Damocha was talking about one of the places his buddies lived and said I should move there, since I make way more than enough money to live there."

"Where were you thinking?"

"The Nic on Fifth."

"Holy shit Karen those are expensive as hell. Isn't a one bedroom there like three and a half grand a month?"

"Yeah, but I don't plan on getting a one bedroom."

"WHAT?" she says not screaming but now very confused." I continue to smudge against the window and stare at everything.

"Yeah I plan on getting the penthouse on the 23rd floor."

"How much?"

"Ehhh like 9k a month."

"Jesus Christ Karen! How much money have you made this year? I did the numbers for Dead Fashion but how much is taken away."

"Well if we actually do decide to stick with the tour and if the listens and sales continue the way they are I will be pocketing a shit ton more than what I was guaranteed on my starting contract."

"So once again, how much?"

"$850,000 and then next year if we do the tour, probably around 8 or 9 mil." Susan slams on the breaks and the car behind her slams as well and almost hits us.

"Let me get this straight... I'm driving you around right now because you don't have a car yet and you're gonna make 850k by the end of the next four months."

"Well... that is before taxes."

20 minutes later

We arrived at the Walmart I needed to go to, to get the face cream. I made sure to do a mobile pickup order so that they would bring it out to us in the car and we could save some time and the risk of getting infected with the Rona. Susan hasn't said a word to me since the car breaks incident so I'm starting to think she is mad at me, so also has been dead faced. It's probably because she knows I make a lot more money than she does, which is just human jealousy of course, but at the same time she should feel grateful because having someone with a bunch of money as a friend means you get $500 amazon gift cards for Christmas. We take spot #2 and I click that I am here and within five minutes a guy wearing a blue vest comes out of an orange metal door on the side of the building with an order on a basket on wheels."

"That looks like more than just face cream Karen..."

"Well hey, I'm going to Walmart, might as well get groceries."

He comes up to the driver side window and Susan rolls it down.

He sighs as he looks at the name "The Akuma?" He says. Susan looks at me and then I shake my head up and down and she says:

"Yes."

"Ok, I just had to confirm I'm in the right vehicle." He says as he steps back and looks at all the items."

"Karen! You put your name as The Akuma on the app?!?"

Dead Fashion

"Well yeah what did you want me to put in Karen, and make him think he was gonna deliver to some middle aged witch, who wants to speak to his manager?"

"Ok well you could've put a real name at least!"

He comes back up to the window and says:

"ok here is a list of some substitutions I had to do, can you confirm if these are ok." he hands the walmart branded phone device to Susan and then she passes it over to me, I look at the list, my texas toast was replaced with wonder bread, pff, figures. My shampoo was replaced with some trash ass brand, however I don't care too much, but then I see it. I saw the one thing I needed, my face cream which was Gojo's non alcoholic sweat-resistant face rub, was replaced with Estee Lauder revitalized daywear, which has alcohol in it. I stare in disbelief that such a trade out could happen, this trade was almost as bad as the Minnesota Vikings trading Stephon Diggs for a draft pick. This is like subbing out Kim Jong Un for his sister who threatens to use nukes against the US. This is unbelievable. I stare dead cold and hand the phone back to him and Susan can now see my face and she has started to pick up on my moods through my face. I look at the guy closer who I know has bushy eyebrows and a mask covering his face, but he can't hide that big ass nose he has with it.

"No."

"I'm sorry he says?"

"That face cream should have been in stock, it was when I placed my order."

"Well ma'am that was earlier today, this is now, it was sold out."

"Ok you know what I don't even care-" I look at his name tag "Kevin, about the brand, Ok? I care about what's in the product."

"Well Ma'am this product is actually more expensive and-"

"Price doesn't matter, you could get a million dollar sports car and this 2016 ford could be better. This product has alcohol in it. Which your smooth brain probably doesn't understand, it dries your face out even quicker, the other one didn't." Susan now looks very confused at me.

"Ma'am you're taking a bunch of time up if you want. We can cancel that item and refund it to your account and give you the rest of the groceries." Susan now mouthing the words do it, with an angry face. I sigh.

"Ok sure, fine, do it."

Ok ma'am and where would you like them?" Susan steps in

"The trunk is fine." she goes for the trunk pop button, but I stop her and say "let me pop the trunk for you, our button doesn't work."

"Karen it works"

"Our BUTTON doesn't work." I step out of the car and he comes around to the back left side of the car. I go to the trunk and as I am about to click the button on the back I stop and turn to him and he looks at me."

"Well?" He says "Can you open it for me?" That's when I decided I had enough.

"Well ya know it's just the fact that-" POW! I smash his face with my fist and he falls back and falls and trips over the cart and the cart falls down to the side with all the groceries spilling out. "That you can't even use your brain to look for another non alcoholic face cream." Susan opens the door and gets out but I get over top of him and grab him by his vest. I punch him again this time, blood starts oozing from his big ass nose and stains his yellow mask. Susan, now out of the car, tries to get me off of him and screams "KAREN! STOP!" I push her off me and punch him one more time as he screams out in pain. Then I lift him up and put him on the orange beam holding the roof of this little parking spot up. And I say to him "Now! When I say I want something on the app, that means I should get it when I'm here. He keeps sobbing,

"WELL!? ANSWER ME!"

"Y-y-yes."

"Ok! So then next time when you're looking for an item, how about you match it PROPERLY!"

"Well I just thought that i- it wouldn't make a difference."

"Well it did, KEVIN!" Now Susan is on me and grabs me and the manager and two other employees run out of the same orange metal door screaming and I release the kid and he runs toward the manager now. The manager comes up to me and screams:

"What the hell is going on here?" as soon as he says this, Susan immediately buts in and says:

"We were just leaving, I'm sorry."

"Oh no you don't, I'm calling the goddamn cops, assaulting one of my employees is not something you're getting away with. You can leave Miss, but she can't." He starts to dial on his phone as the employees make sure we don't leave, Susan now pissed grabs me by the shirt and says:

"Don't think I'm ever doing anything for you again."

Honestly though it felt good to bunch that dweeb, I hit him pretty good.

An hour and a half later at the St. Paul police department

"Assaulting an employee in a Walmart parking lot, that's a first, I've never- Miss Wall please keep your mask above your nose, I would really appreciate it." I reshuffle the mask as the police officer continues to read me a bunch of useless crap. "Miss Wall as far as I'm concerned you're lucky."

"I'm lucky? Oh right sitting in this hot ass police station makes me lucky, do you know how much money I make? Even if you did, you still would not be able to comprehend it."

"Wall don't get smart with me! I've met guys who make four million dollars a year, and guys who make only enough to afford a stick of gum. I've seen all types of guys run through this city, trust me I don't care about how much money you make and even if I did it wouldn't change any outcome, trust me I know first hand. And yes to answer you, yes you are lucky, The kid's not pressing charges and since the altercation was before the police got there and technically Walmart parking lots are public property so it's all up to him."

"Ok so, then why am I here?" He doesn''t look at me, then proceeds to stand up as his white shirt crinkles and his shitty blue clip on tie waves around. He then looks at me and then says:

"Follow me if you would." We entered a room sealed off from the rest of the department, with just a table and some water, three chairs and two cameras. It was easy to tell what this room was, it was an interrogation room. I sat down and then once he left the room I took my mask off to breathe for a second and then a short black woman entered the room. She was wearing a suit more cleaner and fancier than the last bozo and I could start to piece together exactly what type of business I was dealing with.

"Miss Karen Wall, born December 8th, 1998. Correct?"

"Yeah, and why exactly am I here again?"

"Well to be quite frank with you, we normally don't do this but I was very intrigued by a case you were involved in, in Minneapolis."

"What are you talking about?" now pissed as the time is starting to get late.

"Karen, I'm Chief of Police here in the St. Paul district, my name is Kellan Tungavaloa and I'm currently wanting to know more about a certain case." She is trying to get me to latch onto something and slip up, but I am about 10 steps ahead of her, I remember all my alibi's for all my murders this year. She is not going to get anything out of me unless she brings it up first. However I might be able to lead her off on the wrong track if I play this correctly.

"Well Mrs. Toungevold-"

"Tun-ga-valo-a!"

"Riiiight, anyways I am gonna need more clarification like what are you talking about, I still don't know." She looks at me for a solid second staring dead in my eyes, trying to get me to look away, showing a sign of guilt. I'm not falling for that, I stare right back at her and now we are locked into a staring contest almost, both dead faced. My mask is covering

Dead Fashion

my mouth and she isn't wearing one, so much for enforcing the rules.

"Karen a couple months ago a young man named Christopher Stevenson was reported missing and then was never seen from again. I pulled his file from a detective Lars with the MPD, but he concluded that there was no evidence against you because he was seen by himself leaving your apartment through CCTV with a duffle bag. However he never appeared again, McDowell, currently has opened ended, but the search is off, but… I don't buy it."

"What are you talking about, Chris was a boyfriend I had almost nine months ago, what else do you want or need? He was seen leaving my house, like what?"

"The thing is, this evidence doesn't make sense, looking at the footage, why would he be carrying a duffle bag? And how come he doesn't go in the direction of his home or try to get an uber or rideshare?"

"He was carrying some things and- look why do you even care, I mean for god sakes he was my boyfriend, you don't think I was distraught too, I wish he would come back."

"Bullshit, you weren't close with him at all."

"And how THE FUCK DO YOU KNOW?"

"Because I WAS HIS STEPMOTHER!... I raised him since he was 3 years old." She stares, with tears now running down her face and she gets up from the chair and then says "And I'm just trying to find the only child I ever had, for god sake if you did something to my boy and you're not telling me, I need to know."

"I wish I could help you but I don't know anything." I say as I stare her dead in the eyes, she knows it bullshit.

An Hour Later

I am released because simply put, there was no legal basis for the interrogation and the fact I even answered her questions was funny enough. She thought I didn't know the law, however whenever you are being questioned or interrogated without basis, the moment you refuse to answer any questions, it is done deal. They can't do much as the case had no evidence and the main offense I came in for was already dismissed by both parties. They book my info and I get my stuff back and- "Holy SHIT! Susan?! You actually came here?" Sitting in the parking lot Susan sits with her 2014 ford fusion and is standing outside of it.

"Karen in the car now!" Yeeeeah, I'm in trouble. I get into the car and it is pure silence as the car sits idle as Susan has her head on her steering wheel. I think about it before I decide for the first time in a while to genuinely apologize to someone.

"Look Susan I'm-"

"No, No, No, NO! You're not doing this shit again Karen, I don't want to hear it, just… just STOP!"

We drive and after an extremely long drive through the end of rush hour traffic, I watch the sun go down and every once in a while I look over at Susan, only to see her as dead in the face as I have ever seen her. I try to open my mouth, but every time I do I get tripped up.

"You should be thankful I'm even driving your ass home."

"Well you didn't have too, ya know."

"Well I kinda did too as it's basically my job to babysit your ass and make sure you don't do stuff like you did today." We turn to my street and she goes into the parking ramp to the side of the apartment building, she is going to park? Hmmmm.

"Your parking?"

"Karen, I can't believe you did what you did today, I mean seriously, do you have any idea what exactly this means for me and you?" damn way to avoid the question.

"First off, this is risking not only your career, but mine." She now finds a spot and parks "Because this is the thing I was supposed to stop you from doing, having these impulsive problems where you just do things instantly, I am supposed to be the good devil on your shoulder telling you to not do it, yet I can't, which means…" She puts her head down on the wheel again and starts to cry "I can't do my job."

"Hey Susan, I'm sorry. I am, that was so bad of me, and to be honest it wasn't worth it at all, I mean I got no satisfaction out of it and so, I'll take all the blame. If Damocha tries to punish you, I will convince him to put it all on me."

"No, Karen don't, he is not gonna listen." She puts her head up and wipes the tears away, now looking at me "He has a problem with me and he is not gonna take anything, I'm replaceable, you're not, If someone gets hit with it, it's gonna be me."

"Susan, you are not replaceable! Do you think anyone can do this job? Do you know how big of a nuisance I am? Ha I mean you came up with shit and worked around stuff I would have never dreamed of, you're like the one girl from happy gilmore, the one he falls in love with, had the nice boobs, ya know?

"Virginia?"

"Yes, her, you keep me out of trouble and I mean who cares about a little fight, if you are gonna go at him, you aren't doing it alone, I will be there and force him to keep you, any means necessary." She stares at me and I stare back at her before she out of nowhere does the unthinkable. She quickly leans in and kisses me on the lips and put her hands up to my face and then pulls back.

"Oh my god, Oh my god, Karen I-I am so sorry I don;t know what came over me I just-" I lean over and kiss her back and before we know it we are making out in our parking garage. We maybe keep kissing for over like two to three minutes, before a knock on the window scares the living shit out of us."

"Hey You two out of the car now!" It's the security guard of the parking garage. He's a black dude named Jeudy, who kind of just chills, fat guy, super cool. We step out before he looks at me and says "Oh shit Karen? Damn girl, how ya been?" I look nervously as me and Susan are both embarrassed by the encounter and he quickly picks up on it. "Oh I get it now, haha sorry y'all, Karen, look at you girl." he punches me in the shoulder lightly "Bringing home chicks now- Hey I don't judge, we in the city bitch pride all the way, I support yall either way." we both laugh and I reply with:

"It's not like that, she is my manager."

"Damn no kidding, she was managing you pretty well in the car."

"Excuse me, Jeudy, how much did you watch?"

"Oh shit look at the time, I got rounds to make, good luck girl, Karen eats her prey alive, HAHA, see ya." He quickly leaves and Susan then goes:

"Well, now I am really embarrassed, look I'm sorry I-I should go." she turns to go back to her car, But I grab her hand and pull her back hard, I'm used to it and then grab her and say:

"Noooo! You can't, come and see my apartment. You can see how I'm living before I move in a couple weeks, see the now vs. the future."

"No I shouldn't really, I-"

"Please, Please, Please?" She looks at me and bites her lip and then goes:

"God I hate you." and then kisses me again.

My Apartment

The Tour was quite short as I only toured her to my bed until I finally had my makeout session with Susan, who by the way yes I've been wanting to bone since I met her but have always suppressed the emotions and finally got her to my bed. She is really nervous as I take off my shirt and then undo my bra.

"What's wrong?"

"I've never done it with a girl before."

"Ok."

"What do you mean ok?"

"It's fine, do you know how many straight chicks I convince to fuck me? I'm like a sex magnet, it's fine." I try to get her onto my bed but she stands there awkwardly.

"Yeah, but I don't know anything."

"You've never watched lesbian porn before?"

"Maybe once?"

"D-Damn it girl, ok, what does your body usually want from a guy?"

"Dick?"

"NO! Like before that, you want him to eat you out and stuff right?"

"Yeah I guess, I don't do that much."

"Ok just imagine whatever would feel good for you and then do it to the other person, simple?"

"Yeah but you have fucked all these people what if you have a disease or something?"

"Susan, I get tested every month, and when your talking about the guys you've been with, this has never been an issue, do you know what I think?

"What?" I start getting closer.

"I think you're making excuses." I push past her and go to my dresser and grab a vibrator, but I hide it so she can't see. "Just take off your shirt, let me see your titties."

"O-Ok" she takes her shirt off and then her bra off and has ok boobs, nothing special, no birthmarks and nothing big. Nowhere in the ballpark of mine.

"Good step one, now step two, the jeans gotta come off."

"Can we maybe start with just making out?"

"Susan I got you here, didn't I? You think I wanna make out naked? Fuck No!"

"Maybe some wine or alcohol or something, I don't know."

"Ugh fine I have some sexy red wine you will die for." I go and grab the bottle and glasses and undo the cork, I bring it to the bedroom and turn the lights off and light my candle. As I light my candle I look over, only to see her with half the bottle gone. I immediately run over to her and said "Susan! Your gonna kill yourself stop." I grab the bottle and she looks at me and smiles and says:

"DAYUM, that was some fine wine, you weren't kidding."

"Yeah well you aren't supposed to have that much."

"Are you my dad? I didn't think so."

"Ha, you are getting pissed now."

"You can piss on me if you want."

"Ha." She stands up and I go back over and grab the vibrator again and we once again get into the same positions we were in before the whole little wine thing. "Ok take your pants off."

"Why you gonna FUCK me?" she says getting more drunk barely being able to take her jeans off, but she gets them off to reveal a cute pair of light pink panties.

"Yes, that's exactly what I'm gonna do." I then go up to her and push her back onto my bed before she bursts out laughing as I turn the vibrator on "We are gonna have some fun, you ready?"

"YES BITCH."

"HAHA good." Let's just say after this, it was fun.

6:30 AM August 28th

"Good Morning, this is WCCO news, I'm Sherry, your new hostess of the morning show and yesterday was a very odd day in the Twin Cities area. Famous rapper and musician The Akuma was caught on video assaulting a Walmart employee in St. Paul. Karen Wall/The Akuma who lives in the twin cities area was not charged on any accounts as the Walmart employee who has decided to remain anonymous did not press any charges. According to DP Records, the record label behind The Akuma said that Karen Wall was completely in the wrong and that there was no reason she needed to do anything that she did in that situation. DP also says that will end up settling things regardless with the anonymous employee even if they didn't press charges. They also said she will release an apology statement along with counseling over the next few months to get her back into the right mental state. Karen was said to not have been in good health these past few months since the release of her last song Dead Fashion.

Dead Fashion

Despite all of this controversy The Akuma is trending on Apple music still and her numbers seem to only be going up and not down. Now we are going to head over to John Walters at a local Bakery in town called Da Goodies and how they have been managing covid and how they have been staying alive, over to you John!"

The next morning is sunny and I see Susan lying in front of me completely naked. The bed is wet and slowly drying and my leg has a bunch of crusted fluid. I can assume what these are based on last night. I go to get out of bed but Susan wraps her arm around me and softly moans. The cutesness of the situation led me to stay in bed and hold her and I do so gently. I am honestly pissed at the simple fact of how nasty this is, not that I'm not into it, but being trapped in nasty liquids that are RUINING my sheets is pretty fucking annoying. But nevertheless I lay for about five minutes just staring at her. God is she just sexy, easily one of the prettiest girls I have ever slept with, I just admire. Simply because I have a strong feeling this is gonna be a one and done situation. I lay for about another five minutes holding her, until I got bored of it and got up and made some tea. Normally I don't drink tea, I'm more of a water person, but I know that Susan is a big tea person, and I need to get this tea out of the cabinet anyway. I make the tea and then go back to the bedroom and see that Susan is finally awake. I go to her and hand her the tea.

"Careful, it's hot." I say as she rubs her eye and then takes the tea still wrapped in the blanket. I genuinely thought about putting arsenic in her drink and watching her burn from the inside out, but I didn't feel it was the right idea because I care about- I mean because it would be too hard to get away as a free woman on this one. I was last seen with her and I was also last seen at the police station as well. No other alibis on this one, so it ends up not working out.

"What day is it?" She asks

"It's friday" I say to her as she sips her tea. As I say that, she damn near spits all of it out and says.

"Holy shit, really?"

"Yeah I know, it was just a beauti-"

"Oh my god, oh my god, oh my god. I have a meeting at eight, oh fuck, dammit!" She quickly sets the tea down going towards the side of the bedroom and grabs her clothes."

"Chillllll, it's not even seven yet, I mean I never get up this early, like ever."

"Yeah well that's because some of us are adults in this room."

"Excuse the fuck out of me! No way you just said that" I look directly at her and usually this is one of those snappy remarks that Susan has whenever we are talking and right after I respond she will usually say, "I'm kidding" or "I'm sorry I'm just messin with you." but instead she says.

"Well it's true." walking past me now towards my living room with her pants on and no bra or shirt. She either isn't a morning person or she is mad about last night. I mean she did have a decent amount to drink, but it's not like she passed out drunk, she simply did all of that willingly and I think she knows it. Maybe it's just a bad morning or she doesn't like other people's houses. Fully clothed she grabs her stuff and walks out the door before I can even ask where she is going. She quickly barges back in and says.

"By the way you will be getting a phone call from Damocha most likely about the incident yesterday and you will also be getting a email from Mike about some new samples and ideas for when you return in a couple months, I think they want to start recording soon." She goes to close the door again, but I scream just in time for her to stop.

"Where are you going? You still have almost an hour until the meeting and DP is only down the street and aren't all of those on zoom nowadays anyways?" I ask as she opens the door back up a little more.

"It is a zoom meeting, and I am going home to prepare my notes and keep myself looking nice, it's a big quarterly reports thing, stuff you wouldn't understand." Why is she treating me like a child? I know how to do things and for the first time in my life, acting like a dumb zoomer is actually

Dead Fashion

pissing me off and is working too well. She acts like I'm some uneducated broad who just sings and fucks. Fuck her for thinking that, if that's the case. I think maybe acting this way around her needs to change, I would say I would act like myself, but to be honest I don't really know if I have a genuine personality. I mean I guess I could stop acting dumb, but acting like myself? Hmm.

"Why are you being like this Suz?"

"Karen... just stop."

"Look if it's about last night I'm-" She slams the door, I quickly go to the door and open it and she is gone already. Maybe it's time I change up around her. I'm getting very upset at the way she thinks of me, I mean for Christ sake I journal damn near everything in my life. I got a 36 on the ACT, twice because you know they don't believe you the first time. I have probably killed more people than she has met in her life and not trying to brag, but I have almost perfected knife fighting and I go to gun range twice a week and have almost perfected firearm accuracy since the incident a few months back. I mean I am street smart and book smart, I don't know what more she would want from me, maybe I show her up at her own game, maybe that will work, but first I should really let her cool down, I'm sure she will be fine by the end of the day.

End Of The Day

"No Karen, I am not fine. If anything, I'm far from fine actually; I mean for god sake Karen, do you know what we discussed today?" Susan screams to me as she walks into the door. I told her to come over because I wanted to talk about everything that's been happening. At first she refused, but then she changed her mind feeling she could get something out of this.

"I couldn't tell ya, I wasn't there." as I sit down on my couch with the red wine I poured for myself.

"We were supposed to be discussing our talent quarters as Q3 is coming to a close in a month, but instead all eyes were on me and you. About the blow up, it's going viral on TikTok." she says and she starts pacing back and forth.

"What!?"

"YES! Someone recorded it and it spreading like wildfire, even the execs were confused about the big commotion and they are fucking in their 60's. I was bashed and bashed by everyone, do you know how many times my job was threatened? 'I thought you were the big guns who worked with Snoop Dogg and all of these rappers in LA, that's why we put you on this case, would be a shame if you can't get her together and have to look for another job' like fuck you dude, genuinely stick that pen you have in your hand down you fucking dick, probably won't even be able to get his dick hard enough old ass man." Woah she's talking like I am what the hell.

"HAHA, that's dark Susie."

"What did you just call me?" She asks, as she stops pacing and looks at me.

"Susie! I was trying to find a nickname for you and I found it."

"Eh-I- Whatever, for the life of me I don't care, what I care about right now is you Karen. I mean come on what else do I have to do for you to just stop?"

"Susan, I don't know what you want me to do."

"NOTHING! DO NOTHING KAREN! Is it that hard to understand?" She screams at me as she stands in front of me now." For fuck sakes nothing, I need you to stop." I start to hear her voice change and she starts to sound like she is going to start crying. "What do you want from me? I mean seriously Karen, I have done everything I can." Her voice fully breaks down along with herself. "I have taken heat for you, I have lowered your punishments, sweet talked Damocha. When that didn't work I started calling you, doing things with you, I FUCKED YOU and still it doesn't seem like you've even grown up at all. Karen I am only like what, three years older than you?"

"Yeah basically."

"And still you act like a fucking child, you think it cool to be this mysterious bashful, don't give a fuck piss on anyones grave person, well it's not, it shows the old people exactly why

Dead Fashion

they don't trust this generation, even to me who's apart of this I still feel like you are immature. I mean what gives you the right to act like this and be like this? What authority do you have, that you feel like you deserve to be like this?" I sat silent for a moment with my eyes closed and now my nails clenched into my palms making a fist causing my palms to bleed.I hid the fist so she wouldn't see it or me in pain. I start to breathe in and out and try to calm myself down. "I mean cool, you can sing and people want that." She says as she now sits on the other small couch to my left. "But you're acting selfish, you're acting like this high and mighty figure, who because young people think your tits are big and you can sing semi decent thinks she can walk all over every-" I slam my fist on my glass coffee table and my fist goes through the glass and shatters it. The loud crash completely stops Susan from talking and she looks at the table with her eyes wide and her mouth open. I finally break from my shell, I cannot contain myself any longer.

"Do you know what I've been through? Even if I told you, you wouldn't even be able to conceive the things that have happened to me. You think I'm an alt style semi dark girl, because I think it's quirky? Are you actually so GODDAMN STUPID to think that I haven't been through anything in my life?" Normally I just take the bashings Susan gives me and the long talks and let it just hit me, but the months of this happening and it's built up, I cannot stand being the punching bag for problems anymore. "Susan, look at yourself, and then look at me. You're worried about losing your job? HAHA I are fucking serious right now? You lost your job in the shittiest state in all of the US except for Ohio and are complaining. 'Oh boo hoo I lost my 6 figure job, it's not like I can just immediately use my skills from the insane college degree and work experience to find another job.' Little old Susan is gonna have to live in a high end apartment on Unemployment while I look for another six figure job that I most likely will get. Karen could be out of a job at any time and is hated by everyone she works for. Do you know how I lived before I became famous? I lived in low end shitty apartments and ate only three times a week because I could only afford Ramen noodle packs of three each week. I worked from a low end job to another low end job, because I thought I could be a famous Idol in Japan. I saw myself breaking the barrier to bring US pop and rap and Japanese pop and rap to the world. I wanted to be a star. I starved myself. I gave up, I scored a 36 on the ACT, I was a straight A student who was in Choir, I had, could've had so many college opportunities, but oh no, I was some random girl from the middle of bum fuck nowhere, noone gave me a chance, I was forced out of every high school I went to. I dropped out my senior year. I was being bullied so badly I came home and the only thing I could think about was what my lifeless body would look like hanging from my ceiling fan, but that didn't stop me from going all the way to Japan and working my ass off, and do you know what working my ass off living in a shitty one room apartment with drug head neighbors eating only ramen got me?" I stand up and walk up to her and bend over and she flinches, but then stops, I get close to her face, look her in the eyes and then say what I had never told a single person in my life, the thing that started everything. I whisper in an aggressive tone. "It got me fucking raped." I walk away from her throwing my now empty wine glass at my cupboards going to my kitchen. "But oh poor little old Susan, who had loving parents, a great childhood, got a full ride to UCLA, walked out of college right into a sustainable six figure job. Is worried about her life… and her career. Screaming at someone who had to work day in and day out to make what she is making and to be where she is now, but where's her authority right? What gives her the right to be an asshole and aggressive to the world? Living off nothing, being raped, losing her brotherin front of her eyes. Who does she think she is pissing all over everybody else's graves, with her middle fingers high in the air saying fuck everyone, what give her the authority, right?" I walk back over to her after grabbing the entire wine glass. My eyeliner and makeup are running down my face from the tears at which I shed when in the kitchen and well from the whole thing. I had never spoken about that to anyone, not even my brother dying either.. I look at her and say. "Next time you trauma dumb me, at least treat me like a fucking adult." I go to my room and slam the door. I put the wine bottle on my bed and turned the bathroom light on and cleaned out the glass and cuts on my left hand. After that I breakdown. I lose it and cry and cry. I don't I have ever cried like this before and it almost feels like I let go of something big. I hear a knock on the door of the bathroom and I look over and it's Susan. I quickly wiped the tears and said "HAHA this glass is painful ha, brought me to tears." But by the look of her face I could tell I wasn't bullshitting her. I continue to run water down my hand at the sink and look back at it. I try to hold in my cry, but tears want to come down. Suddenly I feel arms wrap around my body. I feel Susan's body press up against mine. I feel her soft breathing on my neck. I stop the water and quickly wipe my hands. I keep my eyes closed for a minute and she continues to hold me. Finally I grab her hands which are around my belly button and turn around to face her and she looks at me. It happens at last and she puts her lips on mine and once again I feel some of the softest lips I have ever felt in my life and this time, they feel even softer. We stop kissing and I say "So this is why you decided to come over." she laughs and says.

"Maybe. But you were the one who invited me over in the first place. Did you not want this to happen?"

"That was the whole reason I invited you over, I figured I could help you blow it over and relieve some stress."

"I figured." She goes in for another kiss and we continue to makeout in the bathroom. We continue for about another two minutes before she says "Well I need to shower, you wanna join me? Your shower looks cozy enough for the two of us." I reply back with a counter

"How about we take a bath, more water and my tub is practically a hot tub in this apartment. I could also light some candles and bring the wine in too."

"That sounds like you want it to be sexy, what do you plan on doing to me in the tub?"

"Everything." We both chuckle and kiss again and then she goes over and starts the water to fill the tub. I grab the candles and then light them. After my little hunt for the candles and then getting the wine the tub is about half full. Standing next to the tub Susan is not getting undressed and for the first time, I really get a good look at her. I don't remember her looking so perfect, but she does, down to the last atom. She turns around and says.

"Well are you gonna get undressed or do I need to do it for you?"

"Contrary to your beliefs I actually am a big girl. But maybe for this instance it would be so much nicer if you could fondle me and take them off for me."

"Haha, fine." She gets done undressing me and says. "Holy shit your tits are so big! My god." She grabs them and starts to play with them before sucking my left tit.

"Woah there, let's wait until the tub." Looking back it's completely full now and we get in. The water is so nice and she is even better, she washes herself a little, but eventually gets too distracted and pounces on me. She starts sucking my tits again and I lay back in enjoyment. Her tongue brushes my tits and it feels like something I have never felt before. Then we make out some more before she decides to go underwater and then puts her tongue on my- Oh Jesus fuck I am too tired right now to write and I have a busy day tomorrow. Long and very sexy story short, basically she tongue fucked me and I did it to her and then we got out of tub and had sex at the exact spot where I lay currently as I write this. Susan has her hand on my tit as she sleeps and I don't care enough to move it, so I will give up writing for the night, maybe I'll finish the full retelling some other time in the journal, when I'm horny enough to. Well tomorrow/today since it's like 2am is gonna be a cluster fuck, it's the weekend so Damocha is gonna go on one of his ramblepages as I call them where he rambles and rampages at the same time, wish me luck... I'm gonna need it. By the way yes this is a journal, I journal, don't fucking laugh at me and call me a loser or whatever. Your the mother fucker who probably bought this, because I'm gonna sell it as my biography, if anything your the loser for buying a book, go watch Netflix or go vape or something... baka.

The Call

I am currently waiting for Damocha to call. It seems as though I am quite shaken up actually; The mess I made has actually really not been good, one of the biggest problems currently is that I am not focused on my career enough. I get it, sometimes I cannot let things get to me, however this was very different, I just snapped. It is not unusual for me to lose myself, but it is very unusual for me to fully lose myself, over something so miniscule. I need to focus, without a career I cannot continue to live the way I live, I mean no offense to any musicians, but it's not exactly a blue collar job. I live great and while I do work hard it's not taxing, I cannot let this slip away, if I did... BUZZ BUZZ! My cell phone rings and it's him, the dreaded call I've been waiting for. I panic and quickly stop and just compose myself, I answer it.

"Hey Damocha, how is the wife, good?" He sighs and breathes in.

"Karen this is gonna work out and you know it." Usually he takes a more aggressive approach and screams but he is very calm. " I have given you so many chances, yet you just keep throwing them away. Karen, if this continues we cannot continue our partnership. I will have to terminate your contract and well you will be gone.

"Damocha, listen, I am... sorry. I messed up and I don't think it's right for me to continue like this without some consequences, I feel I will not learn unless I get disciplined."

"Ok well, I have the perfect punishment."

"Y-You do?" What the fuck is he on about?

"Yes, I want you to make a Tik Tok account." My eyes widened.

"Ahhh" I laugh nervously "Damocha are you sure that's all?"

"Yes, I know you secretly hate Zoomer media, I mean you don't hide it well enough, so how about you embrace it, they are a part of your generation and targeted audience after all."

"A-" I laughed nervously again "Damocha how do you know I don't like zoomer stuff?"

"Karen do you think we didn't do a little research on you, we saw all of your takes on twitter and all of your accounts even @KarTheAkuma stuff."

"..."

"Anyways, I want you to go on there, make some content, since your blowing up all over it right now and then of course issue an apology on socials and you will be fine, but I'm serious Karen, this break isn't just for fun, you need to be working on your stuff AND YOUR IMAGE!"

"There's the sweet old Damocha I know!"

"Fuck you! Anyways take care of yourself Karen."

"Hey it's in the name!"

"Yeah, please don't get into any more trouble, chow."

He hangs up. Wow that was surprisingly ok. Usually anything with that guy is horrible, like bad. Screaming and everything else a person who would want to be a dick would do. But then again I was purposely being a dick to him, so maybe I deserved it. Well I feel accomplished. I feel like I actually am not worthless today, I guess I need to make a Tik Tok, that's gonna be a pain in my fucking ass. I love my zoomer brethren, however there is a certain type which… make me wanna stroke out.

October 31st, There Will Be Blood… and Candy

One more day of this "no work, take it easy policy" and I will blow my brains out. I have been basically stuck in my

Dead Fashion

new apartment since the move and the uh… Walmart incident. Since then I have made an effort to avoid my problems, like any reasonable person in their 20's would do. I did however buy a beautiful bottle of crown, yes I felt like whiskey, whiskey makes me frisky. Jokes aside I have been writing however these bimonthly updates are getting boring. I'm tired of things happening so quickly then these long dry spots of nothing, why is life like this? Who thought someone could live like this? I was telling Susan about this and she told me to "Get a real job." I laughed at her and told her if she wanted to keep me out of trouble, the last place you wanna see me is working another real job. She then told me to get into day trading, to which I actually agreed was a good idea. So I started investing some money here and there, not really day trading, more of just some small investing. I also want to um well make my life a little less boring. Currently it has been exactly 126 days to the dot since I have well taken a life or done anything of the sorts. No torture or Fuck N' Kills, nothing. She is changing me, her as in Susan. I am not the same person I was at the beginning of the year, let alone even before I met her. I was violent, brutal, I had fun, but now I feel like I'm under a thumb and despite having a strong connection with her… It's getting to me. But in all seriousness I am trying to stay clean and hold off until I can get out of the watchful eyes of the production company and still the police too. They still have an unmarked car drive by once a week, I know this because I have seen the same car parked across the street with the tinted windows, it's a fairly regular 2016 Honda Pilot, however the tinted window level is not that of a regular model, or of anything that a normal person in this area would need, considering this is downtown in the nice part of town. I am high up, however the vast window of my apartment is still quite visible from two streets over. If you had binoculars or a strong zoom on a phone camera, you could probably get a nice good look at my naked body and everything I do in my living room at night. However the way the road is shaped on the hill also makes those same vehicles visible to me, and I take a watchful eye. So in the time I had I started to see them show up every day on Friday at 8:30 PM. It was right when I moved into my new apartment, which I love to death compared to the dump I was living in before and way more than the one before that. So I bought an expensive camera with infrared capabilities. Then I pointed the camera to zoom at the car. Strategically place to not be spotted either behind a plant I have. Just as I expected, two others were in the vehicle. One had their phone pointed directly at my window through the tinted window in the back. I can see it was a phone because he was holding something which was radiating heat in a small spot, the cpu was running on his phone because he was most likely recording a video to send to someone. I take my own short video until the car leaves around 8:45 when they don't see me which means they have no reason to watch, most likely they are paid to do this by the only person I can suspect is the police and most likely get bored and drive off because they can just lie to their boss and say yeah nothing was happening so we left. I finished recording and I plan on doing it again next week, piling up some evidence and then saving it for the right moment. I have a more important matter however. For the first time in my life I am gonna dress up slutty. The reason? I want fresh bait. I want a guy to do things to me tonight and then I do things which he has never before felt to him as well, unless he's suicidal, then he probably has felt a small amount of what I plan to do to him. I want it to be a man, because I want dick! It has been months of being very lesbian and I'm not really living up to my nature of taking men and women, the last guy I killed was... well those pigs planning to shoot all those people way back in June or whatever, during the protest.

  I am halfway putting on my Mai bunny girl senpai outfit, a costume I have been wanting to do since I watched that anime Rascal Does Not Dream of Bunny Girl Senpai. It is perfect, it has fish nets, it shows off my ass and my tits and I get to be a bunny! I plan on getting a lot of looks at this underground halloween party tonight at this club, which is supposed to be closed, however I plan on going after hearing about it online on Tiktok. I might even perform, how cool would that be? Well trying to stay out of trouble maybe that's not a good idea. Showing my ass to half the US, which would make the news for sure, would be a tragedy. Speaking of Tiktok, my Tiktok has been blowing the fuck up recently. For some reason the content I post where I just do quick little videos where I do random stuff or react to people who have been doing covers of Dead Fashion and remixes has been popping off. I got over 2 million followers and blew my Instagram and Twitter up big time. I now have over a million on twitter as well after this boom and around 800k on Instagram. So I have been making consistent posts, keeping up with fans and encouraging them to send gifts to our PO box and send letters as well. All these people think I'm some sweet girl who is doing all these things and being wholesome, the plan worked. An easy facade, I am making news articles daily almost and my music is blowing up, I have been radio silent on my music side of things for months and have seen a 35% increase in revenue and a 50% increase in listens.

    I finish getting everything on and finish up my makeup before seeing the clock on my phone say 9:15, I will be there at 10 as I planned, I can already feel my stomach start to get butterflies as I am about to finally release it, it's been building and boiling and has boiled over, I have that feeling of when you are about to lose your virginity right now, that's how I feel knowing what I will do tonight.

    45 minutes later
    I walk into the underground style club, it's fully functioning, surprisingly. Covid had shut all this shit down and now it's back up… somewhat. They aren't allowed to be open, but it's a very exclusive halloween party. Only famous and rich people get to go to it and considering the people and costumes I see, they were not kidding. Everyone here has probably more than 700k sitting in their bank accounts waiting to be spent, it's incredible how much these people actually have. I guess I can't say anything anymore as I am coming to that point thankfully, I have been so tired of being poor, to finally have some money is nice. I didn't get invited here on my money status, rather the

fame I have been bringing. I never really fully grasped until now just how popular I have become and how quickly as well. The place is how you expect a nightclub to look, dark lighting, dark walls and flashing lights and smoke and loud club music as well. There is a lounge area to my right upon walking in and I go there instead of to the club floor to the left. I sit down on a long red and black couch and wait. My costume is really revealing and because of this I'm FUCKING freezing, but I digress. I sit for about a minute before a guy in a tuxedo comes over wearing a mask. He speaks over the loud music.

"Is everything alright? Comfortable?"

"No, actually I came for drinks and food and some of the early snowfall ya know?" He looks at me and says ah yes, what would like for a drink?

"Whatever is the most expensive bottle you have that I can get drunk off of, I am willing to spend a good amount of money tonight, I'm trying to hookup with a rich boy ya know, ya know?" I scream as the music seems to get louder and cheering starts. "And also a bag of the snow and then whenever more people pile in I'll let you know what else?" He nods to me and then proceeds to go away. I presume to get what I asked for and sure enough 5 minutes later he brings me the stuff.

"And because of our new covid rules we no longer are doing tabs and are paying for everything up front now."

"I see three zip lock bags full of cocaine and a bottle of something called Macallan M, which is some sort of imported whiskey it seems, he then says to me:

"That's gonna be 6,244 dollars."

"Jesus Christ here." I hand him my card and it goes through his little machine, I really am living quite large tonight, almost two and half weeks of rent on drugs and alcohol. Soon enough the people enter and as more and more people come in, a few of the rich ones who come sit either want drinks and or to do a line of my coke. About an hour in of about 9 people doing coke, drinking and us laughing our assess off a girl walks up to me and sits down right next to me. Everyone is starting to head

Dead Fashion

to the floor except for a few and then as the waiter or whatever the fuck the fancy word for them are comes over she just orders a shot of vodka. We sit for about a minute before she finally speaks.

"That's a very expensive trap you got there."

"What do you mean?" I say as I laugh and take a shot of my whiskey bottle.

"I mean that is only your second shot of the night and you've been here for what an hour?" I turn and look at her and in a more angry tone I say:

"Because it's fucking six thousand dollar bottle of whiskey, you think I'm gonna chug it down like a little kid drinking a Caprisun after being outside on a summer day for two hours?"

"No, but I would've expected you to want to get a little blasted, also the fact you're sharing it around proves you obviously weren't intending on doing much, I know what you're doing."

"I-I'm sorry, who are you?"

"Someone who wants to get rid of someone, that's who I am."

"What's with the Mary Poppins outfit or whatever?"

"It's Dorthy from The Wizard of OZ actually, I came here as Dorthy, and I need a tornado to come take me to a far away place, that's where you come in."

"What? Look lady, I'm glad you came over and talked with me, but I don't know what you're talking about?" I scoff.

"Karen you're not a hard book to read, in fact I can read you like a children's book. Others might not be able to, but I do." I stare at her dead faced now, my social butterfly face gone now. I try one more time to brush it off.

"I have no idea what you're talking about."

"Yes you do, I know what you do and where you would be tonight, how do you think I knew you were The Akuma?"

"Anyone could've recognized me, it doesn't take some psycho-analysis like you claim you did to me, to know that."

"Ok fine I will explain myself, Listening to your music early on, before you got super famous was easy to decipher the things you were talking about. All the guns and murdering you talked about in Gang Gang Kawaii, which is somewhat unbearable to listen to now, it was obviously real. The detail and how you did it was also hidden in the lyrics, obviously you put them in there for someone to find out. Like the 4chan valentine lyric, all I had to do was put your name into 4chan."

"That doesn't mean anything and my music is completely made up, excuse me I got to go-" I go to get up but she grabs my arm and for a second everything stops and gets dark and all I see is her. The rage builds up, almost boiling over.

"Karen, I know what you did, the pizza place bar, that was Joe's pizza, I need your help, I outsmarted you in your own mind game and so now you're gonna do this thing for me." W-W-WWHAT?!? THIS FUCKING BITCH, THINKS SHE HAS ME ALL FIGURED OUT? OH YOU LITTLE SLUT I WANNA PUMMEL HER FUCKING FACE IN THE TABLE AND SMASH HER HEAD WITH THIS WHISKEY BOTTLE. I grit my teeth and close my eyes and breathe deep.

"I'm giving five seconds to get the FUCK out of my face before I smash it in with this bottle." I say to her trying to keep my voice lower to not make a scene.

"No I'm not gonna go, Karen look around, you won't kill me."

"You wanna bet Poppins?"

"Like I said, it's Dorothy, and you can't kill me. You won't get away with it, to many people, you are too smart to do that here. You are more Premeditated and planned out, you don't kill out of thin air. But that rage you have, I have a way for you to release it, for a good cause finally."

"And what if I don't?"

"I have pictures of you buying coke and consuming it earlier, it would be a shame if the police had some sort of case file on you waiting for you to slip up so they can charge you with anything possible."

"Ok."

"Ok?"

"Yes, but you need to tell me one thing first."

"Hmmm, I guess, ok go ahead."

"Obviously you didn't do that all on your own and from what you said earlier you slipped up and mentioned the police, now tell me are you with the St. Paul police."

"I'm above them."

"How?"

"I work in the FBI. Me and my fellow detective Mcdowell still have your case, however he doesn't know I'm here."

"What?!? Your FBI?"

"Basically I live in the area and work with the Minnesota District, but I'm tired, I plan on retiring… big time."

"That's where you need my help then."

"Precisely, now-"

"Woah, woah, woah, woah, woah. I'm not gonna do shit with or for the FBI."

"This isn't for or with the FBI, this is with me."

"Bullshit, how the fuck can I trust any FBI agent." she sits for a moment and stares at me before looking down and finally saying:

"Because it's the only thing you can do, if you do this I can help close the investigation and once the FBI is off of that murder case you were involved in from a few months back, that bitch Toungevold will have no basis to keep conducting watch parties on you, btw she has been-"

"Have a van take pictures and videos of me, waiting to get something incriminating, I know."

"You really are smarter than you look Wall." I sigh and think for a moment, I am enraged and really want to take it out, my body feels numb and I feel like holding something that I cannot hold any longer.

"Ok, fine, what do you want?"

"I need you to kill my husband."

"HOLY SHIT!"

"Brutally."

"Why?" She looks at me like there is something she cannot say.

"He is, well, let's just say he is the most sinister person I know."

"Bullshit you've seen my file and the rumors, tell me the real reason or it will be you instead of him."

"Okay, okay. He is a growing MLB player, Brady Doyle, have you heard of him? He plays here for the Minnesota Twins."

"No, I don't follow sports and even if I did I wouldn't follow our trash ass teams here."

"That makes two of us, well he is abusive, he's a drunk and all the money he gets from baseball he pours into only himself, fancy watches, new cars, big houses, I don't even know where it is. We are married yet, I cannot even see him half of the year because he is either playing baseball getting his dick sucked by some FUCKING russian bitches or he is partying all night. In fact that's how I got into this party. I need you to lure him in, you are wearing the clothes and everything, you're young and you're pretty. Butter him up, and end his FUCKING PATHEIC LIFE!"

"And I thought I was crazy."

"You are crazy, I don't kill people because they fire me from a job or because I just feel like it. Once he is gone, I can finally lay at night knowing I don't have to worry about him doing all this shit and wasting our money. And I don't have to worry about him abusing me any longer, I can… be free."

"Ok, so why not just… divorce him? If he is abusing you, report it. Get a settlement and take some of his stuff, it's a win-win for you." She looks down, she is hiding something else. "But there is something more than just his stuff right? Let me guess he's got a lot of stocks and money stored away, which you will get along with the life insurance policy and I'm assuming the MLB have some sort of family reimbursement too. Plus if you get him into a legal battle the Twins will drop him over the charges, he will go away forever and then you will still be broke because you chose justice over money."

"Not that it's any of your business but yes, that's exactly what will happen. I want his ass to be murdered. I know you are good at what you do in your music career, but in your true career… You're better." I think about it, I have thought of every possible way that this could be a trap, however despite this being sketchy, I think I might make the stupidest decision ever.

"I'll do it, you'll get your money, but I want something. I want you to drop that case as soon as you can and get that damn bitch from the St. Paul police to stop her from watching parties or whatever."

"That's fine with me, you'll get your wish. But first my end of the deal." She puts out her for me to shake it and as I shake her hand I say:

"You're making a deal with the devil, even a prayer can't repay the sin."

"I don't care, I'm an Atheist anyways."

"Me too. If I wanted to look up to someone for my success, I would put a picture of myself on my ceiling."

She explains to me where he is and then soon I compose myself and get ready to do my job; I walk over to the bar where he is. He is talking with some blonde girl who is in a red dress, cool halloween outfit stupid bitch, didn't anyone tell her it was a dress up party. However she seems disgusted by him and almost as if she doesn't want to talk to him, it's the perfect opportunity.

"NO WAY! Brady Doyle from the-the Twins? Are you serious?!? Oh my god!" I say in a cheery voice, acting as if I'm a massive fan." I look over at the girl in the red dress and say: "And you are?"

"Leaving!" she says as she grabs her drink and leaves the bar.

"WAIT! WAIT JESS DON'T GO I- AGHHHHH WHAT THE FUCK IS YOUR PROBLEM?!? Did you not see I was trying to get with that chick, you delusional bitch! Do you want an autograph or something? Wasting my time for fuck sakes." This guy is a super asshole holy shit, I can tell I'm gonna love shutting his ass up.

"What? No! I don't want an autograph. Don't be silly."

"Then what do you want?"

"You!" I sit down where the girl named Jess sat and I sit down and order a drink to give me a reason to be there.

"What do you mean you? You want me? Hun I'm taken thanks."

"Taken huh? Then why were you trying to get with that girl just now?" He looks at me with a very pissed expression, he then looks at my body predominantly at my chest and then stares for about five seconds, the anger turning to a blank expression before I break the silence.

"Like what you see?"

"Maybe. What did you mean earlier, you want me?"

"What do you think I meant silly?" I grab his leg and start to rub it. "I want you." He stares again and this time I try the aggressive approach to things "What do you think I'm not attractive? Hmph! Fuck you then!" I get up and make sure to turn so he can see my ass. Before I can even get two steps away he says.

"Wait! Come back." I immediately turn and sit down again. "You are very attractive, I trying to figure out how I wanna fuck you!" BAHAHAHA, is this guy for real? Holy shit his rizz is absolutely tragic, he has no game. He doesn't even know my name and he is already saying this? Horny mother fucker.

"Oh yeah? How do you want to fuck me?" I say in a seductive tone, rubbing his leg again.

"Doggy style, aggressively."

"Pulling my hair and making me scream?"

"Yes!" He says slowly, getting enchanted by me. He is now all smiles and giggles and seems super happy. "What's your name?"

"Susan!" I said. "Susan Weckwerth. I'm 26, I work at a record label in Minneapolis, ever heard of DP Records?"

"YES! They are the ones that produced that one girl from here, um um... She has been blowing up after the George Floyd song thing."

"The Akuma?"

"YES! God what a joke. Her music is so bad, no offense but I really cannot stand women rappers, they suck. And also what is with that bullshit situation anyways? A police officer does his job and gets arrested. What has this shit country come too?" Well I guess we know what side of the spectrum he's on.

"I know right! But what if I told you I was her manager of all things?"

"Shut up! Are you serious?

"Hell yes!

"I thought I was the coolest one here, but you, holy shit, you got big tits and you manage The Akuma? Damn you are awesome." Even though he just said my music was shit a minute ago. I'm starting to think all these drinks are starting to take effect, perfect, now we can move on to phase two.

"Uh listen so this is like a big kink of mine... Um like I am really into athletes, I know it's super dumb, but I just have this thing."

"Oh baby, well I have a thing for singers so you are the exact type of doll I want."

"I don't sing, I just manage her, my voice is not meant for that Brady."

"Well whatever, I don't care if you're a doctor or a teacher or a Mexican, you are right up my alley." Well that was random, out of all the things, really a Mexican? I'm starting to think I know what type of guy this is.

"Well... That's a little contradictory, but I don't really care." I lean my face forward and kiss him and he kisses me back. "Wanna leave and go back to my place?"

"Only if you got some booze and a bed."

"I do."

"Well then what are we waiting for?" He gets up and stumbles a little bit, before starting to make his way towards the exit, I follow him. Only about the alcohol... nice.

30 Minutes Later

We arrived back at my apartment. I am settling into the place as I finally moved to one of the most beautiful places in the entire metro area. Not even the Chaska homes are as good as these. I get my door unlocked and the booze is really starting to kick Brady's ass, obviously for being around 6 '3 and I wanna say 200 pounds, he doesn't have a high tolerance level. I sit on my couch as he sits on the other side of it.

I look at my phone as he sits and drinks more booze. Then finally he looks over at me and I look up from my instagram feed.

"So when you gonna let me fuck your brains out?" He says slurring his words almost looking like he's about to pass out.

"I'm not."

"WHAT? Wasn't that the whole point?"

"No I don't fuck guys on the first date, I just wanted to see what you would do."

"This ain't no fucking date, I have a wife."

"Oh yeah I bet she's really proud of you, you're a real stallion."

"YOU FUCKING BITCH!" He quickly gets up and I let him hit me as hard as he can with a close fist so it can leave a mark. He then grabs me and I help him throw my body across the coffee table and I fall to the floor. This is where my acting skills come into play, trust me it will make sense.

"NOOO!!!!! PLEASE DON'T I DON'T WANT IT, I DON'T!" I start fake crying as he gets over top of me and grabs the back of my neck and tries to pull the bottom part of my costume off, I wait until he gets close enough and that's when I strike. I planned for this to be exactly like this, if not very similar, when we walked in I grabbed one of my knives from my collection that I had and set it on the coffee table in front of the spot where I was sitting on the couch. When he punched me, if he tried to do it on the couch I could grab it easily and if he threw me like he did, I could get him off me and grab it. I scramble for a second and then I take my elbow which he was trying to pin down and I smash it into his face and he screams and falls back, guess I got a strong backwards punch, then I quickly grab the knife and hide it.

"You fucking slutty little bitch, think your so tough, you know who I am?"

"Yeah, a loser who tries to rape women who don't wanna have sex with him, what do you think your wife would say now?"

"FUCK YOU!" He lunges at me but I strike him with the knife in his stomach, I quickly punch him in the face with the other hand and then quickly use that hand to grab him by the neck. He winces in pain and continues to scream, I stab him again and again and again until he falls over and I stab and stab and stab and stab. I don't stop, I continue to stab him. Then for my finishing act, I scream out and start fake crying. It helped a lot to cry after that punch. I gotta admit I underestimated his strength when drunk. I should've expected nothing less from a major league pitcher, but still. I continue to fake cry until I go over and grab my phone and then this is where I mastermind everything. I use my phone and call 911.

"911, what's your emergency?"

"HELP MEEEE! THIS GUY JUST TRIED TO KILL ME! HE PINNED ME DOWN AND TRIED TO RAPE ME, BUT I-I GRABBED A KNIFE AND STABBED HIM, I THINK HE'S DEAD! OH GOD PLEASE HELP ME!"

"Ok ma'am calm down." I start to scream and cry again to make it more believable over the phone. "MA'AM I need you to calm down for me, what is your address?" I speak while sobbing

"465 Nicollet Mall, it's the nic on fifth, the penthouse on the 24th floor."

"Ok Ma'am, I need you to breathe, everything is going to be alright. Stay on the line with me until the officers arrive, ok?

"O-Ok ma'am." I say as I go to my apartment camera app and quickly save the video, then I cut the video so that it's only from the time of the killing. Well this is a shot in the dark, I've never killed like this before but my heart is racing like I've never felt, you want a way of getting a discreet killing? How about making it so known, but in your favor that it is deemed as a sorry story about some prick, rather than some cold blooded murder and dumping the body. Let's see how this plays out.

"So you're positive he was gonna kill you?"

"Well what did you want me to do!? Seriously this guy attacks me and then tries to rape me, I grab a knife what did you want me to just push him off and leave? You think I could out power a goddamn professional athlete?"

"Ma'am I'm not trying to make any assumptions, I'm just asking a question."

"Well it fucking insensitive!"

"I understand, I understand. I'm just asking because you are going to court over this, regardless of what intent was, so I need all the details." FUCK! Now I have to deal with a court case too? I wanna kill that bitch now, FUCK!

The officer walks away to go talk to a different officer. I am escorted out of the apartment as it is closed off as of now. The investigators and other people still remain there and I am taken to the police station for questioning.

We arrive at the police station and media and news are surrounding the station, but I just walk past them keeping the messed up makeup and tear trails. They had me put on a jacket and something to cover my bottom so I quickly did that before we left. I get into the police station and I wait for almost an hour before someone comes into the interrogation room with me. It's a blonde man with a casual blue mask who seems to not really want to do this at this time of the night as it is now around one A.M, but he also tries to fake a smile to keep up a good reputation.

"Hello Karen, I'm Jake Smith, the lead investigator here at the Minneapolis police department, and in your case this situation. Umm." He scratches his face under his mask and then continues. "So basically as everything sits, we usually don't ask these questions here but since the location is such a hotspot we needed to get somewhere more private for your rights to privacy as a citizen."

"Thank you sir."

"No problem, so don't feel intimidated by the camera or the room, you're not under any interrogation right now, this is just a basic questioning of the situation from your eyes and point of view. Ok?"

"Ok." I say softly.

"Tell me where did you meet Brady Doyle?"

"I met him at a um, I know this is not something I should say but a party, it was an underground halloween party and I met him and he seemed so charming and like someone I just wanted to know. Then I-" I stop and start to cry and Jake grabs a box of tissues and gives them to me. "I just felt so welcome in his presence, then he was being romantic and I was kind of leading him on, until he said to come back to my place for some more drinks, and I was nervous, but I didn't want to look stupid in front of someone like him, so I let him come to my apartment."

"Ok so then how long were you at the apartment before everything went down?"

"Well we got there and I got really nervous, I hadn't been with someone since my previous boyfriend, um disappeared and so then I was really nervous. I have a video of everything from my security camera, I know you guys are gonna be able to get that anyway but it was only around 10 minutes long, so we weren't there that long. He started to pressure me and I didn't want to, and he kept pressuring me to have sex with him, until I-I… I said I didn't want to, so then he got up and hit me. From there he um-" I stop and cry some more and I can see the guy falling for it so hard. "He um, punched me and then he pushed me over the coffee table and at that point-" This is where I make the mark and get myself scott free. "I felt threatened and scared for my life, I didn't know what this man was gonna do to me. After the struggle it's all a blur but I got out and grab a knife that was on the coffee table, maybe it was an act of god or something that I forgot to put it away, I think it was one I just bought recently, I was messing around with it, but thank god I left it out. I remember feeling rage and anger and I just kept stabbing him hoping the pain would go away." I start to cry even harder now and at this point it almost gets unbearable to be around and it's obvious the investigator doesn't want to be there anymore. He asks me a few more things before leaving the room. Eventually I am greeted about 30 minutes later by Jake.

"Karen I have someone who wants to speak with you, she has a few questions for you and wants to know some more things. She is with the FBI. Karen, her husband is attached to this case and was the man that you killed tonight, but as it currently stands with the PD, you seem to be in the clear after you meet with her, Karen this is-" She walks in. "Karen, this is Detective Kathy Doyle with the FBI."

"Thanks, Jake." she says as she smiles at him and then closes the door. She sits down and is quiet for almost a minute straight as we both look down. "So this is your idea?"

"What, idea?"

"Your plan was to blow this whole thing up? REALLY?"

"What do you mean?" I asked, oblivious to her remarks. "He tried to rape me, I was just defending myself, I understand he's your husband, but I did everything in my power to stop him from doing it. I have video evidence if you wanna-"

"KNOCK THE SHIT OFF KAREN! WHAT WERE YOU THINKING?

"Kathy, listen to me, you want me to tell you the truth?"
"Yes!"

"The truth is, I wanted to have a fun time with him and he ended up trying to kill me, when I forced him off me. I get that your husband is a party animal and can't keep his dick in his pants, obviously, but don't self project that onto me. How was I supposed to know he was married to you? He told me he was married, but I still went along with it, he was just so charming. I'm sorry." I tear up and look at her as she looks pissed as all can be.

"This wasn't the deal!"

"What deal?" Kathy, now visibly frustrated, grabs me by the collar and pins me up against the wall. The tension is high and I know I have now completed the plan entirely.

"You listen to me you little twat… You think this is some kind of joke, I will expose everything and get you locked up forever, you got that you little bitch?"

"And expose how you wanted your husband murdered so you came to a woman and bribed her in exchange for the wealth of your husband and more money. You think you have all the cards but you have none, you take me down and you go down with me, I serve life you'll serve double for being the perpetrator, and you'll get no money, as far as I can tell your lucky I don't expose everything myself and exploit you for money myself." She gets closer to my face, spit comes out of her mouth as she speaks.

"I need this money."

"Then you need to shut up and stop making a scene."

"I will get less money because of this, this is exactly why I told you to keep it private, you think they will pay me money now that you exposed it to the public?"

"No but the MLB should give me money, A settlement more than likely." She lets go of me and looks shocked."

"I did this for both of us, you think I wanted to just kill something? NO! Get your head out of your ass, I kill him I get more exposure in the media as a victim, then I get the money and I give it to you, reap double the rewards and never have to worry about it again, do you understand what I was trying to do or was your thick skull getting in the way of thinking of the best course of action." I start to walk past her now.

"You're sick."

"Yeah? Ain't the first time I've heard that." I look back at her. "And you're welcome for me not going through with your shitty ass plan."

"You think everything is about you don't you? Can't even be someone else's murder plan, has to be yours." I start to walk away again as I say.

"Well then next time don't think of such a dogshit plan and maybe we could've worked better together." I open the door and then she quickly follows behind me.

As I walk to the front desk, I have to do some paperwork and sign some things. I quickly do that before the cop does the usual spiel about how it's an ongoing investigation and that I need to be prepared to answer any questions within the next 48 hours. He then tells me that they are still at my apartment trying to gather evidence and that I need to go somewhere else for the next day or so. I'll tell you what all it takes to get away with murder is some fake tears and a little acting, it's honestly almost funny how fucking corrupted and bad our justice system is.

I walk outside as Kathy holds the door for me I see tons of camera flashes and a bunch of yelling and news reporters. I am blinded and overwhelmed by all of it as it is so early in the morning and I feel my eyes roll into the back of my head as I fall to the ground from exhaustion. Just as I feel myself falling asleep I'm quickly grabbed and jerked by someone, it's Damocha.

"C'mon you damn idiots made her faint, you pricks. Aren't y'all supposed to be six feet away, c'mon move out of the way." He continues to scream, as I see two police officers and Susan coming to help Damocha. Then just as quickly as everything arrived, it went black.

November 1st, A Mocha at Damocha's

Dead Fashion

I wake up in a very foreign feeling bed. The sheet's are red along with the blanket, the attire and decor in the room are something beyond fantasies. I feel the most comfortable I've ever felt in my entire life, the bed is so silky and perfect, must be one of those Tempur-Pedic's or some shit. I lay for almost a solid two or three minutes before I finally got the courage to leave the best and most perfect bed I've ever layed in. I make my way to the door, I'm fully clothed in some sort of pajamas, I can only pray that it was Susan that did it. I open the door and walk into what has got to be the best looking living room I have ever seen. The house is like something out of a dream, it looks like one of those houses you would see in those 30 million dollar mansion tour videos on youtube. Expensive art, white walls, marble countertops, Fireplace with a big portrait over it, a huge vista window that overlooks what looks like the east side of the metro area. Then on the expensive furniture sits Damocha, a woman I have never seen and then Susan.

"Karen, it's about time you woke up." Damocha said. "Want a coffee?"

"Um I normally don't-"

"Nonsense, April, get this young lady some fresh coffee."

"Isaac, you don't have to be so demanding."

"Well I want the girl to be happy, for christ's sake after what she just went through." She stares at him with a mad expression for a couple seconds before leaving to make the coffee.

"Jeez I'll tell ya, when you two find men, don't treat them like assholes will ya?" Me and Susan both stare at each other expressionless after he said that. We both were thinking the exact same thing word for word, if only he knew. I walk over and sit down next to Susan and she smiles at me then hugs me. She continues to hug me for about another 30 seconds and as she does so she whispers in my ear.

"I'm so glad you're ok, Kare Bear." I whispered back to her.

"Don't call me Kare Bear or I'll do the same thing I did to him, to you." She laughs under her breath.

"Jeez Karen, don't you think it's a little early to be making jokes?" Susan says to me as she finally stops hugging me.

"Well I mean it doesn't make the past any different, how I react now, is not gonna change the course of history. It's traumatic, but what? Am I gonna sit and cry over it for the next hundred years? No, yes I'm shaken up but it's nothing I can change, what happened, happened. It is what it is."

"That's a very odd way of looking at things."

"Hey! What are we whispering about?" Damocha said in a very loud whisper.

"Nothing, she is just happy I'm ok." I said.

"Well I'm glad, AH! Finally the coffee is done, Karen please." April, Damocha's wife hands me a cup of coffee and I accept it although I don't drink much of it. "So listen Karen, I get you can't stay at your house, so I talked to the board and we have agreed to fully pay for a week vacation away from the city, anywhere of your choice… Given that you can go there."

"So basically anywhere in the US?"

"YES! Take your pick, and we will pay for it."

"Wow, awesome, I won't do it."

"Excuse me?" Damocha says almost spitting all of his coffee out.

"Not unless I can bring Susan with me." I look over at Susan who now almost spit her cup out as well.

"Well um no offense to Susan, but the board and I, myself included, think that a solo retreat away from society would be good right now, just you.

"I'm good, really. I am fine. I don't need a retreat. I'm going to Washington next month anyway so it would be a little redundant to go on a trip now given in about a month and half I'll be taking one."

"Well Karen, maybe this could help you with touring, I mean traveling a decent amount in a short period of time, that could help you. You've never done it before and I think it would be great for you to travel, plus Minnesota is so cold at this time of the year, why don't you go somewhere warm, like LA or like Florida?" Damocha smiles at me.

"I told you, not unless Susan goes with me."

"I don't get it? Are you so worried you are gonna get into trouble or something when you're not near home?"

"No."

"Then for fuck's sake why do you want Susan to go with you."

"Because I want to fuck her brains out and make lesbian love to her." I say sipping my coffee. Damocha's wife drops the tray with the pot of coffee and sugar and other stuff. Damocha spits out his coffee and Susan I can imagine about having her heart drop down to her feet. "I mean holy shit wasn't it more obvious we are secret lesbian lovers who like to tongue fuck each other?" I look around confused as I sip my coffee. Damocha puts his hand over his mouth and his wife immediately looks over at Damocha super pissed before he looks at her as well and then breathes in and sighs.

"Karen, Susan… I'm gonna have to ask you to leave."

"What I- " Susan tries to say something but then I get up and walk out before staring at Damocha's wife who obviously was the one who had a problem with it, which is exactly why I said it and made it as blatant as possible. I saw a cross on the wall and a Jesus painting so I knew they were religious, or at least his wife was. So I really needed to get out of that conversation and house. Mainly because I was starting to get too jealous of the interior design and location of the house, I wanted to strangle Damocha and his wife to death just for owning such a spectacular place and showing it off to me. And I guess I was a little mad that they wanted to send me away for no fucking reason.

Susan follows me screaming at me to wait, while I can hear Damocha's wife start telling him about why this was a bad idea and how she knew we were sinners. I open the front door and I see Susan's car is parked in the amazing driveway. I immediately get in the passenger side and sit. I looked over at the front door to see Damocha caught up to Susan and was telling her something before she nodded and walked to the car. She gets in the driver seat and the silence is exactly what you would expect. She didn't start the car, she didn't say anything, just quiet, lone liminal feelings.

"Well, where do you want to go?" Susan asks as she presses the button to start her car. I stare out the window, still being an asshole. "Look Karen… I'm not mad at you, at all." She starts to laugh as we still sit in the driveway.

"What are you giggling at you little lesbian."

"HEY!" She laughs again "NEITHER OF US ARE LESBIANS! Your word choice really confused the hell out of them… And me, I promise you that. Gives Damocha all the more reasons to think you were lying." I immediately jolt up from the window and look at Susan and before a pin could even drop I immediately say.

"He thinks I'm lying?" The quickness of my response really caught Susan by surprise.

"No, but he was wondering earlier this morning if you actually were into well… guys."

"What would make him think that I'm not."

"Well…" She looks at me "Ok! Don't be mad at me."

"I already am." I say cutting her off.

"Well I told him that we had made love, just because he had asked me to find you someone who could help you and try to stop you from causing all of these problems. So I put myself in those shoes and instead of finding someone I just used myself. Then I told Damocha that I slept with you. That's what the whole thing was just now outside here. He said that it was ok and to take you to my house, as I was probably the last person you would find comfort with. God sexuality is a bitch."

"No, whose a bitch, is you."

"Hey. What the hell, look yeah ok so maybe I told him about us doing it one time. So what, are you telling me, you didn't tell anyone about us? Oh better yet, what about just now? In front of the man's wife, not even just him in front of the man's wife you said we were sleeping together. What's the difference Karen?"

"FUCK YOU!" I hadn't even realized it, but tears had actually started to boil in my eyes. I quickly wipe them and look back out the window. Susan starts driving away and within five minutes she ask me again.

"So where do you want to go? Wanna grab anything to eat quickly or?" I continue to stare out the window. Not because I want to be an asshole, but for the first time since the incident in Japan, I am getting natural tears in my eyes and I can't control them. My eye glands must be messed up or something, I can't think of any other reason in the world why this would be happening. Susan puts her hand on my back and says "Look yes I should not have told Damocha about us, but I really needed to keep my job and-" I stop her and immediately blow up in rage.

"Oh so now it's about you again Susan. Holy fuck, my job this my job that. When are you gonna realize that not everything is about you. In fact this whole thing isn't even about you. So shut the fuck up and STOP!" Susan looks at me as she continues to drive and I look at her and I see tears coming down her face. Both of us now have tears coming down our faces and once we both see that the tension in myself releases. "Susan I-"

"No, it's ok, I'm selfish, you're right. Even from the beginning all I ever wanted was to just keep my job, there is nothing more to it, I'm simply sick, and I'm sorry."

She continues to drive as we both now just stare forward. I can tell Susan is trying so hard not to break down crying and all I can think about is how I just ruined the one relationship I truly actually had. I haven't even felt this way with my parents before, it was so intense.

"Where are we going?" I say in a soft voice.

"I-I don't know. I'm just driving."

"I've never seen your apartment before."

"You don't wanna."

"Maybe I do."

"Trust me Karen, you do not want to see my apartment. It's horrible compared to your's."

"Mine still has a dead body in it." Susan looks at me and then starts to laugh.

"That's fucked up, but fair enough. Ok fine, I guess I'll bring a murderer to my apartment." I snap at her again.

"Don't ever call me a murderer ever again." I quickly say.

"Ok calm down tough girl, I was making a joke."

"Well it wasn't a very funny one.

"Yeah sorry, OH! I am actually hungry, not gonna lie. Wanna grab some Dairy Queen or something.

"There is no way you just asked me if I wanted Dairy Queen. That has got to be the most vile thing I've ever heard."

"Oh!? Ok bitch! What do you want to have then?"

"If we are gonna get something, get something good, like Burger King or something."

"BLARGH! There is no way you said BK."

"What? What's wrong with the king?"

"EVERYTHING'S WRONG WITH THE KING KAREN! I walk into Burger King and these are the five sins of the Burger King I see. First of all, the wallpaper is ripping off the walls. Second, the floors are always sticky or like the cleaner they use always makes my feet stick to the floor like they just had a massive kid's birthday party and they spilled soda everywhere. Third, don't even get me started with the atmosphere. It's always dead with flies flying around."

"Yes flies tend to do that."

"Fourth, the workers are actually at the bottom of the barrel, I'm talking 'missing a couple teeth' at the bottom of the barrel. I could literally pull up to the drive thru and ask for some angel's dust with my side of fries and get it. And fifth and finally the food is absolute and I mean this when I say it, absolutely garbage. Like can you just please make my food hot? OH! OH! Get this one, the last time I went to Burger King they didn't have any ice, so the drink was warm and the food was cold."

"Bullshit"

"I'm not a kidding you, it was bad."

"Well holy fuck, take me backwards and shove it up my ass then, fine no BK, asshole." I cross my arms. We both sit for about another 30 seconds as the drive continues before we both look at each other and in unison both say the same thing.

"McDonald's?"

"McDonald's?"

"Yeah that's what I was thinking."

"Me too." Dammit I don't know how it does it, but McDonald's wins the fast food question every time, it's almost starting to get annoying. Well anyways at least I'll get a good experience with my mediocre dinner tonight.

November 2nd, 1:30 AM

I'm starting to question whether or not it was a good idea to go along with this manager thing. The problem isn't necessarily Susan herself, rather it's the fact that I'm too attached to her. I simply don't understand why or how, I cannot figure out what made me this way. Despite all of that she makes me too vulnerable, I open up and I do not like it. Everytime I see her, I get this feeling. I don't know how to explain it, but basically I feel like I want to hold her tight and squeeze her. No not death, just enough to show her I care. It's almost primal in a way, like I don't consciously do it.

"Karen, would you stop writing in that damn book, I would really like the light off, It's hard to sleep with it on." Susan says to me as she turns over in her bed. We are sleeping together in her bed, which to be honest is nicer than mine. The silky white sheets are so soft and the fabric softener that she uses... Holy! I must know what her routine is before I leave.

"Sorry." I said in a stern voice paying no attention to her as I finished writing.

"Why do you even still write in a book anyways?"

"It helps."

"With what?"

"It helps."

"Whatever it's too fucking late for this. I was meaning, why not write it on a notepad in your phone, that way it's with you at all times."

"I keep the journal close to me at all times, more than my phone even. It is different when you write it down with pen and paper, compared to a notepad on my phone. The feeling of writing makes the words I say feel more alive and feel like I've accomplished more."

"Okkkk! I don't need the whole breakdown."

"Then don't ask the question." Susan sits up and looks at me.

"What the fuck is wrong with you right now? An hour ago we were literally fucking and now your acting cold and like a complete stranger." I turn back and write one more line, before closing the book and not saying a word. I turn the light off and as I do, I grab my vape pen and take a hit. "HEY! HEY! HEY! No fucking vaping in my house dude! I said this twice already."

"I need it just for this one time."

"Why?"

"Why? Because if I don't I'm gonna smash your head like a watermelon that's why."

"Ok one hit and then open the fucking window, I don't want this place smelling like depression and addiction."

"Ok, King of the castle whatever you say." I put the pen down on the nightstand and then I lay in the bed and finally got comfortable. Within four minutes of the silence and laying Susan rolled over and wrapped her arms around me. I continued to lay not paying any attention, but slowly as I started to drift off I wrapped myself around her too. By the time I fell asleep we were both wrapped around each other hugging each other as we slept, or at least that's what it felt like. It almost felt like a movie scene or a romantic painting, it just kind of felt nice in a way that I normally don't feel it in.

A Few Hours Later…

Dead Fashion

    I wake up and immediately look at my phone. I read that the time is 9:33 in the morning, and with a quick glance to my right, I see that Susan is out of bed. I feel so nasty and gross, I feel tired and almost weak. I was starting to think I had covid or something, but after drinking a little bit of water I felt better. I continue to lay in the bed, as it is soft and warm compared to Susan's apartment. It feels like she has the fucking Air Conditionor on in November. I scrolled through Twitter and retweeted some posts about me and replied to one of them asking if The Akuma was ok.

    "Wage Shooter (He/Him)
@WageShotz12

    I'm starting to worry about @DaAkumaKaren. I know she gets hundreds, maybe even thousands of tweets like this (Especially after what happened this week) but I wanted to tweet this out in hopes that she sees it. I loved the last EP with Dead Fashion and I hope this doesn't hinder any progress on the recovery, keep it up girl. ♥

    6:17 PM ·November 1, 2020
    1,487 Likes"
I replied back with
"Karen/The Akuma"
@DaAkumaKaren

    Lol, don't worry everything is fine. It was one of the most traumatic experiences in my life, but I will not let that stop me from making people happy. I care about the well being of my fans and I want to see them happy. If they weren't happy it would mean that I have failed and that thought and feeling really would hurt more than this experience did. Thank you for looking out for me and caring, Forever in my heart my dude.

    9:41 AM ·November 2, 2020"

    Probably shouldn't have ended it off with my dude, but it fits the character. Do I really care that much about my fans? Well without them I would be a fucking loser, so I guess I have no choice. They are my sole reason I make money after all. I continue to look at memes and other stupid shit until Susan walks back into the Bedroom wearing nothing but underwear and a robe.

"So dressed up, what's the occasion?"

"Shut the fuck up, Karen."

"HEY! I'm not the one walking around my apartment with nothing on at nine in the morning."

"And I'm not the one still laying in bed at nine in the morning."

"Well I like to sleep in."

"Sleep in? Karen you were fucking writing in that fucking Torra or whatever that is for like an hour at like one AM. How were you not supposed to sleep in?

"It's a journal and it's not that old, I got it before I left Japan."

"You went to Japan?"

"I LIVED in Japan. For almost a year. Up until the middle of last year, when I moved back here."

"That must've sucked."

"Why?"

"Well I mean, so many people in such a small area. Unsanitary and having to live an extremely poor life, surrounded by people who are completely different than you."

"I actually loved living in Japan. It was just certain things that led me to leave."

"Money?"

"No, Money was never an issue, I made good money making music and performing in the idol group I was in."

"Woah, you were in one of those idol groups, but you speak English, why would you do that?"

"Watashi wa eigoigai ni mo hanasemasu, baka." You don't need a translation for this one.

"Well I mean I know you speak Japanese, but can you really speak it fluently like 100%?"

"Can you even speak English 100%?"

"Yes."

"What does ostentatious mean?"

"That's not even English."

Dead Fashion

"YES IT IS!"

"Bull, I would've heard it by now. My mom was an English teacher."

"Yeah I bet she is one of those milf's too, who bends over to help a student and her fucking whole package is sticking out."

"Ok. Ok. Stop. I don't want to think about it anymore, I might barf."

"... But does she?"

"KAREN!"

"Sorry… Anyways, what's on the agenda for the old Susan Harris?"

"Actually the agenda is pretty full, we gotta do some interview stuff and some more statements today.."

"Who's we? Like Nintendo Wii or what? I ain't a part of that."

"Well actually you are. Karen it's about you. People want more than just some twitter posts. At some point…" Susan stops and gets up from sitting on the bed as she slowly did over time and starts to walk away.

"At some point what Susan?" I scream to her as she leaves the bedroom. I quickly get out of the bed and slip a sweatshirt over my Akuma shirt that we are going to start selling with the return in two months. I got an early one, it's the best. "At some point what?" I say as I catch up to her in her kitchen. She hesitates for a moment, then gives in.

"At some point you need to put on your big girl pants and start taking some responsibility for yourself. You need to be doing press stuff yourself and not having a statement from me or someone else. Yes we can help you, but it's your job to at least show the fuck up. We can't hold your hand anymore, this time off was supposed to show you that, but I'm getting worried."

"Worried of what?"

"Worried that you're still not ready to take your career in your own hands. I mean you're getting to massive celebrity status, you're the biggest artist to come out of DP and the biggest artist I've ever managed fully myself and I just feel you're not acting responsibly."

"Oh is that right huh? Susan, do you think I haven't learned anything? Since the beginning of the break, I've started to put my career first before anything else and honestly I was before too. And yes sorry as of recently I don't want to do virtual press tours or do any interviews. But it's a little hard to keep composure when all they want to do is get a reaction rather than an answer. I mean I just killed someone not even two days ago, so sorry I'm not 100% there right now." I can feel tears start to water in my eyes again and I quickly know I need to leave the situation.

"Karen I'm sor-" I walk away and go back to the bedroom and put on my pants from the previous night and then grab all of my stuff. Susan follows me into the bedroom and tries to stop me at the doorway back out to the rest of the apartment to give me a kiss, but I push her away and go and grab my shoes. I start to put them on and struggle to get the left foot in quickly. Then as I grab my coat Susan questions me.

"Where are you going?"

"I just need to leave."

"To where?"

"Anywhere, I don't fucking know I JUST NEED TO LEAVE!" I open her door and slam it as I walk out. I don't honestly know where I'm gonna go, but I couldn't let her see me like that. The fact I even shed a single tear fully in front of her scared me and made me want to end everything. Yes I had done it before, but this time felt different and I felt on the verge of slipping from my mask. I can't let that happen. It's still too early to the last one, I can't afford to lose myself right now and do something terrible. That was abrupt I know, but I would rather stain our relationship than the bed sheets with her blood, it simply got bad quickly. I want it to stop.

20 minutes later

After a mile of walking through snow and ice trying not to fall I realized that I had walked way too far. It was a colder morning and my jacket was keeping me super comfy and warm. But I realized that it wasn't a good idea to just walk out like that. I know I was crying but seriously you're gonna cause a big scene because of some tears in your eyes? Get a clue Karen. I see a bus bench that has a cover so it doesn't have any snow on it and decide that I need to sit down and think a little bit. I don't really have anything to think about but I continue to sit and feel the cold air. The nice thing at least is it's not cold enough to deter me from staying, and while it does feel cold it is nice to be fair. After sitting for about a minute I finally indulge into my thoughts.

 Why did you do that? Why did you storm out? Seriously think about it Karen, you only hurt everything that way. You like this girl so why do you not show her everything? But I know why I don't show her everything actually. I know why I run and hide away at every moment of weakness I show. It is because of the things I have done. If she knew the things I had done it would all be over, everything would be lost. Karen, how can you like another person the way you do when you cannot show them your true emotions? Doesn't that make everything fake and impure? Karen you have no right to love someone and make them feel things for you, when you know you can never fully love them.

 There is nothing wrong with you Karen. What's wrong is them, the people. Do you not remember the things those people did to you? Do you not remember how many times you have been used and lied to for someone else's personal gain? How do you expect her to be different? How is she going to be the person that changes you? You don't even actually know her. Yesterday was the first time you had seen her apartment and you claim to be held over heels for her? Don't do this to yourself Karen, don't put your trust on a leap of faith. But sometimes a leap of faith is all you have. Look at DP records and what they did for you. They took us on a whim, with what little you produced they took that blew it up, no you blew up with their help. Sometimes you cannot expect to listen to reason, sometimes you must trust chance and fate. Sometimes you simply won't know what's right, and that's ok.

BZZZZZZZZZ BZZZZZZZZZ

I felt and heard my phone vibrate as I forgot to unsilence it. I pull it out of my pocket to see that it's an unknown number but it's a 952 area code which is in the metro area. I answer it curious, could it be someone I know, a scam caller, or what?

"Hi! Is this Karen?" A woman's voice asks over the phone.

"Yes this is her, may I help you?"

"Karen I'm April with Major League Baseball, Minnesota Twins division legal team. I've been trying to reach you via email and calls by your record label. I even tried the police department but I couldn't reach you until I finally got a hold of your personal cell."

"Yes, um hi, what exactly is this about? Like I know what it's about but what's the deal here."

"Karen I'm going to be blunt, We do not want the bad PR. We have already had issues this year with the baseball team and now this is blowing up. We are trying to figure out a way to do damage control."

"Well then, maybe you should've thought about that before getting a psychopath to play for you." The line stays quiet for almost 20 seconds before she speaks again.

"Yes I understand what happened was over the top and we cannot put ourselves into your shoes, but we can offer compensation. In exchange we want you to make a public statement with the CEO of the MLB. There are a lot of eyes on us right now, this is one of the biggest things in the making of sports television and right now we don't want it blowing out of the water." I think for a moment.

"I mean my listens and sales are through the roof right now. I'm the biggest I've ever been. Am I still completely traumatized and fucked up? Yes, but I'm getting a lot of positive feedback and things because of this, however that situation still haunts my brain almost every second since that night. So here's my offer. I want 25 million dollars, plus I want to sing the national anthem at next year's world series. On top of all of that I want 10 million to go to his wife. After what I endured with just one night with him, I can only imagine what she has endured with him, so I think it's only fair to compensate her as well."

"Karen, I don't think we can meet-"

"Listen to me carefully, When I come up with a number or a solution, I don't come to it with no thought. Everything I think of and thought was well crafted and carefully gotten to. Hours of research and other investigations into things for my numbers. So if you want me to make a statement clearing everything up and trying to die everything down, I suggest you listen to my exact offer. Because that offer is the only offer I have, no higher, no lower. Now I'm gonna hang up the phone, if I don't get a call by the end of the day today, saying you agreed to my terms, then I will not be making a statement in the future no matter what. Even if you guys paid me later on. Thank you." I hung up the phone and decided that I needed to go back to Susan's. So I start the mile walk back to her apartment feeling quite accomplished in what I have just done.

Walking back was very boring, I mean the walk felt longer than it did the first time. The ice is somewhat annoying. I hadn't really given much thought to my surroundings but it is quite snowy. I guess I never realized until now but we had a record snow storm in October. The snow had somewhat dissipated but it has been lingering here and there. I haven't had much time to really process everything around me. Life has been moving so fast lately, I almost forgot to stop and smell the roses. I honestly cannot process anything fully right now, it's been so fast since the start of Covid. I feel out of place, yet in the right place at the same time. It's weird, I almost can't explain it. Like it feels unreal, it feels like a very odd fever dream of some sorts. Honestly it amazes me how much something can change in so little time. My life in the span of eight months has become something completely different than what it was before, it's unreal.

I get back to Susan's apartment building and walk inside. The building is somewhat of a spectacle. I hadn't fully looked at it yet but it has a very nice modern style. They used the inlay of the old brick walls and re-did everything around them and made it look nice. She lives in one of those nice Gentrification projects, where they sky rocket the price and the property tax because they made the place look good. It ended up turning out ok honestly, I like it. My fancy ass apartment building washes this away like a pebble on a beach but it still has a nice little ring to it. I think the location is what makes this place so good. It's in a very nice part of the metro, nothing but businesses and rich people. The surrounding view is almost as good as my view. My view is better but not by much comparing the locations, I mean really this place is good.

As I finally reach the door to Susan's apartment I go to knock but I stop last second. I don't know what or why, but something is coming over me, like almost… fear. The fear of what? I haven't felt real fear since… and that was nothing like this. It doesn't feel like I'm gonna die, no. It feels different, like I'm afraid to see what she's like, I'm afraid of what I did to her. It had only been an hour or two but I could imagine how bad I must have scared her when I walked away. I have to knock, I must knock, I need to let her know I'm safe and that it's ok.

Knock Knock

I hear the fidgeting of the door locks and the knob and then the door opens fast. Susan stands on the other side looking at me then she hugs me and I don't hug her back, I just stand. I'm shocked, I almost can't believe it, I feel warm inside, I feel nice. I feel perfect. Everything feels ok just for the moment.

December 16th, MSP To SEA

After that not much happened in my life. I had my court date and after a very lengthy and media driven court session, I got left off the hook, thank god! I did not need any more problems in my life, was that a stain to my career? For a brief moment yes, but good PR always saves the day.

Dead Fashion

But for the most part, I kinda just moved on. Me and Susan started to see each other more, although she must've felt that I didn't like her apartment or something because we never went there again after that. I am also 25 million dollars richer and I get to sing the national anthem at a world series game. Detective Doyle got her money and the 10 million from MLB (undeserving bitch). Ok so maybe a lot did happen, but it wasn't anything cool to write about, I mean I wanted to save it all up because I just have had such a nice month. It feels so nice I have just been writing a lot of music and talking and now I'm getting excited. I get to craft some new music soon. It was crazy how mad I had become without my passion, it's nice. Mike started to get in touch with me after a long break. It was nice to have a good conversation with someone who has as many brain cells as me. The reason why today is so important is that I am going on AN ADVENTURE! Well sort of, I'm going to my parents' new house they just built outside of Seattle, Washington. I have been to the area before because my parent's love it so much, it's where my dad's dad lived and my dad inherited the lot when he died. He wanted to move sooner but they needed to save up some money and stuff and finally after a lot of day trading and other things my dad could finally retire early and blow some money on their new house. They started building it when I graduated high school, because they wanted to wait until me and my broth- well anyways they built their house and moved in at the end of 2019, coming up on a year there. My mom has sent me pics of the place on snapchat (yes my mom uses snapchat it's weird to get over it), I don't really look at them because I'm not a big snapchat fan but the occasional ones are pretty nice. I actually showed Susan and she wants to go with me, but I would never let her get that close with my family. Maybe if we were fully dating like 100% I would maybe mention it to my mom and dad, but they would most likely disown me. Today is the big day to fly out though. Susan dropped me off at MSP and the goofy drop off roundabout bullshit and I got checked in around 4PM. I have had my airpods in the whole time basically except for when I got some chow at Panda Express, holy fuck it was over priced, but damn I chowed that bitch down. I explored the big ass building a little at my flight left at 6PM so I wasn't worried. Airports always amaze me, like so many people going to so many places and all the places they are going. Millions of opportunities coming in and out the gates. The mask I'm wearing is starting to piss me off though. For a while you forget it's there and then within the blink of an eye it's the most annoying thing in the world, fuck Covid. I arrive at my gate at 5:25 and get checked in. I sit down and a very attractive guy immediately starts eyeing me down. I would totally go talk to him and give him my special treatment but we are in such a tight time slot I can't afford to miss the flight. Oh and if you're wondering, yes I got knives on me, you're allowed to have them, as long as they are not on our person and in your bag and sealed away. I only brought two though because anymore would've been mad sus, so I didn't use that. Yes I used sus, I've been playing a lot of Among us recently watching people play it, AOC played it and that was funny as hell. I've kinda just been watching anyone, it's my little dirty pleasure these past few weeks. Oh and Vtubers as well, I don't know who they are or what they are but they are like these animated 2d girls that have like a tracking software track everything they do, while they play games and talk to each other. It's another little dirty pleasure of mine, that if anyone found out about, I would probably rip their spline out of their body.

   Susan caught me playing Persona 5 the other day on my switch. It's like a role playing anime game and fortunately Susan just bought a switch so she didn't think it was weird. "My animal crossing island is-" I did not fucking care enough to even hear the rest of that normie as sentence. No offense to the very sexy brown hair lady that happens to be my manager and the person I regularly make love to on a weekly basis but buying a switch because it's a cool thing to do during the lockdown back at the beginning of the year is the most NPC thing ever. Yes, NPC as in a non playable character, I saw that joke on reddit. It was pretty good, this guy called everyone

Dead Fashion

who followed trends or acted all stuck up and tight NPC's. I laughed so hard I have been starting to use it more often; Unfortunately he was trying to convert people to very anti semitic nazi-esk beliefs and was talking about how all women are emotionless soul eaters who don't really deserve rights because they are and I quote "Women are just the same as those big nosed baby raping demons you guys call the jews. They are soulless and heartless, they only do things that benefit themselves and will snake you at any time, do not trust those things." Although the NPC thing was funny, that guy has some serious issues, like this guy striked me as one of those dudes that got rejected by a girl one time in high school and then went down this downward path of everyone sucks, everyone is bad. He is probably some fat neckbeard who wears fedoras and has a an anime body pillow that he hugs every night with a hole cut out in it with a pocket pussy in there that he fucks, creep. This guy would benefit so much from a salad, touching a little bit of grass and maybe a blowjob or something from a jewish girl in particular. You could change his entire view of the world in one night, but people like him do not get that pleasure, they chose their options and their hand of cards and now they have to play them.

But yeah Susan is 100% a normie, she definitely does not get the complexities that is the Persona games and the meer fact that she tried to compare her Animal crossing island to my Persona 5 Royal game is disrespectful, not just to me, but to Shigenori Soejima and all the people that worked on the masterpiece that is Persona 5. In hindsight though it was completely my fault, I should have never brought my switch out while she was there in the first place. But I figured I could play a little bit while she showered after we had sex. She has this routine of having a shower after we have sex every time. I mean ok listen yes we don't have super messy sex or anything but the few times we do the deed she always showers right away, and it was in the morning and usually she takes like a 30 minute shower, so I hopped on. Sadly she had something she had to do, so she quickly showered and got out early and caught me with my pants down. Honestly that moment was very close to being one of my 13 reasons.

    The Plane itself is not bad in fact unlike most people who struggle with planes I enjoy them very much. The long flights over the pacific ocean to Japan were very nice and honestly I wouldn't trade those flies for anything. So a nice little flight to Washington will not be that bad. The plane finally took off and since I couldn't use my phone for a while I decided to go into my journal (yes I brought it with me, like hell if I didn't). This journal has been my story and my sanity for the past year. I was told by a therapist back in December last year who I ended up bludgeoning to death because she said I was a sociopath, that I needed to start writing things down. So I got this journal and when I ran out of space in the first one I bought a second one and now I'm halfway through my third. I keep track of all three and bring them with me because I do not want anything in these books to ever be seen by another pair of human eyes. Anyones eyes who has seen the inside of this journal is not living anymore. I look back at the beginning of the journal while I can't use my switch or my phone or anything. I didn't really want to write anything new so it seemed cool and oh my god when I started my first journal after that dinner at Ozymandias I was such a dumbass, I mean wow. Just looking at how I talked and wrote it's almost embarrassing to say that was me. No substance, or structure, just words spewing and spewing. I mean I was in a dark place but this is a different type of dogshit, complete yapping.

    As I flip through the pages over the course of the next half hour you can see slowly how over time my writing becomes better. It's obvious that I got more used to it and got a deeper understanding of how writing works as time goes on. I think it also kind of reflects on my feelings too. I noticed that when I was at my lowest or something wasn't going right, the writing was sloppy and quick, frantic is the correct word I guess. As things progressed and my mind has been able to stabilize over this break you can see how much better I have become at this. I honestly and I say this which I normally don't

Dead Fashion

say often, and am proud of myself. I have worked and worked and improved a massive amount at a skill that was something I used to laugh at people for having. A diary? What are you fucking 12? Want Mommy to make you some fucking waffles and eggs too? Oh no don't be late for 6th grade band class! But now I get it, I understand why people write to themselves, I mean on paper it sounds dumb, doing all this extra hard work, and taking all this time to write a bunch of stuff just so you can never show anyone it. But that's not the point, the point is when you write it down, it becomes set in stone, your brain adds it like a pillar, a new wavelength. It is for self recognition, so you know what you did and the things you accomplished. It's not meant to be work, it's meant to be self-assuring. I am proud of myself. I really am Karen, I can see this as a good thing, your vocabulary has improved, your understanding of deep word constructing and sentencing has massively improved as well, the song lyrics you write are only gonna get better now with all this work you put in. Honestly I do deserve this vacation, I think I'm gonna start this vacay by completely draining my mind of all thoughts of Minnesota, No more nothing, not even Susan. I am going to come out here to this beautiful home at the base of Mt. Rainier Washington and enjoy the decent 50 degree weather and NO SNOW! Thank god, but first a good quick little two and half hour nap on this plane will make a great start to the beginning of this trip. I'm honestly so excited now, wow this is- this is a first. I really am excited to see my parents, I can't remember the last time I said those three words in the same sentence, wow.

  3 hours later...

"What in the hell is an Orting mom?"

"That is the city we live in sweetheart."

"Mom I'm not gonna lie I genuinely thought it was some sort of thing in your body, that has got to be the worst thing I've ever heard."

"Quiet down young lady."

The scene simply is this, my mom and I in a car driving through Seattle, Washington, the home of the homeless. From anti homeless benches, to spikes under bridges with lgbtq+ colors because despite us hating homeless people we gotta support our pride! My god these fuckers still find a way to go everywhere. They trash such a beautiful city, it doesn't matter how many rainbow pride colored spikes you put under those bridges they are not gonna stop anything, it's simply carelessness. Maybe I should become president when I'm older, I mean I could kill two birds with one stone, I know how to solve homelessness and overpopulation and fix the unemployment rate in one simple act. A lot of people would be shocked but hey if it looks good on paper and makes the numbers look good then I'm a good president right? Or maybe I would do the casual lying that every president does, for example I would be in a press conference and when asked about why we are heightening our defenses and funneling more money into military I would simply say: 'We believe that there is an intergalactic wizard alliance that is funneling money into the Greek pantheon of gods to fuel their military forces.' Then someone would reply with: 'Madam President, are the Greek gods a real threat to America?' Then I would reply again with: 'Good question, they are as big of a threat as the ManDogMice that have also traded with the intergalactic wizard alliance to help build the Nazi moon base.' then everyone in shock would say 'NAZI MOON BASE?!?' Then in reality I would then launch a full on assault on the middle east and get so far in over our heads, that it takes four Presidents after my term to undo the invasion.

"I mean compared to all those Japanese city names it ain't that bad, you lived in what Toy-ko or whatever?"

"Tokyo mom, I lived in Tokyo, the CAPITAL of Japan, quite literally the BIGGEST CITY IN THE WORLD?!?"

"For all I care it could be called Ching Chong Bing Wong, I don't care for anything outside the U.S, the other countries are meaningless to me."

"I don't know how you managed to racist, stupid and wrong in the same sentence. Are you ok mom?"

Dead Fashion

"YES! And oh my god Karen you live outside of the United States for one year and all of a sudden you're some geographer? Jesus next you're gonna tell me what the capital of London is and fry me up some latkes." Jesus fuck, since when did my mom become super racist, I mean it's always been kinda a republican family, but this is full blown racism, like genuine stupidity.

"Mom, are you gonna be like this all trip?"

"ARE YOU GONNA BE LIKE THIS ALL TRIP?" She says with a big smile on her face as we stop at a red light. "OH MY GOD! OH MY GOD!" my mom screams as she scares the shit out of me with the sudden loud yell.

"What mom!?"

"BAHAHAHAHA" She bursts out laughing. "Look at their bumper sticker, oh my god, oh my fucking god." I try to look closely to see if I can see the bumper sticker, it says 'BLM, Biden Loves Minors' Very original… Thanks for giving me a mini heart attack over that mom.

"I don't know, I think if you put stickers on your car you're kind of gay."

"Don't be such a debbie downer, it's a funny sticker." I decided it was just better to agree with her then to start an argument. I'm starting to get a sense of how this Christmas is gonna be, god how did she become more racist and far right in a more liberal state?

"Yeah I guess."

We got home and honestly I forgot how beautiful Washington was, everything is so nice, clean air, the birds are still here for some reason that Susan would know and I can hear the rushing of the river just a little ways away. I see my dad and he hugs me like a bear and about breaks my wind pipes.

"Stop dad, I gotta keep these babies to make money."

The trip overall was very much what I expected. It was just a nice way to relax in some better weather than Minnesota and being able to wake up and go outside with just a sweatshirt on in December is perfect, I could almost live here, if it weren't for the two idiots I'm with. My mom and my dad would try to budge their way into my life again and it would just fuck things up, I really like living in Minnesota anyways, I've just started to build up a life there.

A Week and Half later, Friday, December 25th

"So Karen, you really have a girlfriend?! Like seriously you aren't kidding?" My dad says as my mom gets coffee ready while we wait to open some presents in the living room. Yep the cats out of the bag, I told them, I told my now very, very far right parents, that I'm basically a lesbian right now…

"Well sort of I don't really know how I feel about her exactly."

"Want my opinion?" I smile at him.

"No I don't."

"Find yourself a man, a strong man." I sigh loudly. "Karen, I'm serious! You need someone to protect you and make sure you're safe." Like I need that, seriously? This is what I mean, these two have no idea who I am, for God's sake you would think they would know their own daughter. We just opened presents from each other not even an hour again and this is the type of shit we have on the giving holiday? And I am and have always been perfectly capable of holding my own. They should know this by now. How many guys I beat up and defended myself against in high school should have been enough, but I guess they don't listen. I am seriously trying to hold it back, I really am.

"Thanks dad, I'll keep that in mind." I continue to smile although tears and rage wants to funnel out of me.

"You need someone like me, someone who is strong, financially stable and loves you."

"Holy shit dad! I am perfectly capable of doing things by myself."

"No you're not, I know you, Karen," My blood boils as I am about to let loose, I look up about to go off when I see my mom walk in with the coffee and it quickly dissipates.

Dead Fashion

"I got a few extra sugars for my sugarbear!" My mom says as her very cringe Christmas sweater gets stuck on her waist and she has to pull it down.

"Thanks, mom." I put the sugars in and my dad turns the tv on and it's immediately on Fox News, of course. "God do these guys ever take breaks, it's 10 in the morning on Christmas and you can't even be with their families, gotta be reporting stupid news."

"HEY! You watch your mouth young lady! Without the news the government would have microchipped and would control everything like 1984, have you seen that really old movies? Probably not, it's before your time."

"I read the book actually... like three times." I say under my breath.

"What was that?" My dad motions his hand to ear as if he wanted me to repeat what I just said, but I won't. "Well anyways you need to watch the movie so you can understand what would happen. But I mean isn't it sad that these guys are forced away from the children and families for this?"

"Yeah it really is." I finally agree with my dad for this brief moment.

"I mean this stupid Biden Administration forcing these guys to keep watch over everything they do, so they are forced to sit there and wait for news. Fuck those stupid Jewish Baby forskin eating bastards, rigged the election and now just taking over, next they are gonna require everyone to be the opposite gender to vote, god we need Trump to save us." This was the worst thing I think my dad has ever said in his entire life. I am genuinely upset and frustrated right now. Ever since I got here, for the past week and half it's been either this stupid Biden Administration or this democrat thing. Never once stopped talking about politics even on Christmas morning of all things. Like give me a break, are these really my parents? Are these the people I grew up with? I mean yeah this trip has been nice, don't get me wrong. It was a lot of relaxing eating some good home cooked food, but this is the last straw, this is bad. I can't even have one waking moment with my parents where it's not something stupid going on. These are not the people I grew up with and raised me. My parents raised me better than this, way better, and the fact this is how they are acting is the most disappointing thing of the year and a massive virus destroyed the world this year to put that into a perspective.

"What do you think Karen, since you're gay now?"

"Oh Chris, stop it!" My mom says. But my rage boils, my skin is melting, I for the first time in a long time, see the father that let him die, that was too drunk to do anything to help me or him. And for the first time in my life, I can now imagine myself taking his life from him, this has never happened, but it's over flowing now, I can't stop it, I'm going to burst!

"You're really gonna talk to your own daughter like that? First off, I'm not gay! I'm Bisexual!" My dad laughs under his breath as he crosses his arms. "And second I think nothing about the political state right now, What I do think is how bad of parents you have become!" My father stops looking so smug and my mothers shoulders drop, as the air gets tense and there is a brief pause as tears come to my eyes. " I mean seriously this is not how we were raised and if I would have been spitting this type of bullshit eight years ago you would've slapped me across the face and called me an idiot. Now it's all you guys can talk about! Biden this, Biden That! Yes He's the president, people voted for him, that wanted him over that orange idiot!" My dad scoffs again.

"No one voted for Biden."

"I voted for Biden! Is there a problem with the fact that I didn't want a pedophile who can't make good relations with any other country other than sucking off the bald russian fuck and on top of that, he can't keep his mouth fucking shut on anything? Both of them are bad but I would rather have Biden over Trump right now. On top of that, this is the shit that Trump has done, before that 2016 election you would've never talked politics a week before Christmas let alone the morning of it, when we are supposed to be celebrating family and if you're religious the birth of Christ! This is meant to be a day where we can be together, put differences aside, open our gifts eat food and be together and now you've turned it into a massive political debate disrespecting your own daughter in the process, It's heartbreaking and the fact that we can't even be together for one Christmas after I came all the way out here to be with you, just proves everything." There's a long pause of silence from everyone, then my father breaks it.

"Are you done with your feminist rant now sweetheart?" My mom opens her mouth with awe and looks at my father as she taps him on the shoulder. But I don't take it so lightly. I stand up and close my eyes and breathe in and out like Susan tried to teach me. I try to keep it all down but I know even if I sit here for an hour it won't go away. It's like throwing up, once it's up, it's going out. I open my eyes and walk forward and slap my dad so hard across the face, that the hand print will still be there in a week. He recoils back on the couch and the glasses fall off of his face while blood starts rushing to the spot where I hit him to make that tomato red print. He starts to scream in pain and my mom screams at me.

"KAREN WHAT THE FUCK IS WRONG WITH YOU?" I need to leave before things get even worse so I start to walk over to the front door and get my shoes on. My dad screams and gets up and screams something at me, but I dodge his stupid insults. I can hear my mom screaming my fathers name and crying. I don't flinch at all and continue to slip my shoes on. My mom is now trying to get him to sit down, then she looks over at me and with tears and snot coming down her face she screams at me again. "GET OUT OF HERE! GET THE FUCK OUT OF OUR HOUSE YOU PSYCHOTIC BITCH!" I walk over to the spare bedroom and grab all the things I need. Luckily my plane was leaving tonight so I made sure to be already fully packed. I grab my suitcase and the unwrapped presents as I continue to hear sobs and small reassurances that I'm evil from my mom. I walk past them not even looking at them to get to the door. As I open the door I glance semi back at them, but not enough to see anything and in a monotone voice I tell them.

"If I forgot anything you can mail it to me, along with the presents I couldn't grab." And with that I walk out, opening the Uber app on my phone. I'll go hang out somewhere that is open, in fact I'm surprised any Ubers are going until I see my driver's name is Mohammed and then it all makes sense. Yep this definitely was a Christmas to remember that's for sure. I'm honestly surprised it didn't happen sooner in this trip, yet again half of the trip has been laying around doing nothing or taking long walks along the river so I guess it makes sense. Definitely the most weird visit I have ever had.

SHOWTIME, Jan 6th, 2021

This is the happiest day in the world, nothing could stop this day from being such a perfect day. For the first time in over six months, I'm back! The studio smells fresh, the place looks beautiful and everything is so perfect. You know when you have those days where the colors just seem brighter? This is one of those days. The snow is so white the sun beams the tiny bit of warmth it can bring in its big yellow tint, god it's such a good morning, even the Starbucks vanilla bean frappe tastes better today. It's not even 10:30am and everything is so nice. I look over all the work I have written down in the past six months while switching back and forth and seeing my Nvidia stock is up $60 a stock more than when I bought it in June last year making my 5k investment worth around 9k. Then in the mix of everything Susan walks in. I hadn't seen her since before Christmas as she was out of town for New Years and Christmas because I was going to be out, so we just decided to do things our own way. Susan is wearing the sexiest business casual clothes I've ever seen and because of this I can't help but rush over to her and kiss her profusely before she pushes me off of her and laughs.

"This has got to stop, we can't do this in public."
"Says who?"
"Says me, goofball." She hits me on the head softly. Mike walks in of course with all of his files and paperwork shit

Dead Fashion

and of course wearing a mask too. It is obvious that he saw the whole thing because he completely avoids eye contact at all with us.

"I hope I wasn't interrupting play time," he says. Susan goes to respond but I beat her to it.

"Eat a dick Mike!" Susan looks over at me like she just saw a ghost fuck her mom. She taps me on shoulder hard and I wince a little bit as a joke.

"That's the sounds I missed." Mike says as he comes over and gives me a hug which I happily take, because without this guy I would still be a soundcloud rapper. "How have you been Kare?"

"You know the usual, cutting peoples heads off, skinning them alive behind the Burger King on Washington Ave, the usual." Susan and Clemons both laugh, with Clemons almost dying of laughter, he loves that random dark shit, I know way too much about the people in my life.

Working for the first time in months was so good and very fun. We did a lot of brainstorming today more than anything, I ended up recording a song however I don't really like the sound of it. I called the draft As We Fall, but I personally think it's a little corny. After about five hours we decided to call it quits though as Clemons so private shit to take care of. We were the only ones in the studio right now because it was a very snowy day and with covid stuff still going on. It got dark so quickly too it's almost pitch black and we haven't even left yet. Clemons picked up his stuff and hugged me again before taking off too; Susan and I stayed for a while after although we were just showing each other Tiktok for about 30 minutes while snuggled on each other on the studio couch.

"Karen did you tweet anything or post anything about being back today?"

"I actually did, why?"

"Just wondering, I wanted to make sure you actually did what I asked you."

"I always do."

"I know and that's why I love you." Susan finishes the sentence and before she even does is already going in for a kiss. We kiss for about fiveish seconds before stopping and looking at each other and then back at my phone.

"What are we? Like are we dating?"

"I don't know if I would call it that." Are you kidding me? I fucking love this woman and she says this!?

"What do you mean you don't consider us dating?"

"I don't really like the word dating, you're more of a lover if that makes sense." Wow and just like that she reels me back in, that's why I have these feelings, she is so perfect.

Later, 5:00PM...

Buildings roll by as Susan's car moves at a decent pace, I see a driving range covered with snow and completely dead, along with the rest of what looked like a tiny golf course. We are actually in quite a hurry for some reason.

"Susan what's the deal? You good?"

"I'm fine, why?" She is obviously not fine, she looks like a ghost, pale and nervous looking. I don't think I've ever seen her like this. Because of this nervousness I decided to do our hand thing. Me and Susan have this hand thing where when one of us takes our hand palm out and lays it in the middle near her cupholders, the other knows that they want to hold hands, for any particular reason. It sounds really silly and most likely would look stupid as fuck, but it's something we do. I take the palm of my hand and lay it out for her to grab, and she notices it and puts her hand onto my hand and we squeeze ever so slightly. I hope that this calms her down but it only seems to make her more pale.

"Are you sure? You seem on edge." Susan takes her hand off of mine and continues to drive at a very fast pace. This honestly really started to bug me a lot. I semi freak out and raise my voice a little. "Ok what the fuck is your problem, seriously!?"

"I told you there is nothing! I'm fine, it's just been a long day.

"You're keeping something from me." This immediately makes Susan perk her ears up and quickly respond, only proving my theory right.

"I'm not! Why are you being like this?"

"Because it's obviously true, you wouldn't perk up and get upset if you weren't. I'm heartbroken right now."

"WHY?"

"Because you're lying to me and refusing to tell me something, you don't trust me, is that it?

"What? No why would you-"

"Then tell me what's up right now, what are you keeping from me?" We get to the stoplight and Susan closes her eyes and puts her head down on the wheel.

"There is nothing going on, I'm just tired, ok? Can we please just be at peace until I take you home?"

"Ha, you're making um, sound like you aren't coming over tonight."

"It's because I'm not." I immediately shut down into my dangerous self upon hearing that and my smile dissipates.

"Why?"

"I can't."

"Why can't you." Susan seems to get more and more frustrated with me.

"I just can't! IS IT WRONG FOR ME TO HAVE ONE NIGHT TO MYSELF!?" The blow up makes me lose myself and I turn and slap Susan as hard as I can and she recoils and looks so confused as if watching her grandma or someone else she loves die in front of her. I unlock the door and walk out slamming it behind me. Luckily we aren't on a highway and in a residential area, so I can quickly get to the sidewalk. Susan rolls the window down and screams for me to come back, but the light turns green and the people behind her start honking. She rolls up to the nearest opening on the side of the road which is in front of me quite a ways.

Susan gets out of the car and tries to come over to me but I've already turned and walked the other way. She catches up to me and grabs my arm and turns me around, which infuriates me.

"STOP!" I scream and she once again steps back letting go of my arm.

"Karen, I'm sorry I just-"

"Listen... I don't feel right, right now after what just happened. I need you to leave me alone. I will walk home."

"That's still a long walk, I-" I cut her off, speaking in a very monotone voice.

"I told you... leave me alone."

"Why?"

"Because if you don't I feel like something bad will happen." The moment I say that Susan goes dead pale yet again like she was earlier and for a moment I feel like she thinks back to the murder case with me a few months back, and then it almost scares her. She says nothing and looks at me and her eyes water, before turning around and walking fast to her car. A part of me screams and screams to just go back with her and kiss her and make it ok, do something, say something... But I don't. I don't know what happened to that part of me, a few months ago I would've skipped back and hugged her and kissed her, but now I don't, it feels wrong, but I also feel like myself. My parents, then this, I don't know why, but I feel wrong.

1 hour later...

It only took me an hour to get home and by the time I got to my apartment, I was absolutely dead. It was cold and snowy and was just unbearable outside, so to walk home in it was just not as fun as you would think. I was starting to understand why cars became things on that walk and I praise Henry Ford for popularizing them in the U.S.

I got home and tried to warm up by making some hot tea and then turning on my tv. I decided once I had tea I better just stop thinking for the day and just workout. It's just best to just stop what I'm doing and relax and just focus on the workout for the day which happens to be boxing and hitting practice. I couldn't even put the tea on before the news channel pops up showing a bunch of people climbing a wall with flags and all this other stuff. I quickly run over and turn the volume to see that they aren't just rioting a big fancy building or anything like that. They are literally breaking into the capitol building. I almost shit my pants and before I know it I get entranced watching it all, these guys are breaking windows and climbing through them. They busted down doors and they stormed into the building.

I'm trying to figure out why they are doing this until I see it, the hat. I don't even need to describe the hat to you because it's not worth it. But let's just say that it is a red hat. "HAHAHA" I laugh out loud so hard it's actually not funny. Seriously, I fell to the floor laughing when I saw all these "Patriots" wearing MAGA hats and waving the flag, breaking into their own capitol building. I ended up laughing so hard my stomach started to ache and I quickly had to stop myself. This is so funny it's unbelievable, how can you be so stupid as to do something like this. This was honestly perfect, another major event, another hit song it would seem... It's time to capitalize on another tragedy I think.

Back in Black

"I don't have to tell you things are bad... Everyone knows things are bad! We know that the air is unfit to breath and our food is unfit to eat. We sit watching our Tv's while today our local newscaster tells us that we had 15 homicides and 63 violent crimes; Cause if that's the way it's supposed to be, we know things are bad, worse than bad... they're crazy."

"What do you think Clemons? It's a perfect opening, throw it into the mixer, put the beat on over top of it and have it transition into the song."

"Is that from the movie Network?" He says over the phone as I switch it speaker and set it on my counter-top so I can go hands free while starting to make eggs.

"Yes! And I want this song we are dropping to promote the album to be about Jan 6th."

"How is this at all about what happened two days ago?"

"How is it not? The song itself is about how people want us to live a specific life and that we aren't allowed to live any other way. We are supposed to sit by and watch a mockery of the world take place by politicians and people of power. It's a statement, to show that things are not ok with our government and our leaders, including the system too."

"Karen this is really scary to put out honestly, You start messing with this type of stuff you could piss some people off including your audience, I mean some of them are not gonna like that you are fully going in on some of their favorite politicians and on their side. This isn't like it was 10 years ago, you can't go around anymore and have your own opinion. You start to mess with this shit and it could be bad news traveling fast for your career." I stop and look over at my phone.

"Mike I do not care, in fact I could care less if people don't like me or not, it's not my fault they idolize a murdering asshole. I mean the thing about my music, Clemons it's good when it's political, I mean look at Dead Fashion, plus I mean I want to make a statement with my music, this is a great way for my music to be the cause of a great influence in young people."

"Karen Dead Fashion was so successful because people dragged it through the mud, the song blew up because of the fact that you made it about that, you gained a lot of supporters but you also got a lot of enemies that way, especially in the city. Look want my advice, I like the song but just throw it into the album and see how it does rather than making it front and center, I only record the music and mix but being in this game for 20 years I can say-" I hang up the phone, I don't care what he has to say and I'm getting sick of everyone telling me what I can and cannot do, so because of that now I'm going to fully drop this regardless, because of the simple fact I can. Also my eggs were burning and I was getting too focused on the call, my tummy needs breakfast.

Meeting With Friends

Death, it's all I can think about right now. I'm on my way to this bar that just opened back up called The Twin tables, don't ask me why the fuck it's called that, something to do with the twin cities more than likely. I exit the Uber and I am met with a cold draft. I don't even know how it could possibly be cold at the beginning of May, but then again I remember I live in Minneshita and it all makes sense.

It has been two weeks since the last incident with Damocha and I have not spoken to him since and I have not been to DP records either. I think they think if they give me a month of no work or calls I'll mello out, I have already made my decision though. Despite the fact that I am miserable, I will stay on my contract, I don't really have a choice. I have been non stop working out shooting (again finally) and practicing my fighting skills. It randomly came over me after the Damocha incident and so I've been doing that to take my mind off of going insane. I cried more times in the past two weeks than I have in the past two fucking years. The worst part about my life currently, despite me being in great shape and eating well, is my love and sex life. I haven't had sex with a guy or girl in over four months, last time was with Susan. I haven't thought about anyone else except for her, she has been the only person I have been attracted to, I don't look at people the same way anymore. I used to look at people and imagine what they looked like naked (for better or for worse) but I don't do that anymore, I don't really have feelings towards anyone. I've been trying to find a way to cope with everything, Instagram, twitter, watching videos of guys using nothing but their hands and bamboo to make a house out of mud. I've tried every drug I have ever had, like acid, meth, crack, weed, shrooms, DMT, and other than some lousy trips, I have gotten no addiction and no forgetting. It plagues my mind. Susan will not text me, will not answer my calls anymore, that's what this whole thing is about.

Susan has decided to ghost me. I have thought about going to her house, but I really don't have the courage, I know for the first time in my life I don't have courage to speak up, I'm too soft with her. She is just so perfect and pure. When I look at her I look at perfection, from the hair to the lips, to the tits, to her legs. Not to mention she literally is the funniest person I have ever met (besides Adam Sandler) and also she gets me. It's hard for anyone to understand this unless they are in the same position as me, when someone gets you and understands you and will be there for you, it changes how you feel about them. I cannot overcome this no matter what, everytime I close my eyes I imagine how I fucked it all up, how it's all over. I had finally dropped all the hookups, drugs, and parties, and had a relationship, a true relationship, not one like that one faggot whose name I can't even remember. Chris or some shit, that cop bitch freaked out on me for, she made sure to keep tabs on me when I returned, I saw the van again, that fucking bitch. I should show her what I truly can do, but then that would ruin everything.

  Susan has been plaguing my mind so that's why I'm here, I am meeting up with some very close friends who I haven't seen since before I moved. We were always the bad chicks getting in trouble, causing a scene. Never anything like I do now, in fact if I told them about the countless murder sprees I had in Japan or here they would definitely rat me out, they are rats. And on top of that they aren't just rats, they are rich spoiled brat rats, I pity them now.

  Erica, (you saw me on the phone with her, way back in the day) is my Mexican or hispanic friend, I don't really know, she might be from Honduras or she might be from Mexico, I couldn't give a rats ass either way. She is half whatever because her father is this rich farmer who moved up here to buy up a shit ton of land and sell international crops, she used to brag about how her dad would get to meet all these world leaders and stuff because he has one of the biggest trades of farmland in the US. Maggie is my other rich friend but she is white. She dresses like a barbie doll, she is secretly a bitch and listens to grunge and I've even gone to a Five Finger Death Punch concert with her, but she makes herself look like this bimbo, so she can attract men. She's basically a trap, she traps them and then makes them pay for all of her stuff for like a month, even though she is wealthy enough to buy the goddamn Minnesota Timberwolves I swear. And then she uses them for sex and drops them. She was one of my idols, for the longest and even though I laugh at her now, she still is a girl boss. She herself makes up for all the bad shit men did to women by being herself and I can't help but admire it. We are sitting at a high table in this crowded bar. I guess people are excited for a real bar to be open legally and not in the shadows. I am drinking a Truly Margarita mix, I'm on my second can of the night. In front of me Erica has about four fucking white claws, I almost am surprised she isn't trying to kiss me or make out with someone with how drunk she should be, and Maggie is drinking a malt whiskey it looks like it's Grand Teton or one of those weird ass brands.

    Currently the plan is to drink so much I forget what I'm doing and maybe get a night where I'm not worried or stressed. Like I said I've tried everything else, and it seems that nothing works, no drugs or anything, liquor is my last resort. It really is pissing me off because I can't stop thinking, overthinking, I want to underthink something I've always been bad at.

    "Well Ms. Wall, the self made billionaire." Maggie retorts as Erica and I laugh at the statement. "Where have you been? You've ghosted us all summer last year and well ALL OF LAST YEAR!"

    "First off it's now Mr. Wall, I'm a man now, I'm having my vagina repurposed into a fully functioning male junk."
They laugh at the joke, I really am funny as hell.

    "O-KAY Mr. Wall, stop avoiding the question." Maggie sips her whiskey, if you don't like us simpletons that's fine." The fact she called themselves simpletons when they are the two richest people I know is very upsetting to not only me, but real simpletons.

    "Well trying to keep up with pleiades, yoga, eating a balanced diet is hard to make time for friends. Do you know how hard it is in a day to juggle eating lunch and playing video games all day? I'm just too busy." They laugh again and I even chuckle at my own joke this time. "I-I mean guys I really am busy plus I was taking covid very seriously, I had a lot of work I did last year, I mean seriously plus I-" I almost tell them about my relationship but decide not to. I also don't want to tell them I just really have not had the willpower to see them or care about them in the past two years.

"Well if your little incident on Halloween says anything, it says you're a liar!" Erica says. "Your little party you went to did not give me 'caring about covid' vibes." I look at her dead in the face, before smiling again.

"HAHA, another White Claw Erica? Actually, the next three rounds are on me!"

"They should all be on you, you rich bastard." Erica laughs at Maggie's remark.

"Yeah didn't I read in the NY times that this son of bitch made the most money in a single solo performance than any other rap artist in the entire world?" Ericka replies, looking at Maggie. Maggie bursts out laughing and then raises her glass and Erica raises her White Claw and then in unison they both say "To Karen! Thanks, you dumb son of a bitch!" I laugh and playfully throw my Truly can at them, although I guess I wouldn't have minded it hitting a little hard on an edge cutting one their heads open.

Going up to the bar I finally get to see this place in full, it's a massive bar, like I'm talking the size of a restaurant. It is really crazy how big this place is and it's packed like a can of sardines. It's actually quite a high class drinking spot, very nice chairs and tables, of course you got your regular bar and stuff but other than that it could fool you as some sort of nice restaurant.

I order three rounds of whiskey, three white claws but this time mango and I order myself a J&B on the rocks, just one because I wanted something that wasn't in a fucking can. Also it's the drink Patrick Bateman always orders and I admire a lot, I want to harvest that energy right now. Returning to the table I see Erica on her phone looking like she is about to pass out already which makes me slap myself for even ordering three for her, but maybe she is just bored… hopefully. Maggie sees me and her eyes widen and mouth drops like she's a kid in a fucking candy store.

"Holy fuckle sticks Karen, you trying to kill us or something?" She taps Erica "This bitch brought the whole fucking bar with her on that tray!"

"I told you I was going to buy three rounds." I say smiling while setting the drinks down.

"Yeah usually that means cover us, not actually do it, HA Karen I think you are definitely out of your mind." True. "I thought you lost your mind when you went to Japan, but I think you've always been a psycho."

"An American Psycho?" I say smirking at the pun, but I'm quickly shot down by Erica.

"Eww nobody likes that fucking movie, it makes me puke now when I see Christian Bale." then says under her breath. "Misogynist prick."

"OKAY! Patrick Bateman is not a Misogynist, he is literally by definition a psycho. I mean do you even understand the message of the novel or the movie at all? You do know that the book was written by a gay male and the movie was directed by a woman? Not even just that, but the insane sub plots and points made throughout the story to try and mock the disgusting conformity of the late 80's. You obviously need to study up and use your brain the next time you decide to talk about a novel or movie ever again." They both stare at me blankly like I just killed someone in front of their eyes or like when someone thinks they see a ghost. Then Maggie looks at Erica and then back at me.

"Jesus Christ, I'm sorry I just insulted your entire identity, I promise to neve talk about your hubby Patrick Bateman ever again." Erica says as she salutes me like a soldier.

"It's not my favorite novel, nor movie, I just think you should never misjudge something based on a very ignorant point of view like that. Anyways how the hell have you girls seriously been?"

"Other than the fact that you are mansplaining everything I've been fine, it's been so boring these past few months though, I mean all we do is sit around and do nothing."

"Come on Maggie, there has to be something you did." I hope to at least spark something out of these girls, but so far all they have been doing is annoying the hell out of me. I'm starting to wonder if they really are the same people I knew all these years ago.

"Yeah to be honest I haven't really done much either, I mean I guess I did get a boyfriend but…" Erica says, sipping from her white claw.

"Really?" I said actually getting intrigued and putting one leg over the other. "You actually found someone to settle down with? What's his name? Would I know him?"

"Well I don't want to talk about it actually, it's kind of hit or miss right now."

"What do you mean?" Erica looks at me in disgust like I just murdered a puppy.

"I told you I don't want to talk about it. Do you not understand or something?" … What a fucking bitch, both of them. Seriously can we just talk for fuck's sake?

We sit for almost two minutes while I stare at them, my smile now gone and they both continue to drink while sitting on their phones. It's dead silent at our table and it continues to be until I break the silence.

"Sooooo… have you girls heard my new song?"

"Yep." they both say continuing to not look up from their phones. I don't have a new song. I just wanted to see what they would say.

"Oh I actually heard this really funny story about this guy in Wisconsin of all places! Those fucking cheeseheads." I say with a big smile on my phone. "This guy Ed Gein, right he would- get this I'm not a shitten you, would dig peoples graves up, and collect body parts, he even took some chicks head from her body after he murdered her, isn't that just hilarious? I mean what was he doing with all of those body parts?" I say, chuckling at the end. The smile now so big on my face I can feel my cheeks hurting.

"..." it's dead silent, no response from either of them, both of them continue to stare down at their phones, Erica even shows Maggie a video which I assume is a Tiktok or something of that nature and they both chuckle a little.

I out of nowhere feel my mind go blank. It all comes back to me in a massive flash, this massive big burst of rage, anger, pent up emotions I haven't felt since way back then about a year ago are back. They flood my sanity and brain. They don't even give my brain a chance to respond or fight, they take over.

I smash my glass on the table where we are sitting and the glass and a little bit of liquid and ice flies out. Pieces of the glass go into my hand but I don't even feel them, my body is so overwhelmed I forget pain even exists. The loud crash finally catches their attention along with half of the bars as well. They both look up at me and continue to stare me down pale in the face.

"Are you guys deaf, retarded or both!? Do I have your attention now!?" They both look like little sad puppies who aren't getting adopted, they just… stare. "WELL? YOU GONNA STARE SOME MORE OR WHAT!?" They both are visually shaken up and the stress of the situation makes me almost want to gouge my eyes out and cry at the same time. I get up and decide it's best I decide to leave and not worry about this anymore.

"Karen, where are you going?" Maggie says almost offended by the fact I just made this big scene then decided to walk away from it.

"I'm going as far away from you two as I can get." I say now almost out of the little area we are sitting in.

"But why?" She continues. I immediately turn around and get up into her face and then whisper in between my teeth in a very aggressive tone.

"Because if I don't, I might put your head on a fucking pike!" I stare at her for a few seconds before grabbing my tiny purse that I have and walking quickly away, shoving the door as aggressively as possible on my way out.

Outside is a whole different story, I walk and walk and walk for what seems like forever, no rhyme or reason to my walking. I'm thinking, plotting, I'm slowly coming back down to a sane level and I'm now overlooking the situation, it's dire. Maybe it was a bad thing, I mean what I did, but I'm not really mad. It's their fault, they need to realize that life isn't just on a tiny fucking screen, I hope they can realize that on their own because I decide to delete their numbers and unfriend them on facebook as well. They can obviously live without me, so I can obviously live without them.

As Above So Below

As above so below, is the new song that I dropped to promote my new album. Despite what I was told by many people I dropped it anyways because I simply could, I'm tired of people telling me what I can and cannot do. It just simply really pisses me off when people try to make me do things or tell me I can't do it.

The release came with a tweet and small little video I posted to Instagram, it was talking about the thing that happened on January 6th and how sad I was to see people do such a horrible thing. I mean trying to storm your own capitol? That's ridiculous, get some brains my god. The song dropped and as expected it did very well and made a couple headlines because somehow it's a slow news day despite one of the craziest events in United States history just happening. I don't even know who to blame for it, you could blame Trump, you could blame the senators, or you could blame the people, whoever is at fault doesn't really matter, what matters is that it happened. After recording the video and posting it, I do an annual detox. You may be asking what my detox is and I don't blame you, most people don't consider me so health conscious and for a while I really wasn't. I have really forgotten my ways. I was really not in the best state of mind. I was so happy and so pure, I let myself go, I let myself get too far ahead of myself. I had myself convinced I could love and be normal, I'm not and I need to stop acting like I can be normal again. I AM NOT NORMAL! I don't how many times I try to tell myself it never works, no matter what, I am who I am and I didn't get to where I am by being this goody two shoes woman. I am more than that, I'm better, I AM BETTER!

GOD what am I saying I keep going on and on about this shit I need to just calm down and relax, I'm letting myself get to me. There was nothing wrong with how I was for the past six months. Sure you weren't working out as much and maybe you didn't really kill anyone, except for that one guy, and maybe you let your eating habits get a little bad, way more fast food and not balancing the diet. Maybe you were a little crazy with money and spent a little more on things you wanted, But you got to remember it's ok. It's ok to not have your entire day planned out minute for minute. It's ok to just work in the background while just enjoying yourself. It's ok to eat what you want, it's ok! You just got to remember Karen, to keep telling yourself to smile, life is meant to be enjoyed, stop making your life black and moody, it's ok to wear red to your first real concert, instead of black, it's ok to stand out a little, just remember you gotta enjoy it even if it sucks a little. I gotta keep telling myself this, It's ok to not be perfect, everyone has flaws, including Susan… I need to go talk to her before my first show in a couple weeks. I gotta find the courage and time to do it, but I gotta do it, it's ok.

2 weeks later…

The song has received exceptional praise after the first week. At first the people were kind of upset or I guess felt like I was trying to take advantage of the situation (I was) but after of course it gets linked back to Donald Trump and all of those guys all of sudden I'm a hero for giving the people something they can listen to and "connect" with. It's all starting to turn into bullshit, nothing feels real anymore. I don't really care as much as I should. Normally I am super passionate and try my best, but I'm not. I've become so desensitized to everything now, every time I try to do something I don't feel anything or act like I should.

I just had my first concert two days ago and I sang and screamed and did everything but... but... I don't care. I don't really care at all, I almost can't explain it, I'm so uninterested. Normally old me would be freaking out but I'm not. I just did my first live show, my own show, the thing I have been trying and trying and scraping through the mud for, but it didn't feel like anything. My heart never raced, I never got nervous, I never felt like it's what I wanted to do, it felt wrong. My life for the past two weeks has been flipping the switch back and forth between personality A and personality B. The idea of me that I once knew is non-existent, I don't exist like I used to.

Personality A is me dead faced acting on just primal needs, need to piss, use the bathroom. Need to eat, fry up some ramen. Need to breathe, breathe. Personality B has been a lot of the same shit, acting like you're a happy go lucky camper, who is so excited to see everything and everyone. Laugh at everyone's jokes, smile as wide as you can until your lips hurt. Talk fast and energetic, it's tiring, I can't catch a break. I'm starting to think this is all wrong, I don't want to be here anymore, this isn't what I want. I'm starting to make so much money, that even my money is boring. I thought this is what I wanted but I'm starting to think it's not what I wanted. I'm stuck trapped and I can't get out.

April, 2021

It's been a while, a long while. It's been so long I don;t even really care to format anymore, life has been the same constant same old same old. I sleep, I wake up, practice vocals, work on lyrics, eat, then workout, then shower, then perform. With little to no breaks it gets tiring, I mean for fucks sake I can't even hardly laugh anymore, I have to keep up with twitter and all this stuff on social media that I've started to just not engage anymore. I'm getting to a breaking point. Sure, travel is cool, but what's the point of traveling if you don't have time to see anything? For half the fucking day I'm stuck in a hotel, I've seen Susan one time in the past two months and we didn't kiss we didn't even hug, we ate dinner with Damocha when I came back for a week. I was so tired that week I didn't do anything but sleep. If you are wondering why I haven't been writing or journaling or keeping up, it's because I don't have time and to be honest I have no drive.

All my energy goes into being this super excited happy person when on stage and around fans and people, the moment I hit the uber I'm deadfaced. There is nothing real about me, I even tried to go back to my old ways, I snuck out of the hotel in Miami three weeks ago and found some homeless bum and merked his ass but I didn't feel anything. No rush, no thrill, no craving of bloodlust. I didn't get relieved, I didn't get anything, it was a wasted fucking kill. I walk around doing nothing. I'm trapped, stuck, tomorrow is my last show, then I have a plan. I've thought it through so much I don't even think about anything else anymore, not even my passion. I forgot all about music, despite it being the reason I'm like this and living like this, it almost feels secondary, like I'm not really feeling my music anymore, nothing feels right.

April 16th, 2021

Today was like no other. I'm actually talking about today because the writing I did yesterday actually made me somewhat happy again. I think it was more so the fact that tonight was my last show for the tour and the albums. Apparently people have been itching to get back out into the real world, because every single one of my shows have sold out, even though we are booking the biggest venues, they are selling out, every single one. I had a radio interview this morning and for the first time in my life I actually did a radio interview without it going south.

The interviewer was telling me that I'm the first person to come back to doing shows since covid and that me and my camp managed to get the first bookings for every venue. Somehow we either planned this perfectly or got really lucky, either way we talked about my music and I pretended to care, but then the man said something to me that made me start to think. He told me that my shows have been selling out so much that I am competing with Micheal Jackson in numbers for this tour. Yes somehow rinky dinky me, some broken fucked up woman is competing with Micheal Jackson. The more I thought about it the more I realized that the most fucked in the head people become the best, Micheal, Elvis, Kanye, people like that become so popular because they don't/didn't think like everyone else.

   They were crazy fucking weird and did a lot of weird and sometimes even bad shit, exactly like me. I am slowly becoming a legend and I have only been mainstream for about a year now. Somehow in one year I managed to build a legacy so big that it tools other years to get and some people will never in their life get to my status. Maybe it was because of the music and timing of it, or maybe god hates me so much, she is torturing me with success. After all she's done a lot worse for a lot less, remember that Eden chick, bitch ate an apple and exiled. That woman in the sky, if she is real, she really does fucking hate me that's for sure, maybe when I die I'll get to become lucifers right hand woman and come back as one of those Oujia board demons that youtube influencers summon for views, that would be pretty fucking sick. Either way today's show was good and today was one of the first times I actually enjoyed the day along with the show, mainly because it's over and I can finally fuck off into my little shit pit for a few months. First things first, when I get back tomorrow, I'm seeing Damocha, then I need to see Susan, I've thought about it and thought about it and thought about it and decided I'm ready to to own up and be selfless in exchange for her, I don't why but I feel like I want this and it's the only thing I want. I have never felt this way for anyone else and now I know it's now or never.

Memento Mori

Dead Fashion

    The plane ride was boring back to the twin cities from my last show in Dallas. It wasn't long thank fucking christ, and because of this I saved myself from screaming at the top of my lungs. MSP is always nice though, the airport it always so magical for some reason, every time I show up I get flashbacks to when I was younger and we flew to Florida that one time and the airport was just so cool, me and my broth- it was so fun to walk around being in this massive building and how much time it felt like we had. It's one of the only good memories I have of my childhood, the rest are just either dull, bland or make me rage, especially the ones when my mother was teaching me vocals and singing. The amounts of slaps and beatings I used to get, FUCK just thinking about them makes me rage, I thank my mom somewhat for them, but at the same time I also despise her for it, even if she is a semi sweet old lady now, but when we have a kid, me and Susan I should say, when we impregnate her, because I'm not fucking doing any of that bullshit, you better believe my child is going no where near my mother or father. I would rather cyanide the whole family, than force her to see them.

    Arriving at DP Records after a few months really does breathe some life into me, some really good memories, like that time me and Damocha did crack and had sex in the studio, that was wicked, although we made an agreement that if he didn't tell Susan, I wouldn't tell his wife plus chop his lucky charms off. I walked in to see the lady with the big nose, she still works here, great… I walked up to her.

    "Well if it isn't the amazing Akuma herself, Karen Wall, what can I do for you sweetie?"

    "I uh, need to speak with Damocha, I've got some finance stuff I need to work out."

    "A problem?"

    "It could end up being a problem, yes."

    "What is the probl-"

    "Do you need to know everything!?"

    "Okay! Okay! Calm down… Damocha's at lunch right now, I'm sorry but you are going to have to come back later." I look down at this new apple watch thing I splurged on while traveling, it reads 10:41 AM.

"At 10:40 in the morning?"

"Damocha takes his lunch early, so-" I interrupt her as I get closer to her.

"Listen lady, I'm not really in the mood for B.S so here's what I'm gonna do, I'm gonna walk into his office and if he isn't there I will sit in his chair and wait for him, if he is in his chair when I walk in, I will walk back out come to this desk and throw you off the top of the building." I look directly into her eyes, as they start to water, I maybe went a little overkill with the old school way of doing things, but sometimes that's what you have to do.

"Uh… I will let him know you want to see him." she says as her voice gets really shaky and sounds like she is about to cry.

I walk to the back of the main floor where I find his enormous section of the floor and open his door. He is there on his computer on the phone, he looks up at me as he hangs up the phone, definitely was big nose lady. He stands up and just stands near his desk as I stand near the front of the office, he walks over to me and looks at me as tears come into his eyes and then smiles. He proceeds to hug me very hard and I do the hands on back thing to make it more believable.

"Karen, it's been a few months, my god how have you been, do you want a mineral water?"

"No I'm-"

"Nonsense, let's get you some mineral water." He goes to his mini fridge and pulls out a glass bottle. "The best of the best, Mountain Valley is the best on the market!" It's not, it's the best definitely but paying $23 for a 16 oz bottle of water makes it not worth it thus not the best on the market, nobody does it like Life water, simple, cheap and this isn't even an advertisement either, I just simply love that water, built into the classic bottle is the minerals and electrolytes, it's good.

"Thanks, Damocha."

Dead Fashion

"You seem a little off, what's wrong." he quickly quips "I hope there wasn't anything to do about last halloween at my house is it?" I want to talk with him about that but I know he's too simple minded for the conversation I want to have with him about that.

"No, not really that's for another time I think, I'm more concerned with myself… currently."

"Uh… I'm listening." I breakdown a little bit.

"I don't want to do this anymore. I'm willing to give up the contract even if it means paying you money, I've just thought about it and I am not happy."

"I'm sorry to hear that."

"Yes and I'm willing to let you own my music rights and make the same amount of money off it, I just want to be done with the shows, I want to go back to just writing music and producing it."

"Is that so?" Damocha asks as he goes to his mini fridge and pulls out a bottle of brandy.

"Yes it is and I think, well I want to have a family settle down, the touring was fun-" I stop myself and think, I decide I just need to be honest with him "It actually wasn't fun at all, it sucked, a lot. I was miserable the entire time and I just think, that's not the life I want."

"Huh." He sips the now poured bottle.

"So I was wondering how I would go about that, I really want to get back to Susan and see her tonight, I haven't had a chance to be alone with her."

"Well you go about it, by not going about it." I laugh under my breath.

"I'm sorry what?"

"You aren't leaving, is what I mean." He sips again from the glass. "Simply put the contract that you signed states, there is no obligation for you to stay however, if you do decide to leave, the clause on what page was it, fuck, uh… 31, no! 32! Says that any and all products that are made during the time of the contract by you or your party, become property and 100% owned and controlled by DP Records." I stare at him and his wrinkled and fucking disgusting face. He's sick, he's vile, I want to carve his face and get rid of that sick disgusting little smile he has. "Now I know you're gonna throw one of your little temper tantrums now, I've learned a thing by working with you, so before I give you this-" He points at an envelope. "I will tell you this. You are under a legally binding contract, this isn't just a job, you don't get to quit on us, just because you are currently the breadwinner here doesn't give you any leverage or power over me and the board. You are under contract until 2024, you are required to still produce-" he looks up and tries to remember "five more albums for and under DP records. Now you can rush those all you want, but you are still under contract for another four years, maybe you should've read the contract with your lawyer, rather than thinking you are above and beyond everyone else in the room." he walks back over to his desk and pours more brandy into his cup. I stare at him, my face dead, my thoughts are black, cold, bloody, I haven't felt like this in over damn near ten months. This feeling of no control, no emotional control over anything, my mind just works on autopilot feeling enraged, engulfed by all my emotions, I'm losing myself, I can almost feel my eyes ready to cry and my face starting to get red. "The thing is, you think you are better than everyone else, when you need to start cutting the bullshit. Karen, you are young, you are still learning the brain develops fully by 25. You need to accept that you will not always be the smartest person in the room, that's my opinion.

"I will-"

"Do what? Do like you did to that baseball player for the Twins? How you swindled them into giving you money and to sing the national anthem on live television for a murder you committed on self will? God I've been wanting to say this for so long, I can barely contain myself. Do you know what you will do?" He looks at me and I stare at him with tears in my eyes... I don't say anything. "You will do nothing! Nata, zip, zero, you are the breadwinner for DP, do you know how much money you've generated in the past year since signing you? Even if I told you, you wouldn't care because you already

Dead Fashion

know, because you make sure to be one step ahead of everyone, well you didn't get one step ahead of me! We signed you from nothing, the chances of being signed off your work and catalog to a fine established record label like ours is near zero. I signed you personally because I knew you would be the perfect target, the perfect product, and you are. A filthy little poor brat, gets a lot of money and thinks she's tough and all that. You're not. So before I send you out of my office, have this." He hands me the envelope. I open it up and see a check for $25,100,000. I almost fall over, my entire expression changes. I look up at him. "You're lucky I even gave you that. That's your total earnings from the tour you just had. 25% of all sales and profit goes to you. 25% to us and 505 to everyone who runs the events and hosts them and all the workers plus the people who made merchandise like T-shirts and magnets. Karen I understand you are miserable, but look at the money your making, you made 25 million on this tour, that's top 15 in the world, Karen, you are a top artist in the world right fucking now. I've never ever seen anything like this before, maybe Elvis, but that's it. You are oil! We struck you and got the riches; you seem to forget that you are now an icon, I got my phone blowing up from people like Drake and Ariana Grande who are willing to pay 5% royalties for a feature on just a single song. Karen you are something so big, you need to act big. Start taking some fucking offers and let people come onto your tracks and you do the same for them. Branch out. If you decide to continue down this path one wrong move will cost you everything, at least build a connection and legacy. You are selling quicker than everyone else who is making music let that sink in." I look down at the check and the massive amount on it, with my name attached. "Karen, I'm giving you a chance, no one gives chances in this business. Your music is great and you're the first rap artist to be taken seriously by the world entirely. At this rate you could be the Micheal Jackson, or Elvis of rap. So I am giving you one final offer. You can leave, but if you leave, not only will it result in massive amounts of fines and no more ownership of previous work, you will also lose ownership of your brand." I look up at him.

"What?" We own your name, your face and your voice until April 16th of 2024. That means no music with other labels, you can't use your face, voice or brand to make any sort of money including your stage name. You will basically be a money funnel for the company with no say in anything or anyone, you cannot escape until 2024, maybe a bad way to put it, but I need to put my foot down on this situation and you." he gets in my face. "So basically what I'm saying is grow up, enjoy being rich and doing what you love and stop being a goddamn child! Now get the fuck out of my office and don't come in here again without an appointment or so help me god I will tear this contract in front of your eyes and watch everything you've built up burn within a second. Thank you for not throwing one of your little temper tantrums on me and finally listening to what you need to be told, it shows you are growing and becoming more mature, now get out."

I walk out of his office with the check and sprint walk out as fast as I can down the hall, I am about at the door when the front desk lady says: "Have a good day Karen." I look back at her with my eyes so watery I can almost not even see an outline of her, and then walk out. I call an Uber Express. I was going to go see Susan, but I am in so much pain, I can't even hardly breathe right now. I am mentally hurt and I physically hurt myself too. I try to hold off on freaking out so much that normally when I get upset I ball my hands up into fists and just try to gently squeeze them so that I can relax. It's one of the methods I was learning to control myself over my long break from music. But I look down at my hands and see in the palms of my hands 4 massive gouges in a row on both hands. I was squeezing so hard that my nails dug into my hands and caused very big gouges and so minor bleeding, I could barely keep myself composed. I wanted to rip his tongue out and stop talking, I wanted him to feel pain, I don't care how I wanted him to suffer and be in agony, I hate him! I hate him! I hate him so much I can almost picture the exact way I would take his life. That's all I could think about in the uber, I couldn't breathe at all, I rolled the window down, but I still felt trapped, stuck, dying. I need to try and find a way to calm down before I do something really bad, my mask is slipping again, like before, I thought contained it and became better and maybe I have, considering I got this far, but it's getting close, it's on the verge of falling off, I need to stop it. I need to recoup and then go see Susan, she is the only person who will fully understand.

Ragnarok

May 13th, 2021, A day that cannot be forgotten. My day started normally as always when I'm not working or touring. Wake up. Take a xanax or some sort of pill, today was actually adderall, and then workout and make a very good breakfast to balance out all the bad shit I put into my body. Vaping too is a problem but now with these new delta carts coming out with weed and stuff it's like candy. Seriously, I cannot get away from it. I don't think about it, I just start consuming. One moment I am sitting watching a show or writing and then I catch myself with my pink stubby little cancer device in my hand taking rips. Then out of nowhere probably around lunch time I wanna say I get a call. I know the ringtone is her. I set up different ringtones for people close to me, for example if a random person calls me I get the normal standard apple ringtone, but if someone else calls me like Clemons, I have the cops theme. Her ringtone is the chimes one. It sounds elegant and nice, it was the only one that reminded me of her. Susan's name pops up on my phone along with the picture of her kissing my cheek we took right before I went on tour. It was a cold day the day I took that photo and she has her scarf and her brown beanie on and it is just such a nice picture. All the violent and horrible thoughts I've been starting to have again go away. It's like she's the cure to my sickness, my disease. I slide the button to the right and she is there on the other line, I've been too scared and too nervous to go over there and every time I called it ended up going to voicemail at some point. The read on her texts are gone or she just genuinely haven't read them and I made sure she wasn't missing or anything with Clemons, because I refuse to talk to Damocha right now.

"Yeah! Why wouldn't she be? She's just really busy with all the press shit for you right now; She probably doesn't even have time for work calls!" That's what I've been working with right now. So the fact that she is on the other line and I can speak to her is making me get butterflies. It's like the world is brighter or something.

"H-Hey!" I say in short little breath to her as I put it on speaker.

"Hey Karen." She says. I kinda chuckle as tears sort of get into my eyes.

"Where h-have you been? What are you doing? Are you… ok!?"

"I'm- fine Karen. And I've been busting my ass off recently and didn't get the chance to talk to you." That's bullshit and I know it and the angry part of me tries so hard to push through and get to my brain but something about Susan now barricades right in my chest and my heart makes sure that all that vile disgusting shit is stuck in the stomach and below, my heart will not let the blockade go.

"You don't how happy I am that you called me babe, seriously I missed you so much, we need to meet when you're free so I can kiss you so much. God I just wanna hug and squeeze you and throw you around, I miss you so much Susan." Tears are now watering in my eyes.

"Karen, that's what I'm calling about." Everything stops, the fly flying right in front of my face, clock on the microwave, the noise from the street has ceased, all of time is stopped… frozen. The world is stuck in place and the only thing that is moving is my phone and me.

"W-w-w-what are you calling about? What-what do you mean by that?"

"Karen I'm done at DP. I got a job opportunity with Universal music group, to manage this upcoming J-pop singer sort of like you, but in California. I'm moving on from DP, which means I'm moving on from you." I almost fall over, my

Dead Fashion

blood goes cold, I'm now frozen with everything else. "Look Karen, the thing is you're awesome, you really are. You also are one of the most beautiful people I've ever known, but I-I can't do this anymore, You are way too out of my league. Karen you are a popstar now, your an idol like you wanted, you can't have baggage like me hanging around, I'm not getting paid enough to handle you anymore, you have become bigger than me and DP, Karen it's over." everything's blacked out now only the phone is left now.

"What do you mean it's over?"

"Us. We're done, Karen I can't be with you and I cannot manage you, I'm sorry, this will be goodbye Karen, if you ever need to call me or text me... don't."

"WAIT!" I catch her before she hangs up. "Wait a minute just please." My hand is now shaking. "So this is it? Over the phone? This is all you can muster?"

"Karen, I'm sorry but I couldn't get to you, please don't make this harder than it has to be, why do you think I've been avoiding your calls and texts?" Tears come out of my eyes and everything is let go, I cannot believe what I just heard. "Ah shit, no I didn't mean it like that Karen, I just-"

"THIS IS BULLSHIT SUSAN! Are you kidding me? So none of it was real then?"

"Karen I-"

"NO! I'm done, you can't even come to me in person to tell me that after almost a year of love, work, sex, and dinners you're done with me? What am I just some sick fucking pocket pussy for you to fuck? Is that what you think of me? Some doll that you used and just threw away?"

"No Karen it isn't-"

"Then what is it then? I'll wait, I will wait here until my grave, you wanna know why?"

"Why?" I get close to the phone on the counter and point at it "Cause you're a filthy lying sack of shit!" mucus and snot and tears are all destroying the little left over makeup on my face. "All you do is lie, that's all this was wasn't it? HUH?"

"Karen-" out of the phone very faintly in the background I hear a male voice, I have never heard this voice before and it was so faint it sounded like he just walked into the room or something.

"Babe what is all-" I believe he said all that noise, but it's so faint and I'm so worked up I can't even process it fully, all I hear is that. That sick voice. Disgusting. Vile. Arrogant. It sounds like the worst sack of meat to crawl out of a hole.

"Who the fuck was that?" I say now with my face almost on my phone.

"Karen, I gotta go, please don't make any trouble, continue to do good things, you'll always be in my heart."

"WHO THE FUCK WAS THAT SUSAN!?!?!?" But the phone hung up before she could hear anything. I storm around my house, snot tears and anything else dripping everywhere. I currently have no shirt on. I only had my black bra on and some shorts. I pace my house looking for clothes, while being so angry my neck has veins popping out of it, I can feel the anger, the hatred, everything, It all loose, it's all gone. I'm shaking, I wanna throw up, it's all so fast, I can barely think I'm just acting, blurry vision, all of the emotions are all on the table. Shirt somehow gets on me, Pants go over the shorts and next thing you know I'm puking all over my nice concrete kitchen floor. I lay in the puke and cry. It finally all hits me and I hate… I hate her. It's bad, so bad, I lay for maybe five minutes. Then finally I get up, it's time, I can't be a baby anymore, I have to do something other than cry like a little bitch, I'm not like that. I get up, throw my shirt off and get a new shirt, one of the black ones that has very thick wool lining. I somehow get my air force ones on in a matter of seconds with no hands. I go to the closet in my room and pull the shirts away to reveal the hidden compartment I made. I open it up, grab the 12 gauge shotgun out of there along with 15 shells and put them in a sports duffle bag, before walking out of my apartment. I don't know what I'm going to do, but I know it won't be pretty.

Dead Fashion

My Last Day at DP

My last day at DP was a shit show. Yes I know Susan, aren't you the one who can contain yourself and always look positive yes I am, but that doesn't mean things can't go bad. I checked all my stuff into the office and then had a ridiculous phone call with Karen when I got home. I didn't have the heart to tell her about my Fiance, Tyson who I have been seeing for over 3 years. He finally proposed in February and he decided to move in with me, until we leave for California. He finally got me pregnant after three years and I'm so happy, I can't contain myself. I finally got the baby I've been wanting for years and then because of it, Tyson proposed.

I'm about five months pregnant and now Tyson and I are going to be moving to LA where I'm getting a new job. Look… nothing against Karen, but I cannot deal with her anymore. After all the murder shit and freakouts I finally got an opportunity to leave and I will be taking it.

Nothing will stop me from getting out of here, seriously I'm completely and utterly fucked up from her. Me and Tyson agreed that to save my job I could sleep with Karen, in exchange I make sure that we make love double the amount I did with Karen. The plan was simple, the only flaw was trying to break off, Karen didn't take that lightly. I didn't think she got so attached to me, am I really that special? Tyson also wanted me to call her and cut it off directly because it was the best course of action, I didn't think so but I decided to anyway. It was bad… really bad. Tyson walked in right as I ended it.

"Was that her?" He asked as he brought me a cup of coffee as I hung up.

"Yeah it was unfortunate it didn't go well, who would've thought…"

"Well hey babe, don't be mad at me, it's not fair to her to just leave her."

"Fair to her?" I laugh "She's a fucking monster! The only thing she should get that's fair is a trial. Once I saw all that shit about the baseball player I almost got sick everytime I saw her. She's lucky I didn't turn her ass into that police bitch that was questioning me."

"Why didn't you." I didn't have the heart to tell him. I didn't have the heart to tell him after three years and during our relationship I did get feelings for Karen. She is sick, she is vile, I can't deal with her, but every time I see her I get sick, but a part of me doesn't. A part of me wants to turn her in and tell them about all that sick shit and I would be a witness, but another part of me wants to hold her touch her talk to her kiss her, I can't explain it. Everytime I think about that nasty stuff she did I feel odd. I enjoy it, I enjoy a psychotic woman, It's why I put up with it for so long. It took a baby and ring to realize who I wanted more. At one point I almost thought about it. Yeah it, leaving Tyson and dating Karen fully. I really liked her and still I hate to admit it, I still do like her. I like her enough to not turn her in and cause trouble in her life even though she has caused so much to others. Karen Wall is an enigma. I can't understand her, as that one detective said, his name was McDowell. He stopped by after the time of his partner's husband's 'murder' and that's what he said. She is an enigma, she is hard to understand, you could never try her in court because there is no ulterior motive. There is nothing, there is no clear video, no evidence supporting any type of reason to kill. He said there were maybe 10 or 15 people he believed were murdered by her in the city since December of 2019. He sat me and Damocha down and told us everything and that we should talk to the board and terminate her. Of course DP didn't because she is making enough money to pay for every single person in Minnesota to go to college, and that's going to the pockets of the higher ups. It's so strange, how someone who is so high up with the FBI can't do anything. How is it possible? Karen is something above motive, there is no motive to her I've seen the shit she's done, it's horrible. She is horrible. It doesn't matter what they get on her, it always seems that she can never be caught. No matter how hard they try, it seems she slips through every single fucking time.

Dead Fashion

Because there is no motive, plain and simple. She is not a stable person and that's why I ended up leaving her and all this behind. Plus well I guess I get a good fresh start with Tyson too, which is extremely nice. I'm more excited to see what life has in store for me. I've been so screwed this last year. I almost think God is mad at me for something and is punishing me. She does have her way of doing things I guess.

    I'm currently on my way back from the store. I went to Target to grab some things. I needed some new lotions because my old lotions were disgusting. Tyson hated them and so did I, plus I need vegan lotions and luckily I found some there that I can use. I also was struggling to eat. With being pregnant now it's time I start eating healthy. I don't want to have my child have problems or disorders. Tyson and I did a lot of research into the topic and found that children can develop better traits depending on what you consume. For example if you smoke a lot or do a lot of drugs, there is a high chance your baby might be autistic or have mental problems. It's imperative to keep the mother's body as healthy as possible. God I'm so happy, I smile every time. I'm gonna be a mother, an actual mom, I'm gonna have a child like I always wanted. I hope it's a girl, I want a little me running around causing a little chaos, it would be better for the world. I'm so excited that it's with Tyson, for a while I didn't know how I felt but now I know how I feel. I love Tyson, I love him a lot. I love him so much I can't even express it. He is my everything and I'm his everything. Just being gone for a while makes me so sad, I want to be around him all the time. Maybe I'm being a little clingy but I am just excited to be married and have a kid with this man, he's perfect in every way. His nice brown curls and his perfect facial hair and shape. Second softest lips next to only one person who I despise. He's also super fit and has a very big cock. Just thinking about it makes me want to pin him down and make him feel good. He also says I give the best head in the world which makes my body feel so warm, I just love feeling needed or wanted, I love just being loved I guess.

The drive back from Target is always slow, especially at this time of the day, it's rush hour and in the Twin Cities rush hour is about as fun as stepping on legos barefoot. I saw a homeless man and woman at one of the stoplights and gave them a ten and they were so happy I felt so good about myself. It's also a beautiful day, it's sunny and it feels like the perfect day. It would only be more perfect if Tyson was with me. He had some business stuff to take care of at home on his computer, he is still working from home sadly and so I had to do this myself. God it is just perfect, she is finally blessing me after that long punishment, maybe it wasn't a punishment. Maybe it was a test, maybe she was testing my strength, and I passed.

I finally reached home, my place of comfort and solitude. I can finally see my husband again, I hate not being with him. I open the door to my apartment after taking the elevator and walk in and it's very quiet and peaceful. I set the groceries down.

"Hey babe I'm baaaaccckkk!" I say in an almost musical tone. I walk towards the office door and open it.

Their Last Day At DP

Today is her last day at DP records. I'm not fucking dealing with this anymore, I've tried and tried and tried to hold everything in. I've tried so hard, but I can't do it. I decided before I went to see Susan I wanted to go pay Damocha a little visit and his bitch wife too. Damocha's house is far away but I wanted to go there first and make sure I got payback. I'm tired of being defenseless, I'm tired of being weak and holding back. I'm pushing through, my mask has slipped. I took a Xanax for the first time in four months. Ever since I met Susan I stopped taking drugs except for vaping and alcohol, all hard drugs are gone and detoxed out of my system. The stress and anxiety caused this, I took two Xanax and have almost gone through a full vape cartridge too. It feels weird but feels normal again after this long break. The uber drops me off down the block a little bit and I get out and walk to his house and to the front door. I'm about to ring the doorbell. Luckily I know he's home because today is a day he works from home.

    I look at the window with the curtains shut to the right of the door and can see my reflection clear as day. I see myself and my chaotic nature, I see the draped nasty black clothing I'm wearing. I look at myself and I see tears boiling in my eyes. I stop myself from ringing the doorbell and turn around. As I turn around I hear a voice. Not Damocha's or his wifes, it's a familiar voice, a loud and powerful voice. A voice so disgusting I want to shoot myself in the face with this shotgun. It's my own voice. It almost sounds as if it is coming from outside of my head, in the real world, like there is another me. I look back at the window and see myself staring, it's not me though. It looks like me but it's not. It's me but in some other dimension behind the glass. It doesn't move with me or my actions, it is it's own being.

    "What are you doing?" it says to me or I say to myself.

    "What?" I replied.

    "Where are you going? You came all the way here and you are gonna leave now?"

    "FUCK YOU! This is for the better, I can't be here, I need to leave, I-I need to go!"

    "Can't and shouldn't are two different things Karen, You are supposed to be here, doesn't mean you should be but you definitely can be here, you are here now."

    "Stop it! Just stop, I'm going." I say as I walk away.

    "Going where? Back to your apartment, to cry like a little bitch, is that what we are now Karen, a little bitch? You don't deserve to be out there." I walk up to the window and look myself in the eyes as close as I can.

    "Shut the fuck up! You don't know anything ok? I'm out here because I make the decisions, not whatever you are, you don't make them. I'm bigger than you, I'm stronger, the strongest thing I can do now is get over myself and leave."

    "I am you! I know how you think, I know how you feel, I know how you act. I know you more than you could ever know, I know how he treated you- how she treated you. You don't deserve to let these faggots walk all over you, It's not right and sure as hell is not us Karen. You are a psychopath."

"I'm not!" I say as tears are now pouring down my face.

"YOU ARE! Whether you like it or not you are batshit crazy." I am now fully crying looking away from the window. "Look at yourself, you're pathetic, you Karen, you are crying like a bitch. You don't deserve to be out there."

"I'm done… I am done! DO YOU HEAR ME? I'M FUCKING OVER IT!" Suddenly the front door opens and it's Damocha's wife who stands in the doorway looking confused. She is in panic and in awe of my presence.

"Karen! Look at her, she is scared of you, you can tell. Look at her face, look at her body, she is. She thinks you're a monster Karen. Did you hear that? She thinks you're a monster… prove her right." She looks at the shotgun in my hand and then back at my face and now horror overcomes her. She quickly screams and is about to slam the door as she screams. I don't think I just do, I don't even use anytype of precision, I quickly pull the shotgun up into my shoulder and pull the trigger and the pellet smashes into her head causing her head to explode like a watermelon. The shot is loud and the scene is bloody.

It's all happening so fast, everything is, time itself is moving at 2X speed. I can see brains and blood splatter all over the entrance of the house and the lifeless body is stuck right in the middle of the doorway, I enter the house. I quickly make my way to the bedroom and in the process I'm knocking over small stands and desks in the hallway as I'm being very frantic and in a panic. The rush is back, I haven't felt it in so long, it feels- it feels… perfect. I kick the door to the bedroom down and see no one in there. I checked their massive walk-in closest, but no one was found. Then just as I am about to give up and search a different room I hear a man's scream, it's him. He tries to swing a golf club at me but my reflexes are too good. I turned just in time and leaned back and he missed the

Dead Fashion

swing with the driver and hit a bunch of shoes off a shelf. Things are tumbling everywhere and scattering and he swings again and I dodge once again. Then he tries to swing over his head like he is gonna hit me with an axe but this weak old fuck-face has no idea how strong I am and hold the gun in one hand and grab the club with the other stopping him in his tracks. You may be wondering why I haven't blown his brains out and that's a great question with a very great answer… I want him to suffer. I want him to feel the pain, I want him to feel how I felt when he took my freedom, I want him to know what it's like to be trapped.

  I pull the shotgun up and shoot him in the thigh and he lets go of the club and falls backwards as he screams in pain. He tries to grab his bleeding leg but the hole is so big that way too much blood is coming out. His hands are bloody and his blood oozes all over the floor of the massive walk in closet.

  "YOU FUCKING BITCH! YOU HAVE NO IDEA WHAT YOU HAVE DONE!"

  "Oh I think I do Mr. Damocha." I laugh frantically and almost in such a psychotic way you would think I'm a psychopath.

  "FUCK YOU. YOU KNOW HOW POWERFUL I AM, WHEN PEOPLE SEE I'M MISSING WHAT DO YOU THINK THEY'RE GONNA DO?"

  "Mr. Damocha, you really are silly. I love self confidence but you really aren't terribly important." He looks up at me with all of hatred and anger. His eyes are watering, his face is bleak and his blood is boiling, I love it. I lean down over him. "I mean seriously how did you get in such a bad situation? You're bleeding everywhere, this is gonna be one massive mess for your wife to clean up Mr. Damocha!" I say with a big smile on my face as I close my eyes. "Why don't we go and call her into here and show her the massive mess you made?" I get up and walk to the doorway and look back at him and then scream in a light hearted tone. "OOOOOHHHH MRS. DAMOCHA! YOUR HUSBAND HAS MADE A REALLY REALLY BIG MESS IN YOUR CLOSET." I wait to hear a response and put my ear up to the door and really exaggerate listening for a response I know will never come. "Huh that's odd, must not be a good wife huh Mr. Damocha." This infuriates him enough and he quickly is trying to move around but can't get up and has lost so much blood his body is almost not functioning. He is pissed, very pissed. I can see the anger in his face, it looks like he is about to pop a blood vessel.

"AGHHHHH!" He screams and tries to grab at me but I am just a little too far out of reach.

"Hold that thought for just one second let me go fetch your wife for ya, ok?" He says nothing as I walk out of the bedroom and grab the nasty bloody mess that is his wife and then dump it right on top of him. He sees the body and immediately gets enraged but cannot do anything. He just breaks down. He starts to cry. He cries like a little puppy dog, I almost feel bad. I see him grab her lifeless body and hold it close to him and he closes his eyes. I let him lay for almost 30 seconds and just when thinks he will go in peace, I grab her body from him and push it off him and then put a shot into the chest and then another one again.

"NOOOOOOOOOOOOO!" He screams as he cries and then when he tries to crawl to her remains I hit him with the butt of the shotgun and he falls onto his back. I get overtop of him and put the whole gun down over his throat and push as hard as I can. I can feel it boiling, it's all rising, I can feel everything pushing to this moment and I feel the enragement. I think about every single little thing he ever did and every single time I wanted to rip his head off and put it on a stick.

"AUCK! P-P-PLEASE!" He cries as he is being choked out. Suddenly he starts coughing up some black liquid, just a tiny amount spits up and over his face. What the fuck is this? EWWW. I've never seen anything like it! I decided to ignore it and continue on.

"I'm sorry, what was that Damocha? Did I hear a please? Oh am I hurting you, I'm sorry! Here let me-" I stop choking him and he coughs again and tries to grab me but I hit him again in the head. "Looks like you're just gonna have to suck it up right? I know it sucks but you signed up for this didn't you? EVERYTHING! Was perfect, it was great! But nooooo, you had to go and FUCK IT ALL UP! Because of your greed and ego, you couldn't let someone else be better than you, well guess WHAT… I won! I FUCKING won!" I squeeze harder on his neck. "You think you had all planned out, how you were gonna use me and my talent and treat me like property huh? Well look how the tables have turned, you pig. You old fucking pig. You're sick! Your wife paid and now you will too!"

"You-" He tries to say but I only lay the gun harder against him and I can feel the life leaving his body, I can feel everything go cold and feel his soul leave.

"You what? Speak up!"

"You-you were my biggest failure." Then he finally lays dead. I spit on him. I can feel nothing left in him anymore, it's all over.

I sit. I reflect on everything I just did and all the blood I have just shed. It's horrible, it's brutal, it's sick, it's… great.

I love it, I can't stop thinking about all this blood I need to spill, I NEED TO KILL A LOT OF PEOPLE! But I can hold off, I think that urge is just so big because there is one big target, someone who really needs to be bloody. Maybe that will suffice and if it doesn't then I don't know what will. But before I leave I need to dust my prints and get rid of the security camera footage! Burn it all, I would try to fix this mess, but I want them to be found, I want people to see how these pigs were slaughtered.

One hour later

I'm walking down the street concealing the blood on my shirt with a small pullover I found in Damocha's closet, I'm assuming it was his wife's. It is gray and has a picture of a goose on it and has a joke written on it that says "What is a goose's favorite city? Honk Konk." Is it the stupidest thing I've ever worn? Yes. Is it concealing the blood stains? Yes. So as far as I can tell it will have to do. It feels so weird to be in someone else's clothes walking down busy streets and busy roads. Luckily I didn't have to cross any highways to get HER apartment. The apartment building is so nice honestly, I really like how simple and cozy it is and I almost wanted to move in with her so badly until all of this has unfolded. Another nice thing about the pullover is that it helps conceal the shotgun very well and I have holstered between my tits and it goes down past my pelvis and into my leggings. I'm wearing baggy enough stuff too, that it is hard to notice anything but a tiny bulge.

    A few people stopped me right outside her apartment and asked to take pictures, which I said yes too and put on my mask to hide my true self, the job always comes first sadly. After sitting taking photos, wanting to break these two teenage girls' noses, I finally went inside the apartment building.

    I love the modern aesthetic of her apartment building and after a little walk I reach her apartment. The smell, the feeling, it all feels wrong. It feels off. I love this place, I want to stop, I want to stop, I want to stop… but I can't. I break the lock on the door, I don't want to do it, I want to stop entering the apartment, I want to quit and go home. STOP KAREN, STOP KAREN, GO HOME YOU'RE OVERTHINKING.

    I enter the home and see it as usual, it hasn't changed. It is so nice and clean, the wood floor looks so sparkly, it shines so bright it almost looks like a bald man's head after a shower and a wax. The smell is so beautiful and is so nice, it smells so elegant, sweet, pure, perfect, so… Susan like. It reminds me so much of her, everything reminds me of her, smells, TV shows, the feeling of touching myself, even looking at an arby's roast beef N' cheese sandwich reminds me of her. I can't escape her I- What is that? What is that smell? It doesn't smell like her, it smells foreign, something that doesn't belong, it smells impure. It's coming from a room near her bedroom, I have never been in that room before, the door is closed. I walk towards the door from a distance.

    I pull out the shotgun out of my waistband and reveal it from underneath my hoodie and walk to the door. I knock on the door.

"Susan, is that you babe? You're home already, that was fast!" A-A-A-A man's voice says. A vile voice, disgusting putrid. A voice of a man who seems to have taken something from me, deep within me. I knock on the door again.

"Babe, will you stop, haha." he says as the voice gets less muffled as he comes to the door and opens it. The pure shock, horror and disgust in his face all at once is amazing, it feels so perfect for the situation he is in. He now has the expression on his face that I have on my soul. The moment feels slow, very slow and feels right. I feel almost like the flash, like I'm fast but everyone else is slow. I raise the shotgun up to my chest and swing it from the barrel of the gun as hard as I can, almost as if I was trying to hit a homerun with a baseball bat. He tries to block it but I easily go right through his arms and the arms hit his face and he drops to the ground. He tries to scramble up to his feet by going backwards onto the ground farther into the room. He puts his hand on his chair and tries to lift himself up, but I turn the shotgun around and shoot the chair and watch it explode into pieces with a big hole. With the sudden chair being dropped from his whole body, he slams onto the ground and his face slams first and puts a big red bloody spot on his head or maybe it was there before I don't really know he turned around on the ground so I couldn't see. I quickly got over top of him and hit his head into the ground with the butt of the shotgun again and this time massive amounts of blood oozed out of the head onto the floor. I am making a big mess, maybe a little cleanup on aisle four is needed here. I grab him by his nasty longish hipster hair and sit on his back.

"PWEEZ!" He screams, with it being very unintelligible because his mouth is bleeding and his tongue is swollen. "PWEZ STOWP!" Maybe a couple important teeth are missing too, I hit him pretty hard, probably too hard.

"What was that? Sorry I couldn't understand you?" I saw in a softer light hearted tone, getting closer to his face. "Repeat what you said I'll try to really listen this time, it's kind of hard with all the blood in your mouth, you're speaking like a retard."

"I SWED PWEZ STOWP!" He starts crying heavily while he speaks and now the blood is running out of his mouth and off his face and mixing with the tears, kind of nasty. I turn him over to face me. I laugh.

"Look man, maybe if we were in the bedroom right next to this room, I wouldn't mind the baby talk, I like a little submissive bitch who talks like a baby. But this… In this situation, I just don't see how this is gonna help you my dude." I get really close to his face. "Here you know what, maybe if you ask me without talking like you can't pass a third grade spelling bee, I'll consider keeping you alive long enough to see that cheating whore bitch loser Susan again so I can put the bullet through both of your heads at the same time, What'da say?" He doesn't answer, he just lays there crying and coughing a little blood. "I could lay by the bay, make things out of clay, I just may!" I laughed and smiled while looking at him and he only continued to cry. I get agitated and my demeanor changes, I quickly punch his face this time with my fist and his head hits the floor and cocks back up. He winces in pain and continues to be a little crybaby bitch, stupid millennial ass, Susan really choose this fag over me? Am I being homophobic? Am I being very disrespectful? YES! Of fucking course I am! I need to check his pants. I need to see how big it is, why is she with him there has got to be some reason. I see the bulge, but there is no way it's big, judging from the size of the bulge only lifting the blue jeans up about 1/4 of centimeter which deducing the math we can assume if he is half chub which most guys are when a girl beats them, it's a psychological reflex that primates have, all male primates secretly get aroused with pain as a coping mechanism. I'm guessing it's maybe at most six inches long going that he's at about three at most right now.

I take his pants off and he screams and struggles, but I get them off just enough and I look and see it, yep about three, it's tiny though, holy shit! This guy is a freak! I bet he likes to do some dirty stuff. If he is fully hard off this, then that means he has a submissive type, Susan likes submissive little boys is that it huh? God that is so like her… KAREN! What are you saying stop, she is horribly, and he's a disgusting small dick baby who deserves to be punished for taking her from you and she also deserves to be fucked, metaphorically and maybe one last time physically. With her soft lips and her perfectly shaped vagi- STOP! DO YOU NEED TO SHOOT YOURSELF TOO WHEN YOUR DONE? God damn girl, pull yourself together and get a clue.

I whisper into his ear. "Now you listen to me, Don't think I have any reason to keep your sorry ass alive, the only reason I haven't killed you yet is because I want you to hear what I have to say first."

"NO!" He screams and the blood is everywhere, over his face, into his hair and even onto me. I laugh.

"Well, Mr. StealYourGirl, I don't think you really have a choice, I mean what are you gonna do?" There is silence. "I mean look at yourself… Well not physically look, but mentally look! Your hands and arms have been untied and unguarded this whole since I flipped you over and you haven't even tried anything other than struggle when I took your pants off. Were you hoping this was some massive sex gag thing where I beat you to a bloody pulp and then sucked your dick or something? I bet you got really excited when I took your pants off, I beat you wanted my nice big fat red lips around that tiny little boy cock didn't you? Let's face it, you're worthless, nobody likes you." I say bluntly with a very neutral face.

"Susan Does." He says softly. My entire personality changes, from the light hearted murderous girl to The Akuma, the darkest, blood raged version. The rage I felt when I first heard his voice.

"Take that back! You take THAT BACK! SHE NEVER LOVED YOU, IF SHE DID SHE WOULDN'T OF LET ME FACE FUCK HER WITH MY PUSSY AND WOULDN'T OF STAYED ALL THOSE TIMES WITH ME!"

"She- She-"

"SHE WHAT HUH?"

"She said sheownly did with you for the-the job." My eyes start to water badly and my entire face which is now facing directly over him with my hair now flying all downward toward his face is wet with tears.

"Take it back. Take it the fuck back." I say as I try not to cry. He spits blood in my face and smiles. I see the blood around his lips and the stained blood teams, the smile of someone who has won, someone who has accepted their own defeat and in that time has overcome life and won, he is happy and he is satisfied with life.

My face scrunches up with rage and anger and I quickly lift the shotgun out of my one hand and put it into both and smash it into his face. Then I smash it again, and again, and again, and again, and again, and again, and again. I smash it so hard as I scream at the top of my lungs blood getting everywhere all over my face, my clothes and the back of my gun. I feel the rage build and build, it doesn't relieve like normal when his face is unrecognizable. I still feel it all boiled up inside, ready to come out, it isn't gone, it's terrifying, my own rage is terrifying.

I hear the door close out front and I quickly peak out the door which is half open to the room and see her. That witch, that bitch, I want to do everything I can to make her pay- I must wait! I quickly scramble and shut the door quietly as she is really looking around and isn't paying attention. I grab his body and position it in the swiveling office chair and then I look for a spot to stand or sit and I notice in the corner of the room a beautiful nice luxury chair, one of those bigs one that doesn't move or ever get sat in and I quickly make my way to it and put my leg over my other leg with my shotgun in my lap. In that split second the door opens and all that anxiety and that rage ceases for the moment, and I look as cool as a cucumber, minus all the stained blood on my face and clothes of course.

Till Death Do Us Part

The room was silent, dead silent in fact. The look on her face was something I wish I would've taken a picture of. It was perfect and I mean perfect, down to the smallest, minute and minuscule detail. Her lip was quivering, her eyes tearing up the look was priceless. But as I was looking I paid no attention to my own expression, the bleakness was gone, I too was full of emotions that I shouldn't have been expressing. I could feel water in my eyes, I tried to stop myself but I couldn't. I was completely and utterly out of control.

"Well…" Susan said in her soft and I mean soft voice. "It's been a while." Her eyes are now so full of tears, that I doubt she can even see properly anymore. I stare at her, I can do nothing more than just stare, the reaction she gave was not what I was expecting, I think maybe the shock is so much that her brain is scrambling to keep sanity, but so is mine.

"Y-yeah… it has." It's awkward and tense in the room. She could've tried to run away and I probably wouldn't have stopped her, but she stayed. She finally breaks and gets skittish, it's almost a moment of victory for me as if I won the emotions contest and beat her, I controlled myself better than she did.

"Look Karen, I'm sorry. Ok I am and I-"

"Save it." I interrupt her and the silence goes again. I speak and break the silence and staring after about 10 seconds. "So… that's him huh?" Her face quickly changes to tears and anger with a frown coming across her face.

"That was him, yes. That was my fiance. Who's blood is all over the floor too I'm assuming, you pig." I respond quickly.

"DO NOT CALL ME A PIG! You wanna talk about pigs? I'll give you a pig to talk about, look in the FUCKING MIRROR!"

"Karen, why? Why do all this?"

"Get out of the doorway and close the door… NOW!" I point the shotgun at her and she quickly gets into the room and shuts the door.

"Seriously Karen, you're fucking sick!"

"Sick? Me… sick? Nooooo never haha, your husband's face isn't in a million pieces or anything and Damocha and his wife are tooootally fine right now."

"You killed them too?" I burst out into laughter, almost manically.

"No. I didn't kill them… I massacred them! I mutilated their bodies until they were unrecognizable."

"Karen, listen to yourself. Do you hear yourself speaking right now? And look at yourself! You are covered in blood, You're not just a monster, you're a villain, you are inhumane." I quickly get up and she flinches and I hit her in the stomach with the butt of the gun. She falls to the ground and starts to cough. I picked her up with my left hand by the shirt and threw her into the chair I was sitting in.

"No, no, no, no, no, no, NO! I-I am in touch with humanity. I'm the closest thing to a real human as there is! You walk around and act like you are better than me, better than everyone else, and you think we're sick and monsters. You are no different than me."

"I AM TOO." I slap her with the back of my hand, and get in her face.

"YOU ARE NOT! We both are horrible creatures spawned onto this Earth to make other people suffer, you made me suffer. Do you know what you did to me? Do you know how much you hurt me? I was in pain, I was in shackles to you, I was your slave, I would've taken on anything for you and you threw me to the curb and spit on me with your pretentious and perfect life, with your nice apartment and a handsome rich husband, who by the way has a very small dick and you should be ashamed of ever choosing him over me."

"So that's what this is all about?" She will not stop standing up to me, most people break down and give up, but she won't, there is something driving her. "This whole thing is about because I stopped fucking you?"

"IT WASN'T ABOUT THE SEX! It was about us!"

"WHAT US KAREN? This is no us, ok?" she does a back and forth point. "Karen there never was an us, we had a thing, yes, we did, a lot of people have things like us. Karen we were never fully together and never for a second did I believe we were going to be together."

"LIAR!"

"It's the truth."

"That's bullshit!" I say balling my eyes out. "BULLSHIT!"

"Yeah it is bullshit, wanna know the truth? The truth is I slept with you and kept sleeping with you to make my job easier. It was the only way to make you calm down. I didn't want to and I never ever wanted to sleep with you, but I had no choice, you and Damocha gave me no choice, I was left with that. Karen I tried to make it work and make things nice and simple and I hoped that with your personality you would've moved on. I got scared of you. I couldn't handle being around you anymore."

"WHY?"

"Because I knew who you were, deep down. I knew of all the horrible things you had done, and how horrible of a person you are. Karen listen to yourself, all you have talked about was me this or I that, never once did you consider someone else's feelings."

"I would've been fine if you would've told me, if you would've told me after the first little fling that you didn't want to go further I would've stopped and nobody would've gotten hurt!"

"See you're deflecting again, I cannot be with you, first you TAKE my husband away from me and then you act like it's all my fault. Fuck you!"

"Are you asking to die? Do you want me to put a fucking bullet into your dense fucking brain?"

"I'm saying this because A. This is how I feel, and B. Because I know there is no hope for me. I knew the moment I saw you in my house I was dead, I just figured if I could at least try to make you understand how horrible of a human you are maybe you would walk out of this apartment with some sort of changed mind, but now I just want you to rot in the deepest part of hell and I hope they lock your ass up for so long you forget what the sunlight looks like you fucking bitch." My face is boiling and everything in my body is on fire, I want to do some many disgusting things to her, I want to make her bleed.

"I want you to suffer as much as you made me suffer."

"Go ahead I had nothing, oh and by the way thanks for more than likely taking my child away from me too." I stop.

"What?"

"When you hit me in the stomach, yeah I was pregnant, for the record, since you were wondering why I fully decided to go with him and why I love him, that's a big reason, he gave me something I have always wanted."

"Congratu-FUCKING-LATIONS! Does it look like I care about that? No offense Susan, but all I ever wanted with you was what you had with him, that's all! I didn't want just a fuck fest I wanted to love you and be with you. I wanted us to have a child, I could care less if that limp dick loser gave you a child or not. Why do you feel the need to say anything?"

"Because I know what makes you tick. I know well enough to know that you will be forever pissed that you never will get that opportunity."

"Fuck you!"

"I'll see you in Hell."

"I fucking hope not because I don't want you anywhere near me." I raise the shotgun up to her skull and put the barrel right on her forehead. For a moment, just a brief moment I catch a glimpse of something fascinating, something so unnatural and something so fucking awful to me, that as my finger pulls the trigger I have the nastiest feeling ever. The thing that I saw was her smile. Just moments before her own death she smiled and stayed smiling until I pulled the trigger and exploded her head into pieces. Her body recoils out of the chair and falls forward and onto my feet. Her blood oozes all over my air force ones and I do nothing for almost a minute as I just stand there and reflect, tears swelling up my eyes. I see the mess I have just made and the horrible things I have just done. All the rage is gone, all the feelings are gone, I finally feel at peace, I feel complete.

I walk to the bathroom and clean the blood off my face making sure not to get fingerprints anywhere and then after cleaning myself up, I grab another hoodie from her closet this time and walk out of the apartment and make sure to take crowded streets so as to not be seen. Just like that I am away hidden by the shadows of the metropolis, I return home to get myself fully cleaned, today was one of the best and worst days in my life and I hope I never live another day like it. P.S to myself, never ever get attached to anything or anyone other than music, it's not worth it, Music will always be there for you, they won't.

May 14th, 6:00AM

"Good morning to the beautiful state of Minnesota! The sunrise was absolutely gorgeous today over the WCCO tower! What was not beautiful this morning was the mass murder spree done yesterday, the three victims names are not released as of now but all have been suspected to have been murdered by a coworker of the famous record label in downtown Minneapolis, DP Records. The police made a statement this morning right at the brink of dawn claiming that the SPPD is working closely with the Minneapolis police to solve this investigation along with the FBI.

The Minneapolis police who were involved in the death of George Floyd last year, are receiving backlash for the investigation, because of their failure to act last year. Will they even be able to find the murderer or will this terrible tragedy go on to be an unsolved murder? John, what are your thoughts?"

"Hey Christine, I'm standing just outside of DP Records, which is completely dormant this morning. There is a small crowd of people here along with a police squadron. They say the murders are 100% linked to DP Records and in fact may even be linked to the superstar The Akuma.

The Akuma/Karen Wall broke into stardom last year after the George Floyd murder and riots in the city with a hit single Dead Fashion. Since then her Album American Psycho which mimics the elusive novel under the same name, has been in the top 10 albums for the past five months. Her 'Breakout' tour was also record shattering with crowds that topped those of Queen, Micheal Jackson, and more recent successes like Drake and Beyonce. Akuma has yet to comment to us or to anyone on the matter, but until then she is a key suspect in these presumed murders. Back to you Christine!"

"Coming up, a look at the new Vikings themed bar, which just got a whole new look during Covid and Vikings Quarterback and Minneapolis resident Kirk Cousins, will be at the grand re-opening of the bar this weekend, to promote the bar and his contract extension to 2024! The Vikings, who came off a struggling season this year, hope to bounce back and take home a super bowl, but for now you can get a super bowl… of NACHOS! At the Vikings Bar located on 4th street here in Minneapolis! Come for a chance to win a signed jersey by Cousins himself!"

Tied Hands

What am I supposed to do is the question that plagues my mind. I have had the feds knocking on my door with the police searching my house for any sort of evidence and despite wanting to be caught I'm just so above these pea brained people, that I managed to not leave any trail in my house. Even the security camera footage is too blurry and can only confirm it was a woman, there are about 3.5 billion of them floating around so that narrows it down a lot, you dildos! God I can't believe they would storm in like this, what could provoke this, they just immediately knew it was me? Did everyone who was a female at DP get their whole house searched while being detained? Just as that thought crossed my noggin I see her walk in, that noir bitch, with her stupid fucking look and short hair, it's the lady from the Police in St. Paul. Of fucking course, this was all her idea and now she has any opportunity to ruin my life because I ruined her sons life. What even is either of their names again? I couldn't remember if I tried, and believe me I am trying. Tunguey-Tungme-Tongue my asshole? Something like that. I know it started with a T. She walks into my house with two other officers and approaches me.

"Karen, you're in deep trouble girl." She looks at me then back at an ipad.

"Tell your cops to get off me. I didn't do anything! Why do you always assume something is my fault, you hag!" She looks at me and her lip quivers and her face gets stern and she looks like she wants to rip my guts out… good, exactly what I wanted, internally I'm smiling like the Grinch.

"Because it is your fault, not only are you the key suspect with motive, but your prints are found all over the crime scene of both places." Lies! There is no evidence of fingerprints at all, I was wearing gloves the whole time.

"I don't even know what crime scene you're talking about!"

"Ok sure girly, it's been all over the news! You can't lie like that, it makes you look more guilty."

"What news? Lady I was asleep up until I heard my doorbell ring like 1000 times, plus massive amounts of alerts from Ring for movement then the pounding on my door. You fuckers woke me up you indecent asshole, you could've waited until after I was awake!"

"Bullshit the guys got the warrant at 10:40 this morning and were here at 11:30."

"Ma'am to be fair I was one of the first people to show up here and we did drag her out of her bed." Said an officer standing next to me keeping an eye on me since I was detained.

"Then why is she wearing those clothes?" The Tongue lady asked.

"Well that's what she was sleeping in, she was sleeping in an AC/DC shirt and gym shorts." HAHAHAHAHA! This lady will try anything to lock me up, what's next I'm not allowed to eat pudding in the kitchen because it's not normal and makes me guilty of murders? This lady can go to hell.

"We'll see about all of this, we're taking her to the MPD."

"No don't, the last time Dr. Richtofen touched that thing he went insane and tried to kill a little girl and her father." I said, looking serious.

"Mark her down for insanity as well."

"On it Ma'am."

One And a Half Hours Later

We are in another interrogation room, similar to the one in St. Paul, except it smells less like bitch and more like racism in this one. She enters the room and tells me her name, Tungavaloa! That's what it was. There is a camera on a tripod pointed at me plus the usual CCTV cam in the top right of the room. The room is white and has crappy lighting like always and makes you feel like they can see through you, maybe they do.

"Can you tell me your name?" I'm being very unresponsive and bleak unlike when they first got me, I don't know what has come over me, but I am feeling very bad almost, I feel unsettled and feel as though my whole facade has been pierced and destroyed. I am sweating badly too, thanks to the heat outside and in the room. My face is turned down as of now and I am refusing to speak. I didn't even notice the other hefty balding guy come in and sit in the other chair. "Karen, please just answer our questions." She says softly. I reply still looking down.

"You seem to know it pretty well, why don't you say it?" I say as I slowly look up at her, and smile a little. She looks aggravated.

"Karen Wall, born December 8th, 1998. 22 years of age currently living at The Nic on Fifth, Was detained at 11:33am this morning, the current time is 1:07pm. Is the main suspect in a homicidal killing connected to three people all brutally mutilated beyond belief, did I miss anything?" She tried to throw that in at the end but I caught it and didn't bite.

"For the most part, except I'm not a part of any suspect list, this is the first time I'm hearing of three people, who were they?" Also I believe there were four of them, weren't there? Two at each place. Maybe she wants me to correct her, but I'm not.

"Either way Karen, can you tell us about last night?"

"What do you want to know?"

"Where were you from around 12pm to 6pm?"

"Well let's see I woke up around 11 or so. I took a pill I'm prescribed to not lock me up, then I had coffee and worked on some songs while watching GameGrumps. Have you ever heard of them? No? Thought not, they are these two dudes, Mrs. Tongue you would get along really well with the one guy he's jewish, on Youtube, and right now they are still locked up for Covid so they have been doing these reactions things, you wouldn't understand how the zoomer brain works, just know that it works differently than yours. Actually in fact they're latest episode was pretty funny, the one guy Dan-"

"STOP!" Tungavaloa screams. Slamming her hand onto the table.

"Hey take it easy Chief." says the hefty guy.

"Take it easy? When we have a murderer in front of us and we're supposed to take it easy?" She stands up. "Girl, do you know what type of trouble you're in?"

"No." She walks over to my side of the table and leans in and whispers into my ear.

"I know what you have done you sick bitch, you deserve hell and not just prison!"

"Why are we whispering?" I snarked in a whisper. She looks at me for about five seconds and then starts to choke. I actually can't believe what is happening, she is actually attacking me.

The hefty guy tries to get her off and quickly three guys come storming into the room and grab her away from me and separate her from my neck. I gasp for air as one guy has his hand on my shoulder as the other two drag her out. The investigation continues without her with some no name loser and the hefty guy, and was nothing special. They finish and I am stuck in the room for a while, bored out of my mind since I'm not allowed to have my phone. Oh and for those of you who are wondering why this is so short it's because you can simply go fuck yourselves. I don't really care to go into the details of my interrogation so just know that I pissed her off and that I was pissed. I mean seriously this is bullshit, I know they don't have anything on me and then they do this shit, yeah sorry not really in the mood to describe what color panties the hefty guy was wearing (probably pink) or anything about the rest of the interrogation. Go fuck yourself.

After what felt like an eternity, someone comes in, and it's a guy in a suit and a very nice tie. My lawyer perhaps? Gosh I don't even remember getting a lawyer, must be some big wig that helped get Trump out of trouble or something. He looks to me like he could use a shower though, his hair is a little greasy. I'm not a fan of it. He sits down across the table and pulls out a big brown briefcase.

"Hey Karen I hope this big fiasco hasn't affected you too badly, It was really stupid how they brought you all the way down here and took you ILLEGALLY! It doesn't really

Dead Fashion

happen, even for these cops in Minneapolis with their track record." I look at him blankly.

"Un-huh… Umm, who exactly are you, might I ask."

"HA, Karen great questions you have a keen eye, that's good to have. My name is Hubert Harker, You can just call me Harker."

"Harker, like from Dracula?"

"No, it's a very common English last name actually that spans centuries before the book, good question though." He says in a very uplifting and nice tone as he smiles, I don't like it that much.

"Ok pal whats the fucking deal here, like with you, like what are you doing here? You, my lawyer that I hired when I was high or something or a public attorney? Like you kinda just waltzed in here acting like I'm supposed to know you."

"Karen, let's just say I work for some powerful people who have your best interest at heart."

"The Jews?"

"NO! Not the Jews… at least I don't think, I don't know. Look DP records is kinda in the drain right now, whether it's thanks to you or someone else they are scrambling without the CEO, soooo…"

"So what?" I say crossing my arms.

"So let's just say I am your designated lawyer that YOU hired-" He winks at me. "Because I'm the best lawyer that YOU could find. Ok?"

"Can you get me out of this situation at least?" I say with a sigh.

"YES! But…"

"But what?" I'm now kind of agitated.

"But that depends how committed you will be to joining us."

"So you are working for the jews!"

"NO! Karen, just quit with the antisemitic jokes for a second. I was sent here by my company to get you out of this, in exchange the deal is that you come sign with us, I mean you are going to need a new label more than likely because DP is riding on you and spoiler alert they are about to go bankrupt and you don't want to be on that ship. On top of that I got a hold of your contract, don't ask me how please, and I found a loophole." My eyes lit up when he said that. A chance to get out of DP is exactly what I needed and wanted, this is like a gift from God herself.

"I'm listening." I said as I put my leg over my other leg and started to fully engage in the situation.

"The loophole is this, without Damocha here, you know what I mean right?"

"Yeah they just told me earlier that he was the one who was murdered along with my-" I pretend to shed a tear "My old manager."

"Yeah I'm sorry Karen, that's gotta be tough on you."

"It really is." I am being truthful here. I am very upset about everything with her, I didn't want her to die, but it just kind of happened, am I feeling regret?

"Well essentially without him here your contract holds no merit because it's signed to his name, not under DP records, I looked and nowhere does it say you belong to DP, you just have to do stuff for his signature at the bottom, sure it mentions the company but it's assigned to the company."

"Wait, are you serious?"

"YES!"

"Why would he do something so stupid like that? I mean surely he would want the company to own my rights."

"Well actually he was using you." You don't say... "He was using all of his talents and secretly putting the contracts under his name, that way if he needed to overthrow the board if they tried to kick him out or he wanted to make a few extra dollars off of you and your music, he owned you. If they kicked him, you were going with him. And with no heir to the contracts, they are essentially nothing but a piece of paper, no legality to them."

"HOLY SHIT! FUCK YEAH!" I say as I jump out of my chair, I run over to the other side of the table and hug the man, he smells heavily of Geàu cologne, yeah he definitely

Dead Fashion

hasn't showered today. "This is great! You have no idea how bad it was there, he used me so badly, gosh look I'm not saying that I'm glad he's dead but between you and me I am glad in a way. I still don't know who would do something that heinous to another soul." I go over and sit back down. "When I was younger I remember first breaking into the industry, in Japan, how I was used and abused, I don't know what would bring a soul to that point that would be so crude and disgusting to make another human have a tragedy."

"Yeah, no kidding, well Karen, will you jump off the sinking ship and lead a new crew through the seven seas?"

"The joke is bad, but Fuck it I will." I shake his hand. "You aren't some bum ass record label though right?"

"Oh-ho, definitely not!"

"Good, I already did this dance once, not doing it again. Ok! So what is the situation? Can you please just let me go home?"

"Well, there is some great news actually. Number one you don't really have any evidence as of now that would force you to be a prisoner, except for the fact that you were close to them, which is not punishable by imprisonment. Second, you also were barged in on, with what turned out to be an unjust warrant, which will now have leagues of consequences for the judge who authorized it, and on top of everything, the big cherry on top of it, the way they handled you and this situation with the attacking of you here and at your home, with the false imprisonment and with the interrogation, basically means even if they had a tiny bit of evidence that pointed to you, with the police's track record here and with all of this, it's gonna get thrown out in court with a good lawyer, with no evidence, they more than likely will not take you to court especially if I decide to send a subpoena about a potential lawsuit, Karen, you are scot free in this situation, in fact I will more than likely get you cleared to walk out of here by the end of the hour. Just sit tight, I will take care of this, Karen, thank you!"

"No thank you Mr. Harker, I just want to go lay in my own bed, it's getting a little late. Yes it is, well good news is it sounds like the president is flying to MSP by 6 PM so you'll be right on time to meet him! I gotta talk with the police, then the press and then they will more than likely walk you out of here."

"OH!"

"Yes Karen."

"One thing to add, the person who attacked me, is not only the chief of the St. Paul police, but also has history with me, and thinks I killed her son. Will that change the case at all Mr. Harker?"

"HA! Are you kidding me? That is like the final Trump card, That is gonna look so bad on them, they will have to drop this investigation and case."

"Nice, thank you!" I say with a smile. He pretends to tip a hat to me as I see his nasty black greasy hair again because I looked up at it during the weird fake hat tip thing.

Forty-Five Minutes Later…

Time passes and finally the lawyer walks back in with two police officers and they come over to me and unlock the handcuffs which have been hurting my wrists and more than likely leave a rash for a few days. They both look dumbfounded, maybe because they are pea brained cops or maybe because they have never seen such an attractive girl like me. I also am very famous now too which changes a lot.

We walk out of the room and through a bunch of locked keycard doors, before reaching the main hall of the police department where a row of police stand watching as me and my lawyer from this company walk side by side. A few people from the press are just near the big entrance doors snapping pictures, and as we get closer the lawyer starts to block some of the flashes. We open the doors and hear nothing but camera clicks and shouting and people trying to shove microphones in our faces, he tries to swat some away and manages to do so, it reminds me of the time at the St. Paul station too, this time without that weird nice side of Damocha. He was only being nice because of how much money I made him, prick, I will go spit on his grave once it's finished. The press are trying to ask me tons of questions and as we get closer to the street, a big black limo is waiting there for us, really fancy and flashy geez. But as we almost get to the limo, something catches my ear. That voice, it sounds so familiar. It sounded like... Susan.

I snap my head over and look directly at a lady with black hair and a microphone and for a second I scared the living shit out of her, because she almost jumps back and then goes back into press mode. She has an iphone just recording the situation, and must be independent. I know, I know, you are never EVER supposed to fuel the flame, but hey... I'm The Akuma mother fucker! My job is to fuel the flame. I walk closer to her and Harker tries to grab me and stop me but is too late as I get close enough for her to ask her a question.

"Uh-uh,uh" there are now so many people crowding her trying to get an answer from me as she tries to speak.

"What are you gonna say, I only have a couple seconds girl."

"Uh- Are you guilty of those murders linked to DP Records?" It gets really quiet over on the right side of this walkway as everyone wants to capture my response. Me, my response, all these people are waiting for me. They want to hear from me, they are controlled by me at this moment. I finally gave her an answer.

"Just because I play a character and fuel it up for the audiences and the generation of people, doesn't mean I'm a murderer. So because I talk about murders in my song, I am immediately a murder? How disrespectful of not only me, but of all artists. This police department has proven time and time again that they cannot handle and control situations and are just flat out horrible people, my statement is this, No! I'm not guilty, the guilty ones are in that building." I point to the station. "These people are out here blaming me for a murder that just happened close to me and they sat in there and interrogated a poor girl, to try and confess to something she didn't do, I shame people like that and I hope they can learn to treat people who are struggling with emotions with some respect and I hope they can stop trying to just frame me for the murder and actually go find the sick son of bitch who killed those people, it's sick the lengths people will go to just get a paycheck, I pity those pity." And I spit on the sidewalk towards the police station.

My statement was long and probably made it the quietest it's been out there since I got here. The crowd got fired up badly again and kept trying to ask more things, but I retreated to the limo with Harker and left the whole scene behind and let my mind clear a little bit.

The limousine was very fabulous. It was nice and the air was cool too. There was a little flat screen tv that popped out of the ceiling and champagne that was at least a thousand dollars. There was a nice dark and black coloring all around. A massive table in the middle with food and assortment of goods and stuff. The back where we were was nice, it was like a little private car with two benches, one with one chair and walkway to the rest of the limo, and another on the back of the car fit for two people. I sat on the bench with the lawyer Harker, who has been somewhat not the worst somehow and he sat on his phone while he pulled out a cigar and chopped it, then lit it. I just sat and laid my head back and let my mind clear of all the bullshit that has happened today. To think that bitch caught on so quickly, it almost is scary, and I will more than likely be watched on my every move, but if I'm signing with a new company, one who is by this limo, obviously bigger than DP, I probably will move out of the apartment and build a cool mansion like Prince, and be a recluse for the rest of my life while just making music and doing tours. I also have been getting a shit ton of money from the tours and since my contract with DP is technically considered complete I have free reign over my music and everything I own right now. So I will be careful when making this deal, which by the way, we seem to be heading toward the airport, which more than likely means we are meeting this president. I am almost feeling excited, I feel full of life in a way, I feel like I have everything back in my control, it feels… nice.

Dead Fashion

We don't stroll all the way into the airport as traffic would be too intense, but we take a back way into an open tar lot to a hangar that is obviously privately owned. We sit in the car and I let the cool AC keep me from losing my sanity. I don't mind tight spaces, but with other people it really pisses me off. After some time we see a private jet touchdown and stroll around and make it's way into the hangar and then after about five minutes a couple people in suits come out and walk towards the limo that is on the side of the hangar. Two bigger guys and a semi tall, less buff and skinny guy all enter the car. The two bigger guys go up towards the front, while the skinny guy sits in the single person seat across from me and the lawyer Harker. He gets situated and we start to drive, as we do so he grabs the briefcase from the lawyer and then looks in it and then at me and then smiles.

"Ms. Wall, What a pleasure to finally have the ability to meet you!"

"Yeah um I've heard that a few times in my life." I say now paying full attention to him.

"Well I just want to say first and foremost your welcome."

"For?"

"For getting you out of that bad situation you were in, do you know how much bribe money was needed or did you not hear about that? Look anyways point is forget about it, you were in some trouble and we got you out of it and now I hear you do want to sign with us and join our label is that so?"

"Yeah, you could say that, umm who are you guys anyways." I say as I grab a little bit of the champagne and pour it into a glass and then take a swig.

"Well, we're Universal Music." I spit out all of my drink onto him and he semi chuckles and then wipes it off.

"Holy shit are you serious?"

"As serious as those murders you committed."

"Uhhhh, dude I didn't kill anyone. I don't know what you're talking about."

"Oh please don't bullshit me or my company, yes we are Universal and we are interested in you and your music. We also know of your past including in Japan, thanks to our friends over at Sony, which by the way most people think we hate each other, spoiler alert we don't! We are like bread and butter and help each other keep an iron grip on the market. We also know about that baseball player you murdered plus these people, Karen. I saw the photos and let me say you must have had some pent up rage, young woman."

"I told you I don't know what you're talking about!" I say firmly and look at him.

"Ok look, in my 13 years at Universal, I have never been wrong about my talents, whether it's getting them hired or fired or what to do with them."

"Well you're wrong about me, look guys I'm popular but I'm telling you now I can't be cast into a mold, I don't follow rules nor will I follow rules… and I don't do managers." I scoff.

"Well that's exactly what we want from you. We want you to be rebellious and be crazy on twitter, as long as you stay within community guidelines. We want you to produce your own music and do your own thing. We are here to help not create. Look, when I was assigned to the R&B and Rap Division, I didn't know what to do, I mean at that time there wasn't just a set division for it. I made the standards and created the guidelines for the company and my standards are when it comes to rap and commercial rap, it's not authentic if it's not fully produced by the musician. That's why our rap department took off, and now I wanna branch out to your J-Rap fast style hip-hop. I want your music, your way and I want to produce your music for the world to see. You saw what a little company like DP could do, now imagine having the entire world at your fingertips Ms. Wall! That rage and heart you put into those bodies, I want that into your music. I need that from you!"

"LOOK I DIDN'T KILL THOSE PEOPLE FUCKFACE!" I say no red in the face.

"THAT! That's it right there, that's the energy I want and need." I look at him and grind my teeth and after a few seconds of my imagination showing me how it would look like to run him over with the limo a hundred times, I calm down and get back to my normal self.

"Look I am willing to sign with you, I suppose."

"Great, well let's just-"

"But! I have some conditions."

"Well with the situation you were just in, you're not really in a position to negotiate, but I want to hear them."

"JUST! Listen… please. I want a non binding contract, which means at any point I can retire, you can continue to sell my music and I will get you x amounts of albums and songs, but so help me god at any point after that if I want to be done, I will be done. Number two, I don't want to tour outside western Europe and the USA and Canada. Despite my J-rap I don't do shows in Japan anymore unless it is for a special occasion. Number three I want full say over every final touch to my song, I don't want to be making music for you, I'm making music for me and the people. And finally number four. I want a signing bonus large enough that will pay for me to build my own mansion just outside of the cities here and I will refuse to move to anywhere else. I will go to California to record and do all that, but so help me god if I have to live in cesspool we call a state, I will Kurt Cobain myself and blame it on you, got all that, I hope someone was writing that down, because when my lawyer reads the final contract, if I don't get those benefits I will not sign and I don't care what type of leverage or anything you have on me."

"Geez, you were right, you will be difficult, okay!" He says as he smiles and claps his hands. "Let's get the contract done, so you will sign with us if we give you those benefits?"

"Yes 100%"

"Great, shake on it, to make it official?" I shake his hand and make sure to wipe it off when he isn't looking. "Well this calls for a celebration. A good dinner?"

"Actually I am quite starved." I say for some reason talking like a character out of a novel from the 1890's. "I know a really good place actually, it's called Day Block, great fries and beer is cheap as hell. Good little brewing company."

"Look at you being a business lady!" He says in a pet like manner which really pisses me off and I almost want to cause a ruckus, but that would be bad with those two jackholes up front. "We can discuss more stuff over dinner. How about that?"

"Ok, sounds fine to me. Oh one more thing though for you Mr… well shit I don't even know your name."

"BAHAHAHA, oh my goodness how silly of me! How did we forget such a simple thing? Mr. Martin, please and thank you."

"Ok Mr. Martin, tell me one thing if you think I killed all these people, why still go out of your way to quote on quote save me and do give me a contract?"

"Ms. Wall, I'm a businessman, business isn't supposed to be easy or ethical, sometimes the best way to make money is to get a little bloody, at the end of the day your little escapades don't matter to me, for as long as they paint you in the public light. You're a money making machine for yourself and everyone you touch. Do you think I would let such a great opportunity like you pass by? Once you understand that, you understand my motives."

June 3rd

Did I format this the same way as I have been? God I don't remember nor do I care. The past three weeks have been somewhat agonizing despite all the good things happening to me, I don't quite understand it all. I don't get it, I just signed this deal last week and it made headlines, I was on the BBC, I was on FOX, CNN, and apparently my social media presence has become somewhat immaculate, especially for the liberal left side of the media. My little masquerade on the police really has pushed me into a spotlight that I don't care to have, but I also don't want. My biggest problem as it sits is that all these people like ShitYouShouldCareAbout and PocketNews have been fangirling over me like I'm Taylor Swift or something, which has caused a lot of my fans to have this cult-like following. I don't mind that but I don't want these fucking little shits all over me talking about how they always knew I was gonna blow up and shit and they listened to me on Youtube when I only had 12k subs. I HATE fake fans, especially these ones that have been all over me since the signing. The funniest take I heard from anyone in the media was Tucker Carlson, he called me and I quote "One of those fake queerbaiting pop artists who only pretends to care about politics and their fans for views and money." I love this take because out of all the people to ever talk about me in the media, he could not have been more right and wrong at the same time. I am somewhat using my political views for money and I don't give a shit about politics at all, What I do care about though is my fans. DON'T EVER SAY I DON'T CARE ABOUT MY FANS!

    I will have you know I care about my fans more than I care about my own family at this point, which by the way I haven't spoken to either of my parents in over five months now. Ever since Christmas, I have dodged all their calls. I read my moms texts talking about how she and my father were sorry and so proud of me for becoming so popular and having such a successful tour, but that didn't matter to me. No one's words matter to me, I don't care if Sleepy Joe Biden walked onto the stage at the next Union address and sucked me off like a MILF on Brazzers, I wouldn't care. You simply can't care when you are at my level, I am at a point now where I am topping charts and still am, despite no new album in six months and I am banking on it. I have done in the span of a year what artists dream to do in their entire lives and you expect me to care what my parents think about my work or matter of fact, what anyone else's opinion of me is? If you think that you are simple minded, you are below success and there is a reason you aren't where you want to be. I got to where I wanted to be, by simply being the best and constantly fighting, you get knocked down? GET THE FUCK BACK UP, you don't have time to be worthless and nothing, you are a human being born into the earth, spawned of life, you creation (while unknown) is magical. If it's by a God or by the universe either way we are one in a quadrillion, you were given this beautiful opportunity, Don't fucking waste it. Take your life and do something with it. Look at me, look at what I did and see how far I have gotten. I now have so much money I don't even know what to do with it, while just last year I was barely able to afford heat.

   Despite all of that above, I don't feel complete. I have nothing, yet I have everything I ever wanted. I had a love affair (didn't work), I'm making music, I am currently building a very large and beautiful house just outside of Chaska near Hazeltine National Golf Course. I also have bought a very, VERY nice car. I sold my last one and got an Aston Martin Valkyrie Spider, one of only 82 in the world to own one. I got it as a gift to myself for this massive signing with Universal, overall it was around 2.3 million dollars, but I knew a guy and because I am the motherfucking Akuma, I got a massive sale on it and got it for super cheap at only a million dollars. I also got it in a custom color and got it in a nice glossy hot pink and it looks stunning. My life has so much substance and so much worth, but I still am missing something. Journaling like this has helped me, but that isn't what I'm missing. Maybe I will figure it out but I haven't wanted to do anything, I have worked out, worked on music, and watched all this media shit and paid attention to that. I am supposed to go to California in August to record a new album but I don't really care, it's a new experience, but for some reason, I'm not excited, I don't understand it. I will try to figure it out, hopefully my house should be done in September and I can move in before October and enjoy the winter in my new home.

July 5th

I know it's not a month on the dot but here is my monthly update. The psychological analysis I had to take yesterday really pissed me off and I'm contemplating going back to that place and burning it to the ground. It was apparently some test I now have to do every three months as a requirement of Universal and so they ask me all these very intrusive questions about my mental health which I lie about, because I know what the correct answers are and not what my answers are. The lady did ask me a very odd question and I remember it quite well.

"So Karen, now we have passed the entrance question portion, could you please answer these next questions about yourself?"

"Yes, go ahead."

"Ok, so the first question I have is… well do you have any thoughts about suicide?"

"Just the normal amount." I said not really paying attention while grabbing my water bottle off the floor and taking a drink.

"The normal amount is zero, Karen." I looked up at her with a dead sad face and then proceeded to give her a fake smile.

"Oh right, of course." I said hitting my forehead softly with my hand as if to gesture I'm an idiot.

This was very interesting to me because for the first time in life I have thought about suicide. Not in a sense that I plan on offing myself or anything, but rather in a sense that the thought about that act has crossed my mind. No matter how low life got in the past I never even had a thought of any of that, sure I've joked about jumping off buildings or killing myself when something pisses me off, but never have I seriously thought about it. Now I know what some of you may be thinking, why lie on the test, you seem like you need help, and maybe I do. But my goal isn't to allow that to happen, I will not and never will let anyone know how I truly feel about anything ever again, not after what happened before. My writing has also ceased with me now only doing a monthly update which even though I don't want to write, my house is going good and is coming along exactly how I wanted it. I also have almost all my songs finished and I'm quite proud of my work. I'm celebrating by grilling an impossible burger and taking a Xanax, yay me. That is all that has happened in my life that is interesting, sorry. I wish I had more going on but I don't, and if I did I don't really wanna write about it, that is all I have to say.

October 2nd

My house is done… Fuck I guess I should write something else, ok fine listen up. Life has been extremely boring, I have been nothing but tired and no amount of pills will help me right now. I am curious to see my doctor that I decided I need to go to annually now. I never wanted to go to one before, but I feel I need to. I also have to check up with that psychiatrist soon too, which I will again lie to and say everything is fine, however I will actively seek help from my doctor soon. I have a meeting on the 4th and will be hoping for a quick fix. I'm sure once I get fully settled here and get back to touring and stuff I will be fine, but right now I feel so weak. My eyes are always half shut and I always feel like I'm one second away from passing out.

I guess the house is nice though. It is massive, there are over 25 rooms in the whole house, two bars, a long indoor pool, a rehab center, a hot tub, and a six car garage too. There are two master bedrooms and four regular bedrooms as well. A completely built studio with insane modern equipment, and there is a theater in my house that all I have to do is climb up these steps and pick a movie for this digital projector and I get it all there. I have requested one room to be a nice cozy study with a tiny collection of books with a fireplace, simply because I like to work in a nice room like that and on occasion when I do media stuff or when I just simply want to read, I will sit in there by the fire. On top of that with it getting colder and soon the snow will be here I have requested a nice big glass window that looks out over the yard in the room, so I can see all the snow and feel so warm inside. I also noticed that it makes me feel more intelligent and sophisticated, and I feel like I have a place I can retreat to when I need to get away from everything. It's nice.

October 18th

I know I have been trying to write less and less in this piece of junk but I decided I needed to write this morning despite just writing in it about two and half weeks ago. It's about 9:40 AM and I think I am having a schizophrenic attack or at least I did in my sleep. My dream was horrible, it was so bad and it was so vivid, I remember almost every detail!

I started off alone in a desolate space of reality which seemed not part of the world. It wasn't like the weird dreams I used to have last year in those hallways with bad lighting, no… this was weirder. I was in a place with nothing but black around and what seemed like far away balls of light which looked like stars, but now that I think about it, that wouldn't make sense. Anyways I was standing on a see through bluish white platform and it was terrifying to look down and see nothing but space below, if I fell through I would drift endlessly for eternity and never come back. That isn't what makes the dream weird though. The dream was weird because I remember walking on these platforms/pathways and what felt like an hour later I was confronted with a deep fog or smoke. In it a silhouette of a person stood. I walked closer and as I did so the figure emerged out of the fog and I couldn't believe my eyes. It was of all people… Susan. She stood there looking at me with a dead face, but she was alive looking, she wasn't dead like she is supposed to be. We stared at each other for what felt like an eternity, before the silence was broken.

"I know I'm probably not the figure you expected to see here, but alas here I am."

"Why are you talking like that?"

"It's probably because this is how I was perceived to be in your brain. Some high class speaking lady, somebody of great importance, is that true."

"No… No you got it wrong, unfortunately."

"Karen… I'm in your head ya know. I can see everything you see and have seen, I know everything about you."

"Look here you stupid bitch! I put a bullet through your skull, does that speak of respect to you? I respect no one, but myself, everyone is either greedy, self centered, or some weird pedo/horrible person."

"And Karen… you aren't any of those?" I stare at her and she looks at me and I finally notice that she is wearing the clothes she was wearing the first time I saw her way back last year over the zoom call. It is almost disturbing to see something in the past playout and act in front of your own eyes, it's uncanny in a way.

"Look, it's not about that, the point is I never had respect for you, you cheating asshole."

"Karen, how was I cheating?"

"We were dating!"

"We're we? I mean think about it, sure we did stuff together, and sure we had sex… a lot, but does that mean we were dating? Plus I was already in a committed relationship with another person."

"WHICH YOU DIDN'T DISCLOSE TO ME MOTHERFUCKER! You think you come into my head and try to make me feel bad about putting a bullet through you! Huh? Is that what this is? Is my conscience trying to make me feel like a dick because of the stuff I've done? Well if that's the case go fuck yourself! After what this world has done to me, spit on me, kicked me in the nuts, it's only fair I fight back and show it what I'm made of, what I am! I am what I am and no matter how wrong it is I won't change. Plus go take your stupid talks somewhere else, because I'm done." I start to walk away and then turn around for a second to speak again. "Oh and by the way I have only killed one person since your death and he was a bum on the street! So you're welcome!"

"Karen stop, where are you going? You don't know where that leads!"

"I don't care where it leads, I would rather be by myself than with you, you liar!" I continued to walk and kept walking, forever and ever and ever, until I saw a door at the end of the path. It was a wooden white door and for a moment it reminded me of the doors I used to have at my old house when I was younger. I got closer and when I got to the door I felt the handle. It was round and felt so familiar, like I had touched it before. I was sure I shouldn't open the door, but curiosity beat me and I opened it slowly.

When I opened the door I was greeted with a cityscape. At first it all looked foreign but, slowly and surely I remembered it. It was Minneapolis! Not the city I walk through and murder in today, no! It was an older Minneapolis, not ancient, but just felt older. The colors were more vibrant, the city felt more alive despite probably having less people in it. The buildings were taller, the sky was dark and crowds of people and I'm talking crowds of people are walking. Which is unusual, even for the memory. This many people, surely it would be less. I also started to notice the snow, it was coming down heavily, and as I turned around, I saw nothing but a massive stadium. It was huge! So foreign to me, but huge! I couldn't believe the size of this place, I felt like an ant! I looked all around and slowly the dread which had been building up in my mind came all the way through as I recognized this night down to a tooth and nail.

January 17th, 2010, a day I cannot forget. It was so snowy, the snow was coming down so hard, I felt almost like I was stuck in a way, like no matter how hard I tried I cannot move myself, I'm moving on autopilot. I remember the reason for being out so late at night at such a young age, I was only 11 after all. I am standing outside of the place now demolished, and long gone, called the metrodome. Few don't remember it, and few have never been there in the area. It was where concerts were, baseball played there and most importantly the reason we were there, football. The Minnesota Vikings played here, my father was a big Vikings fan and this was apparently "Our year" just like every other year, except the further the season went on, the truer that statement became. They were winning, big time and the Vikings had reached the playoffs. This is why we were there. We were watching the playoffs, and they actually had won. It was a huge celebration and of course a huge win means huge amounts of drinking. I remember my father was so drunk he was stumbling out of the stadium. The crowds were massive and all of sudden my drunk father was gone, lost. I felt scared yet at the same time I wanted to be brave, I had just turned 11 and I wanted to show my parents I was a big girl. I was grown up, in reality I was not, but it's what I thought at the time. There is a factor I am leaving out which I don't want to remember, I block out that piece, for the life of me I try to forget. The piece I'm leaving out is I am holding someone's hand… a small person's hand… a small boy's hand… my brother's hand. Joshua was only 5 years old, but like me, was scared and didn't want to show it. I remember I decided to walk by ourselves, all we had to do was take the train from the stadium. to the mall of america, and then ride the bus that stops there every hour and a half. My mom told me this information. If I somehow ever got lost in the metro area, all I had to do was get to the mall of america, the biggest mall in the world at the time. If I got there I would take the bus that stopped near the front entrance of the mall and that bus would always go to our town Minnetonka, where our house was. Then we could make our way home. Of course we were told that was never a good option, and that it would be better if it was a backup plan, because the chances of us getting kidnapped were massive. But I was determined, I was gonna get me and my brother home safely, together we would take the train on the other side of the street at the train station, and then from there, we would take the bus around 10ish, if we were on time, I had a tiny spongebob watch, that I always checked for the time, because I wanted to be on top of everything. We were about to

Dead Fashion

cross the street, I remember there being so many people and traffic was still flowing because the traffic control was not a big thing at this time, I remember everything happening so fast. I looked down at the watch, I was trying to figure out the route and go home, and then all of a sudden I remember looking up and before I could act all I saw was a silhouette of his body in the heavy snow and the lights of some jackass trying to leave the stadium on the road my brother most likely couldn't see and all of sudden I hear a loud crash! I watch the car hit the silhouette and then fly through and continue to go through almost hitting more people near the cross walk. I remember the sidewalk feeling so pact, yet he somehow had a clear shot at the road.

    The body laid there and all I saw was a crowd surrounding me and my brother as I ran to him who was now laying on the side of the road on the curb, due in part to the impact. It was so horrible. I just remember seeing so much blood and feeling his body it was limp. I didn't need a doctor or an adult brain to know that my brother was dead. A police officer got to us and people started freaking out and I remember everything feeling so chaotic. I can't even remember anything after that. The other thing I remember is the funeral in the snow and how cold it was and how much I cried. I tried to tell everyone it was my fault, but in reality everyone blamed my father. For once in my life I don't blame my father for this, even if he was tried for child neglect and a bunch of other stuff I don't blame him. Neither does my mom, she just always told me to not feel sad, because "It was his time and God wanted him." If God was real she wouldn't have killed a young child, she would have let him live and grow old! She also wouldn't let me be so stupid as to not pay attention to him and my surroundings. She would've been better. The point is this scene happened in front of me again, my mind was forcing me to watch it again, it was agonizing me, tormenting me of my biggest failure.

    I woke up in a sweat and then drank about as much water as I could as I was hot, despite it being around 30ish degrees this morning. I tried to sleep again, but couldn't so I got up and ate toast and then wrote this now. I hope I can figure out why my mind is tormenting me with these dreams. I hope that maybe I can figure it out. I think I will stop writing in this thing for good now too. I think this is the last thing people need to read of me, and my life. I have nothing left I want to put onto paper, I want to live my life and try to start fresh, less killing, less smoking and drugs, more working out, and more concerts and music. My goal is to go for another 20 years. If I can do that, I will retire at 42 I promise, until then I will live my life. I don't want to continue this journal or my stories of my life anymore, I'm done. Oh and by the way the Vikings lost the next game and didn't even go to the Super Bowl that year, story of my life.

As The World Caves In

Well… It has been a while hasn't it? I'm looking back at this thing and see so many things I wish I wouldn't have said. But to be honest, I'm glad all of this stuff is here. It was like a journey down a memory path which I had forgotten well. I almost wanted to go back and rewatch everything, the drugs, sex, murders all of it. It has been four years, I think, and well… today is my birthday! Yep December 8th. I am officially 27 years old today and I celebrated by having a cake sent to my house via Uber Express, a new experimental service which flies things to your door within minutes of ordering it and yes it was an ice cream cake, because today is the hottest December 8th of all time for obvious reasons. Even if it was still not too much, it was 61 degrees today. Not close to the record high, but still incredibly warm for December. Looking back at the past three years was incredible, I mean this was such a small sliver on my life, yet was so impactful on me as a person. Since then I have grown… I have been less chaotic, more controlled, more subtle in my ways and actions. I have decided that I no longer need to be an egregious nasty teenager anymore; I am an adult, who acts like one. I act like my age. Now the impact that I had

Dead Fashion

on the people and the world around still stands as an accomplishment I take credit for. We now have critical thinkers in this world who don't just believe every single thing an old person tells them to think. Somehow out of all of my teachings and the things I've said to my generation, we still are electing old people into office, however, don't worry because that will change soon, I promise. We have another four years of Joe Biden, but honestly I realized how little that changes anything in the world really, it's all still a fucked up mess.

    My good deeds came with great greed however; Over the past four years I did a lot with my life, which I'm proud of and some of which I am not. I released my first album with Universal in March of 2022 which was incredible, I called it The Scheme of an Akuma, all written by me and composed with you guessed it, the one, the only Mike Clemons who I had requested to come aboard and since he was looking for a new job, because of obvious reasons. He ended up signing with us and helped produce this masterpiece of an album. The biggest song on the album titled Quit Killin' My Vibe hit number one of the charts and would've been there for almost the entire year however in October that asshole Taylor Swift knocked me out of the top 10 entirely! EVERY SINGLE SONG ON HER ALBUM WAS IN THE TOP 10! Like are you fucking kidding me? Are you serious? My tours, my music, it was killing it that year, I was gonna win so many awards and then this beautiful, sexy blonde hair son of bitch steals all of my awards. I did actually win an award in 2023 however after two years of being mainstream and people bitching, I finally won an award. I still don't know why I never was even considered for a grammy up until then, I can only assume it was because of all the controversy and all the stupid shit about me and how I was just some bozo woman, which by the way spoiler alert, a girl is gonna come along in 2022 later that year as well and she is gonna win a bunch of awards pretty much doing the exact same thing I did, which was blow up on the internet and then sign with someone, the only difference is that hers was all english rap and she had an ass so big you could throw a baseball at it and it would get shot to outer space. Also that reasoning is bullshit because Billie Ellish did the exact same shit I did and she won all the awards in 2020, so that really pisses me the fuck off, but whatever I won three grammy's that year and while I could've won all the general field ones that everyone cares about, Taylor stole all of them… she is lucky she is so pretty. I won "Best rap song" "Best Rap album" and the only general field award that I won was "Songwriter of the year, non-classical" which was actually massive and I had to build a trophy case for them. Then in 2023 I got busy, I dropped another album again, this one called American Psycho. The album cover had me mimicking Patrick Bateman on the album cover and this was when I realized I really like to have awesome album covers and they are some of the best parts of music. I had a couple themed songs about the novel and a couple horror slasher films and then I did a bunch of really cool music videos for it too, which my music videos had always been the same old, same old rap stuff, but I changed it up and decided to be different. This paid off massively as I ended up winning a grammy for that as well. 2023 was also the year I got into cinema. I always liked movies, but now I was making lists, analyzing them and because I was in Hollywood a lot for the recordings now, and because I was super popular and rich, I started to hang out with actors and big wigs in the scene and I would watch them make films and do movie shoots when I wasn't recording. I even got to meet the man himself, the sexiest man on the planet, the man everyone wants to meet and or do things with, RYAN RENOLDS! I love him so much and he actually I'm not making any of this up I promise, he was a fan of my music and wanted me to cameo in Deadpool 3, which I was so into I almost kissed him. Then of fucking course the dumb writers strike has to happen and then of course the actors have to go on strike, so all of sudden I was halted from the filming and seeing everyone. There were protests everywhere in LA and picket lines and all of that, it was crazy, kind of reminded me of a more civilized version of the riots in 2020. Eventually that ended in September and I got my cameo in Deadpool 3. I played a store clerk who Deadpool runs into during a fight and I say a quippy one liner before he gets thrown back into battle, it was super fun! Oh and I forgot the best parts about all my trips during this time to Los Angeles, were the murders. Yes I cut back on them, but I still had my fair share of fun. I murdered some up and coming actor who wanted to have sex with me so badly that I actually felt sorry for him and let him do it, then I murdered him, instead of just doing it. The homeless there are a big problem and I helped get them off the streets and clean them up. Like I always said my solution to homelessness and world population control is one and the same. After 2023 was over I stayed home for a while and decided to continue workshopping from home while indulging into my murderous tendencies occasionally and yes if you are wondering, I stopped having those weird dreams, thank God herself.

  2024 was a very odd year and I was really unsure about it but after landing another cameo and getting back to LA, I found a new inspiration for life. I dropped another funky album this time focusing solely on J-rap/my roots called A Necessary Evil. It was an ok album and the best song on it titled Ace In the Hole. The song was number one on the charts for about two months and I was overall happy with the success. 2024 and 2025 were the years of touring. I wanted to focus more on touring and with the problems in the world with the Chinese-Korean war going on which had now had US involvement, and the AI malfunction which scared a bunch of people into thinking Nuclear winter was coming. I figured the world needed some light hearted Akuma music. However this came at a major cost to me and my mental health, because I got into a state similar to how I was when I first started touring. I took a month long retreat in October of this year and I decided I want to fully step away from music and touring for a while. I might come back or I might not, I haven't decided. My music is very much a product of it's time and if I continue to make the same old music it will lose it's touch. The same problem is happening with Marvel and superhero movies right now. They were a product of the 2010's and they don't have that same feeling anymore, which is sad yet makes the old Marvel movies feel like gold. It's nice to re-watch them and that's how I want my concerts and music to be. I want it to be re-watched and re-listened to. I want it to be the statement it was and continue to garner success for the time. On top of this, I have made so much money, my kids wouldn't even have to work if they didn't want to, but I won't have kids. I don't have a husband, or a wife, or any kids. I sent a christmas card to my parents last year and I plan on doing it every year just so they know I'm alive, although I'm sure they know that, it's just the right thing to do, it's the best thing to do. All this money and fame and nobody to share it with, huh… it just still feels all wrong. I thought this was what I wanted, but now I'm not too sure. Any-hoo… I have an interview on 60 Minutes tomorrow about my life and the music I made, I also announced that my last show I will be doing for a very long time, maybe ever will be here in Minneapolis on the 12th at the new renovated U.S Bank Stadium, which got a new look and a size upgrade so it can now fit 100,000 people! It sounds like every seat is sold out and it will be a massive event, I will probably make over 800k just off this one event. I was asked in my retirement to play a Super Bowl halftime show with Drake in 2026 at the 49ers stadium in San Francisco, which I declined, however I did say I would do the halftime show at the Christmas home game for the Vikings, just because I have always wanted to do a Christmas concert and it gives me a chance to just do something like that, so that will technically be my last concert, however it isn't a true concert I guess, I don't know.

  I'm excited for the future, retirement is something that seems like an old person should do, however retiring at 27 will be amazing. I plan to spend that time messing with new sounds, playing video games, watching the stock market (which is more fun than it should be) and just traveling. I know going to that area right now with the massive war going on between China and North Korea, which in the long run will be good, because despite China being a fascist horrible country

Dead Fashion

they are still more than likely gonna wipe North Korea off the face of the planet and it sounds like all the nuclear bombs have been hacked thanks to A.I, crazy world we live in, I'm sure that's a lie, but that's what I heard on CNN. But no sorry for going off topic, I want to travel to that side of the world and go back to Japan again, I swore against it, but I need to fight my demons, it's only fair as a demon myself. I then want to go to Indonesia and I want to go to Australia, I have a friend I met online who lives there. Her name is Ballie and she is an Aussie who has such a sexy accent. I love accents (except French and British) and I would love to just see the world as it is. Gosh it will be so exciting! That's my life update, wow, it does feel so nice to write again!

The Next Day

60 minutes is something that was always strange to me. I was supposed to come on this show four years ago, but the timing just didn't work out. This show was always intriguing because I would never guess to be the star of an episode considering the type of people who they usually have on this show, but I became somewhat a national news headline with my stepping away from music announcement, so much so that even that sleepy old man in the office offered to give me a "National Medal of Arts" For my amazing contributions to Rap and Japanese music in the United States. I was also offered a medal in Japan but I declined that one as it didn't seem fair to me that I would take something that definitely was deserved by a person of the nation. However I am taking this medal from Joe because I do feel I have earned it in a way and I will be having a ceremony on the 10th at the white house, where I will get to meet that son of bitch and shake is decrepit hand and then get a cool medal that I can put in with my seven grammy's hopefully I get an eighth soon. Anyways my schedule is packed and I will hopefully be able to deal with this all. I'm in the makeup room waiting to go out and be interviewed. I think

it will in a way be very boring, but fun, we'll see! I met the old guy who will be interviewing me and he seems nice.

"Karen, I am interested in something from your past."

"Uh, yeah I'm pretty interesting you could say."

"No I mean a particular thing, the murders of DP Records that were linked to you back in 2021, now of course we know that they were done by another member of DP records, Shelly Akers (Jew Nose), but how did that affect you as a person, not as a brand?" I thought about it for a second and then spoke.

"Well you know Bill… It was hard… It was. All of this work and all of my life I had thought was going to be gone in an instant for something I didn't do. And you know I was scared… I was scared I was gonna lose everything, I still get threats from the police about it, I'm scared to call them even if I'm in trouble and need help, because of the amount of distrust I have in them, it scares me. I feel as if I don't have anyone to support me and for a while during that time I thought my career was over. I thought it was gonna be game over, I was going to have to go back to flipping burgers or some type of minimum wage job. Luckily the people understood who the true cause of chaos was."

"But being blamed for something so terrible must have ruined you mentally?" I look at him and pretend to tear up a little bit. I nod my head up and down a small amount in hopes of making it seem genuine.

"Yeah, it was bad, I woke up a lot of mornings, well I still wake up a lot of mornings and think about the feeling of being in such a position. How I was looked at, how I was treated, it scared me, it scared almost more than coming into this industry of Rap which is predominately men and english speakers, I mean I speak english as a first language, but I wanted to use my voice the way I knew how, and that was scary."

"That was going to be my next question, you are being awarded by the President the National Medal of Arts. Do you think your contribution to rap and music as a whole was big enough to deserve such a medal?"

"Honestly I do. I think personally that I was an inspiration for young women in the United States and the world to show them how to stand up to people and how to make something out of nothing. Don't let someone tell you can and cannot do, you are stronger than that and I wanted to show that in my music, even if my music is intended for a more mature audience, I think it speaks to everyone properly. It's a struggle to try and be the best you can be while still providing a good example for the world, it's tough, it really is."

Dead Fashion

Trying to wake up on such a morning is incredibly hard. It would be like waking up to go to your own grave, I mean just think about that for a second. Think about how horrible that would be knowing that your end is near and there is nothing you can or want to do. It's almost tragic in a sense, I didn't want to get up at all. I had my alarm set for 6:45 which I missed and then I missed my 6:50 and my 6:55. I finally got up in time to stop the chaotic nasty beeping of the 7:00am alarm and went to the bathroom. This is the most descriptive I've been in this since writing in it again because of obvious reasons and I pissed so loudly it sounded like someone was frying chicken in my bathroom. I looked in the mirror at my face and how it was already aging more than when I was young. I look old, and tired and it's due in part to all the stress I've endured in my life. I mean for fuck's sake I have been working nonstop for the past four years, I would assume I'm dying faster than most. I do a little bit of eye makeup because I also need to look sexy, before going back to bed and touching myself for a little bit, but I am not in a mood so I just stop and lay in bed for what felt like an hour, but was really like 25 minutes. The day is slow and it's because I am on vocal rest and I am not allowed to use my voice and or consume acidic things. I am so groggy and tired still, it's kind of annoying.

I made myself oatmeal with a little sugar and then grabbed a bottle of water to go with it and watched Youtube at my work station while writing a manuscript on the influence I have on society. It's a biography and I'm hoping to be done sooner than later. I finally am starting to wake up when I get a buzz from Jeudy. Yes, the security guard at my old apartment, I hired him to work as my gate security guard because I actually trust him and he came to me begging me for help because he needed support from his family and they were not paying him well. So I gave him a job as a security guard for me, he essentially just sits at the front gate and reads, occasionally tells me someone is asking to come through, who I usually know is already coming. We get along really well and I sometimes ask him to come inside the house and have lunch with me when the private chef comes to cook every other day. His buzz is odd because I am not expecting anyone considering I have to leave in about three hours and get to U.S Bank Stadium and get ready and rehearsed.

"Hey Karen, there's a fellow sister here, who says she doesn't have an appointment, but that you might know her." A fellow sister, so she is black... hmm, I don't really know who that could be.

"Jeudy, I am not supposed to be talking at all right now." I say in a soft tone. "What's her name?"

"Hold up... She told me you know her just by Tungavilila or something." No... Fucking... Way... I haven't heard that name in almost four years. I almost am laughing at the sound of her name, oh my god what an idiot that woman was, and she is trying to come here? Right now? Why? I want to let her in just so I can laugh internally at her struggle, but I don't think I should... Ah fuck it, let's light this candle.

"Go ahead and let her in and tell her to park in the roundabout shit in front of the front door."

"You sure Karen?" He says with obvious concern in his voice.

"Yes."

"Roger roger." Jeudy says pretending to be a droid in Star Wars which makes me chuckle a little.

She drives up the longish driveway, and parks out front of the house in a nice Chevy Impala. Maybe I wanna say 2020 or 2021. The snow is really bad right now and it is coming down pretty good and fluffy. It is a true winter wonderland out there and I watch her grab her coat and hold it together as she exits her car and makes it to the front door semi quickly, deciding to keep her car running. I wait at the door until she gets to it and open it to the wind blowing coldly into the house and a massive howl rings through the door. She enters and I grab her coat from her.

"Welcome! I am so glad you decided to stop by Mrs. Tungavaloa!"

"Yes-yes, it is a pleasure too. I'm sorry, I should've made an appointment." She says as she rubs her boots off on the rug and then just takes them off.

"Pffff, oh please I am not that important, I don't need big appointments and such, I am a simple girl."

"Well this house doesn't make you seem like it, Weren't you in DC yesterday might I ask?"

"Yes, I was." I say as I walk towards my kitchen and she follows. "I flew back last night on a private jet, to try and get a little bit of sleep, probably why I am so groggy right now. I also am supposed to be on vocal rest right now, but fuck it, I'll be fine."

"Oh I hope I am not being too big of a nuisance to you." She says as we now reach the kitchen and I go to one of the cupboards and open it.

"Oh please, I'm not like my younger stupid self, I like a little bit of company these days, Tea?" I say reaching for the tea bags and keeping an eye on the stun gun I have taped in the cupboard on the side of the wall as an emergency.

"No thanks."

"Coffee?"

"Again, no thanks."

"You sure? I can always make some."

"I'm good, this is just a congenial visit in a way." Uh what? Is she really here to see how I am doing? No way this... can't be, she can't be here for something like that, I just don't... believe it.

"Really?"

"Well, not exactly I guess, I do want to see how you're doing, and make sure you haven't been in any trouble, you old lady!" We both start to laugh, but mine is very fake and I want to rip her eyes out and feed them to a dog at this moment.

"Hey come on now I ain't that old, not compared to you, you gotta be pushing 70."

"Oh jeez girl, stop that. I don't look a day over 50."

"Sureeee." I say as she walks back into the hallway and starts to look at some photos on the wall of me as a child. "So why are you here really?" I say walking back over to her looking in the dark hallway.

"Well for one thing I guess there is news you would like to hear."

"Oh yeah? Is that right? What is it?"

"It's news on Chris." Oh shit, who was that again? Was he her... son right? Oh jeez, that kid I murdered, come on really you old hag. This bitch just cannot leave shit alone, that was almost 6 years ago, holy fuck just stop!

"You're son Chris? The adopted one?"

"Yes. We found some evidence that points toward someone and..."

"And?"

"It isn't you." She says now looking over at me, as I hide the kitchen knife I grabbed before walking over here behind my back. I didn't know if she was gonna pull something and I always have to be cautious, you never know. "Karen, I am so sorry for ever accusing you of all that." She says as tears start to boil in her eyes. I walk back to the kitchen and put the knife away and grab a paper towel to offer to her, which she refuses. "Seriously girl, I just- I just wanted to find my son, I wanted closure, I want him back." She breaks out crying now.

"Hey, hey, hey, it's ok, it's ok, look I am sorry, I really am, I wish you would get the justice you deserve. He was a great kid, and I liked him a lot, And I gave him all I could in my time with him. I really am sorry Mrs. Tungavaloa, but now is a time to be strong." She stops crying and looks at me. "Look, you guys are close to solving this case. I know it, I hope you find justice, so you can rest easy. If there is anything you need, a donation to the police, or some comfort or anything, just ask, I can see what I can do, I want justice too."

"That's very kind Karen." She grabs my arm forcefully. "You're too kind, Thank you so much, I am so sorry. I hope I didn't hurt you, I know I got physical with you and stuff, I can't even believe myself for that." I pull her in for a hug and we hug for a good long while.

"You didn't hurt me, it's ok." The hug ends and then she wipes her eyes a little.

"Well I need to be going, thank you so much for everything Karen, I just needed to close this out with you, sorry for the intrusion. But, I heard you were retiring."

"I am… In a way." I say as I smile.

"Well, I wish I could retire as young as you, but we all live different lives, congratulations." She walks towards the front door and I walk with her and open the door for her. She puts her boots and jacket back on and then starts for the front door, but stops. "Oh and Karen."

"Yes?"

"Have a great concert tonight, and have a Merry Christmas!"

"I always try to." I say as we hug once again, but the door being open is making me so cold that I stop quickly and we wave as she walks towards her car and I shut the door. What an odd experience that was, I must not let this distract me, I need to continue to prepare for the concert.

Three Hours Later

I walk out of the house and get into my uber which I ordered because I don't like to drive in the winter. The drive is playing Christmas music, and it is actually somewhat soothing to hear. The arrival at the stadium took about 30 minutes and when I got there I was escorted downstairs and had to rehearse a bunch of shit. I also had to try on clothes and a bunch of makeup, I felt like shit during that. After hours of bullshit on bullshit, everything was finally ready and I walked out onto the stage at 7:03pm. The crowd was so massive and all around me were phone lights and a bunch of people. So many people in one area, if a bomb went off it would be the biggest catastrophe in U.S history… would it?

  I started my song list as rehearsed and after almost two and half hours of singing, dancing, playing piano, playing guitar, laughing, and screaming I was to the end, but I didn't want to end, I didn't want it to. It was so perfect, everything, it was the best I couldn't believe how many people were cheering me on. I almost fainted at some points. I was wearing my first ever merch T-shirt along with a hoodie and my Akuma hat that has little horns, and seeing everyone wearing my stuff, cheering my name, it all felt unreal. I don't want it to end, but I know it does. I have to let it end, I need to end The Akuma now.

  "Well this is it. This is the time I have been waiting for, I think everyone has been not waiting for it but still I have. You know, I was so close to giving up at one point in my life. At one point it was so close to being over, I had nothing, no job, no money, almost no house or food either. I was so close to being on the brink of death, it was calling my name, all I had to do was just reach the other side. But something pulled me away from that. It pulled me back, it brought me back to the Earth and kept clothes on my back and food in my mouth. I always thought that maybe I had grown too attached to a certain person in my life and I was right. I needed to take that energy and attach it to something greater, more beneficial, something that was worth my time. Well, I did just that!- I did everything in my life I wanted to achieve with The Akuma. The Akuma was a product of it's time, it's place. I was a product put out to give you guys hope and make you guys happy and I would say

Dead Fashion

I did a pretty good job at it. John, can you come roll the piano out one last time? I have something special for you guys. It's not really my normal style of music, but I wrote this when I was 16 and I have never felt a time more perfect than this, to sing it. I love you guys so much and I can't think of a better way to send myself into eternal paradise than this last song in such a big venue. It is all surreal to me, how I have all of this, I-I love you guys." The crowd screams and cheers so loudly that you could hear it from a mile away. The piano got rolled out. And plugged back in and I walked over and sat down and the microphone got situated for me. "I don't think I could have a better audience, seriously, thank you guys, now! It's time for The Akuma to be gone, let's send it off with one last song, you're gonna love it, I'm a little rusty bare with me.

I play the opening piano part to a song I wrote so long ago, I barely remember it, but slowly it all comes back to me. The song is called Dark Hearts. As I continue to play the intro melody, the crowd goes berserk, they scream and slowly I see the lights on the phone cameras turn on and start to sway all around the entire stadium.

♪*If I cannot fly, then why do I try at all?*
If life puts me down, and I feel like a clown then why?
Life makes me feel so bad all the time! Why do I do or why do I don't, I couldn't tell!♪

Wow it is surreal, this entire thing is impossible, my entire life is impossible, I have seen things, done things, I wish I didn't. I was a victim, I was a killer, I was a terrorist. I was a lot of things in my life, and some of those I am more proud to call myself than others. My entire life never fully started until 2018. My life at that point was fake, it was barren, it had no meaning, well I found my meaning. I found what it means to be alive and I found my purpose in life, I found out that I wasn't just a nobody anymore, no matter the circumstances I was somebody.

♪*But you know you can't test me and especially*
Best me, so why do you try at all?
It always made me... feel so crazy, like WHY?

But one afternoon, in the middle of June it came!
♪

Because simply put, the Akuma didn't die, and it isn't being sent off tonight. The Akuma will always live, it will always be here. Because the real Karen Wall is The Akuma. There is no Karen Wall, she doesn't exist, she's a fairytale, she's… not fucking real! The realest thing about Karen, is her ability to be herself, the ability to be The Akuma, there are no inner walls of her head, you can look into her eyes, feel her flesh, feel her anger, but they are all just an illusion. An imaginary thing crafted to be the perfect vessel of chaos and destruction. I am not Karen, I am The Akuma, I will always be The Akuma.

♪*So sennnnnnnnddd me away!*
And taaaaaaakkeeee alllll that I have!
Make me feeeeellll so small and bad-
But see that's what they do, all them you-know-who's, those guys!
They're hearts are dark, oh so dark, it's a shame!
♪

Even in my last breathing moments there still will be no regret for those who have come between me and dream, even her. Those monsters of society think they knew what was best and how to control things, when in reality they haven't gotten the smallest of an idea in their tiny little heads. Their minds are more dull than an acorn and they think like sheep. This entire time, there has been no recovery, no signs of it getting better for me. I had that opportunity and I had to cut that weakness out of me. I had to destroy what destroyed me, because if I didn't, I wouldn't be able to be myself.

♪*So darrrrrkkkk, so dark!*
Black as black and mean as can be, what's the point that they see?
Ruining me and killing me, I'm done!
That's right, I am done!
With the Dark Hearts!
♪

Dead Fashion

When I started this I was nothing. I was an amalgamation, I was a husk. I didn't breathe like normal people, I didn't talk like normal people, it was all fake, complete and utter bullshit. Bullshit designed to trick and deceive even the smartest of people and give myself an opportunity to consume and kill people at a higher level. There were roadblocks and problems, but I was achieving my goal, I was being me. Over the course of this I lost myself, I was "getting better" but it wasn't true, I was getting worse, I was setting myself up for failure from the start. Someone like me can never be better, I can fake it, pretend to be better, pretend to be stupid or dumb and sane and quiet. But on the inside; On the inside I am sick. I don't belong. I don't fit into the mold of anyone, one category or person. I realized in re reading all of this my truest form and self was lost. I was no longer being a parasite, but being a contingent. I was relying on others to allow me to live, when simply put that just isn't fucking right. I am and will always be a monster. The violence, the drugs, the sex, it will always be with me, even if I pretend and lead it on to not be the case, it was and always will be the case. I am Karen Wall, The Akuma, I am the illusion of the normal human, I am the embodiment of success and power. I am someone who you feel you can talk to and have a genuine conversation with, I am someone who you can rely on or trust. I am the friend who is always there for you, I am your boss, your neighbor, I am you. I am tired and sick, I am worn out and used up, I am no longer in fashion/style. I am death and I am life. To answer myself in saying there is only one word to describe me is simply wrong. I can be described in more words than you or her or anyone ever could think of!

At the end of the day it is all a lie, all of it is fake, all of it doesn't and won't make sense. My life never made sense, because I never had a life and I still don't. My actions cannot be justified and you can pretend to like me all you want, but deep down… But deep down you know, she knows, I know the truth. I know what I am, I know there are endless amounts of words to describe me and while that is true, my statement still stands. For there is one word, one thing that everyone knows about me, deep down. No matter which way you slice it or put it or try to say it, it will always be the same, mean the same. It will always be not right. You already know that one word, you know what I am. I am Karen Wall and I simply am *sick… Sick*. I'm proud of that word, in fact I want to copyright that word, I want to own it, although it won't matter. At the end of the day, nothing will matter, so what I do this or do that, want to know the true reason for my leave from music and the shows and the singing, it's because I'm burned, I'm sick but mentally, I'm ill, I'm not right, I have no idea how to fix it and because of this, it's time to say goodbye. Just like when you say goodbye to an old friend, or someone you meet online, on a video game in 2011 and know you won't ever see them again, it's a goodbye like that. It's a goodbye that quite literally means, good-bye, I will never see you again, and I hope we never see each other again, because as you can tell from what you have learned, most who cross me don't get the satisfactory of a long vital life, that's what I am, and that's what I mean by sick. I'm a sickness that can't be cured or contained, I can't be fought against and I can't be killed easily. Sadly my time has come, mentally or physically? I do not know, what I do know is how you should picture it, picture it like this so you can remember me until the day you cross river styx, picture me as more than being, picture me as an entity, more so a star if you will, picture me as a dying star, watch the light of the star in the sky, and watch it fade. That is me, a dying star on its last flicker of light.

Dead Fashion

About the Author

Jayson Nichols is a young author who was born in Montevideo, Minnesota. He is 18 years old and is currently studying at Lyon College in Batesville, Arkansas. Dead Fashion is the first of many novels to come by Jayson Nichols.

Thank you WMD symbols for the skull and bones cover art. Variant vertical.svg: Fastfissiontpa2067 (Allô...), Public domain, via Wikimedia Commons.

Dead Fashion